T0157093

"—YOU'RE NOT STRONG ENOUGH FOR THIS, OWEN," Harley's voice said.

Owen looked up from the first-aid kit. The telephone was where he had set it: on the table in the galley.

"I should be there," Harley's voice said. The voice was not coming from the telephone.

"Harley?" Owen said aloud. He felt the presence of his brother as if he were aboard the *Nepenthe*. He sensed a heaviness as Harley moved among them.

"This is the way that it is. There are those of us who know, who can move like this. And the rest . . . most of the rest are going down, Owen. Like Kate is going down."

Owen stepped over and picked up the phone. "Harley?" he said. Harley laughed at him.

"No, it's not the phone, Owen," his voice said. Then, over the phone, Harley said, "It's not the phone, Owen. The world's changed. Some of us are doing better. Most people are doing worse."

JOHN DE LANCIE

SOLDIER OF LIGHT

JOHN DE LANCIE AND TOM COOL

POCKET BOOKS

New York   London   Toronto   Sydney   Singapore

This book is a work of fiction. Names, characters, places and incidents are products of the authors' imagination or are used fictiously. Any resemblance to actual events or locales or persons, living or dead, is entirely coincidental.

 POCKET BOOKS, a division of Simon & Schuster, Inc.
1230 Avenue of the Americas, New York, NY 10020

Copyright © 1999 by Bill Fawcett & Associates, Inc.

Originally published in hardcover in 1999 by Pocket Books

ISBN: 978-1-4767-3069-1

First Pocket Books paperback printing May 2001

10 9 8 7 6 5 4 3 2 1

POCKET and colophon are registered trademarks of Simon & Schuster, Inc.

Cover art by Jerry Vanderstelt

Printed in the U.S.A.

Dedicated
to
Alexander Thomas Cool

"As I fall, one shall rise, stronger and more true."

ACKNOWLEDGMENTS

The authors would like to thank Jim Baen, Bill Fawcett, Carol Greenburg, Steve Lefevre, and Linn Prentis for their contributions to this project. Special thanks to Vernor Vinge for his cosmological inspiration, used with gracious permission.

SOLDIER OF LIGHT

ONE

As the city of Oakland crossed the terminator into night, Owen and Harley Keegan departed the store and entered the street. In the gathering darkness, they heard the first noises of a riot. From around the corner echoed a man's shout, a shotgun blast, and a child's wail. Harley muttered a curse. As he and Owen looked up and down the waterfront street, the rioting grew noisier. Men shouted in fighting anger; like a string of firecrackers, dozens of pistol shots popped in quick succession.

"We better get going," Harley said and headed for the truck, parked next to the nautical hardware store.

Owen grabbed Harley's arm. He stood, listening to the gunfire. Perhaps it was a trick of sound, but Owen thought he heard gunfire from the hills.

He shook his head. "No," he said. "We can't go driving up through Oakland. We better cross over to the island."

"Alameda?" Harley asked.

"Yeah."

"What are we going to do there?"

Smiling gently, Owen jostled the arm of his older, bigger brother. "Survive?"

Harley returned the smile. "Survival is good. You drive, then."

They climbed into Harley's truck, a midnight blue Ford Bronco with black windows and over-sized tires. They dumped the bags of nautical hardware behind the front seats. Owen started the motor and backed the truck out of the lot. Harley popped open the glove box, revealing the flat metallic form of a Glock 9mm pistol. His hand moved toward the pistol, hesitated, then slammed shut the glove box, leaving the weapon inside.

Owen headed west, away from the sounds of the rioting. At first, they encountered no problems and little traffic. In minutes, they put several blocks behind them. Owen stopped behind two cars waiting for a light to change.

"Run the light," Harley urged.

Owen wrenched the wheel over and drove the truck up onto the sidewalk. The big tires bounded over the curb and over cement parking stops. He cut through a gravel parking lot, tapped the brakes to allow a car to flash past, then pushed through the intersection. Horns blared.

Owen clutched the wheel and upshifted into third gear. He gunned the motor. Moments later, they crossed the old drawbridge over the estuary, tires humming against the steel grid of the bridge platform.

At the farside of the bridge, three men spread out to block the way.

"Go around them if you can," Harley growled.

Owen glanced at the three men, who now stood, blocking the way, their hands empty. Owen braked, stopping the truck a few meters short of the men. Harley flipped open the glove box, but he didn't reach for the pistol. Instead, his hand rested atop his knee, very close by.

"Watch them," Harley said, softly.

One of the three men walked up to the driver's window. Through the dark window, Owen could see the weatherworn, deeply lined face of a laborer who had worked outdoors all his life.

"Do you need some help?" the man asked. He had sad, rheumy, bloodshot eyes.

"No," Owen answered.

Through the dark window, the weatherworn man studied Owen's face.

"Don't be killing anyone just yet," he said, with a glance at Harley.

"No," Owen said.

"We didn't make this world," the weatherworn man said. "We just found ourselves in it, just like any mother's son. So have some consideration."

"What do you want?" Owen asked.

"I was going to ask for money," the man said. "But now I wonder what's the good of that."

"I don't know," Owen said, wondering whether the three men were on drugs.

"Maybe you could explain," the weatherworn man said. "Maybe you could tell me what's going on."

"I don't know," Owen said. "All I know is that there's a riot behind us, and we'd like to get going."

Puzzled, the man looked up and studied the sky.

"I don't know," he said. "It feels like I don't know

the world anymore. Didn't much like the way things used to be, but I thought I understood them, and now I don't know what to think."

Harley muttered at Owen to drive.

"I feel so old," the man said. "I feel like I'm a million years old."

He stepped back from the truck and raised one hand to his forehead as if pained. With the other hand, he gestured for his two fellows to step back. Owen gunned the motor, slammed the shift into first gear and roared past them. The truck sped down the decrepit road, past the aluminum-sided warehouses and tool shops.

Harley flipped shut the glove box. "Nuts," he muttered. "Nice of you to stop to chat with them."

"What was I supposed to do? Run them down?"

"You tell me, Owen. What if they had had guns in the back of their belts?"

Owen looked over at his brother, disturbed by his unusual bloody-mindedness. Lately people seemed more tense than usual, but his older brother had always been steady in tight situations.

"Haven't killed anyone yet," Owen answered. "Don't know why I should start today."

"The whole world's going nuts," Harley said.

"The world's been nuts for as long as I can remember," Owen said. "But I must've been sick the day they were handing out the licenses to kill."

"Christ on a crutch," Harley said, disgruntled. "Who needs a license?"

Owen looked askance at his brother, trying to determine if he was serious. At first, Harley ignored Owen, but then his eye gleamed, a dimple appeared in his beard-roughened cheek, and he smiled mischievously. Together, the two brothers laughed, as if the riot was a backdrop for a private joke.

Without further talk, they drove down the length of Alameda Island, taking the Bayshore Road, with its scenic view of the San Francisco Bay. By now it was twenty minutes after sunset. Across the bay, the hills of San Francisco had grown dark and shapeless. The highest reaches of the clear sky still held light from the set sun. Reflecting this light, the waters of the bay glowed as brilliantly as if electrified. The water clung to the failing light long moments after the earth had accepted the darkness.

By the time they crossed over to Bay Farm Island and passed the Oakland airport, it was fully dark. Owen drove with the headlights on bright. He was worried about Kate and Constance, alone in the house high in the Oakland hills. He crossed over to a residential street that climbed the hills through a peaceful suburb. Twenty minutes later, they arrived home.

Waiting by the door, calmly, Kate embraced him.

"I was worried," she said, her voice sounding close to his ear.

"There was some trouble," Owen answered.

"Half-a-Keegan's worth, if that," Harley said. "Two Keegans were overkill." Then he shouted, "Princess!" and strode past them.

Owen and Kate's daughter, Constance, was sitting in her playroom off the front hall, studying the patterns of water cascades in an executive office sculpture. It was her favorite pastime. Harley scooped the ten-year-old girl into his arms. "Hello, princess!" he said, too loudly. Constance ignored him in a way that was far more profound than an ordinary child's distraction. For Constance, it seemed that her uncle simply didn't exist. Harley kissed her neck. Face averted, Constance struggled until Harley let her down to the floor. She returned to her study of the water patterns as if the interruption had never taken place.

"There's riots," Kate said.

"I know," Owen said. "We had to dodge one. What started them this time?"

"No one knows," Kate said. Slowly she withdrew from the embrace. She was a solid, powerful woman. Her long and oval face and large dark brown eyes were framed by long, black hair. Her full lips were set now in a serious press. "But something happened a few hours ago."

"What?"

"The vice president shot himself."

"The vice president?" Owen asked, in the stupid way of the shocked.

"He went for a walk in his garden and shot himself in the head."

"What? Why?"

"He mentioned something at a meeting this morning," Kate said. "He complained about people reading his mind."

"The vice president lost it! I can't believe it."

"It's just getting too crazy," Kate said. "We're leaving just in time. Did you get the parts you need?"

"Yes."

"I'd like to leave tonight."

"In the dark?"

Kate nodded seriously and leaned against the doorway into Constance's room. Harley was sitting with Constance, watching the fall of water between the sculpture's panes of glass. The older brother was larger and more muscular than Owen. He slicked his hair straight back. Today he was wearing a tailored white cotton shirt with a stand-up collar. His pants and his boots were black leather. Harley was maintaining a steady stream of commentary, which Constance didn't seem to hear. Like many adults, Harley had determined to act as if Constance's condition did not exist.

"We should take Harley," Kate said.

Owen felt a jealous twinge.

"Why?" he asked. "Don't you think I can take care of you?"

Kate shot her husband a look. "No," she said. "I know you can. I was thinking about Harley."

Owen leaned through the doorway. "What do you say, Harley?" he asked. "Want to circumnavigate the globe?"

Harley laughed. Lately his laughter held a false note, as if forced. "I'll leave that to you guys. I own too much of this town to let it go to hell."

"You should come," Kate said.

"Nah," Harley said. "I'm going to wait until they burn down the joint. Then I'm going to buy up the land dirt-cheap. Chaos and war. That's when real fortunes are made."

"This isn't a game, Harley," Owen said.

"Oh, I think it is," Harley said. "And it's just starting to get interesting."

In lifelong satiation with his older brother's self-confidence, Owen turned, worked the childproof latch, and stepped into the living room, which was stacked with the supplies for the voyage. He picked up the checklist. Something important was missing.

Shotgun shells, double-ought, two cases. Bang-stick.
Compass and sextant. Carpentry tools, the same that I
used to build the Nepenthe . . .

Owen saw a flash of himself: a medium-height
man, young, fit, brown hair, brown eyes, from the
outside so ordinary. He saw himself surrounded by
his supplies and he thought himself ridiculous: a
paranoid, a garden-variety survivalist. The kind of
man who destroyed his family in an absurd attempt
to save them. He had a special responsibility, too,
toward Constance, but he was about to embark on a
circumnavigation because no country met his stan-
dards of safety. Because he thought his family
would be safer at sea than anywhere ashore.

Then confidence surged up within him. He knew
himself. He trusted his eyes to see and his mind to
think. The world was deteriorating in a strange and
dangerous way. He was a man. He could take the
responsibility. They would go. Anyone who tried to
harm Kate or Constance would have to go through
him.

Owen lifted up the box with his wooden bowls.
He had packed five: *Thirst for Air, Continuum,*
AnNautilus, Mourning Star, and *Rondulus.* Spalted
wood turned and carved and polished along the
lines of a Zen form. A Japanese collector had
offered his agent $15,000 for *AnNautilus.* Although
Owen enjoyed some prestige within the American
fine art community, his most ardent patrons were
Japanese, who seemed to connect with the simple
elegance of his work. In any case, Owen had
rejected the offer. Constance sometimes studied
AnNautilus for hours. Owen turned it in his hands

and gazed at the convoluted shape, which seemed to invert upon itself when seen from different perspectives. As delicate a thread as it was, it was one of the few connections between his world and the world where Constance lived. He would take it with him.

The childproof latch rattled and the door swung open. Kate walked into the room and began to reorganize the medical supplies. She worked in the emergency room of downtown Oakland's Mercy City Hospital as a nurse. She had helped to save hundreds of lives, including the lives of children with bullet and knife wounds. Owen had never seen her cry, even when the doctors had told them that their daughter would never lead a normal life, when they had labeled her still undiagnosed condition as autism. He had asked Kate why she never cried.

"Someday the world will stop," she had said. "And then I'll have all of eternity to cry."

So Owen believed that deep within her, his wife had enough tears to fill the well of eternity, yet while she was able to fight, she had no time for tears.

Harley joined them. Owen looked at his big brother.

"You should come with us, Harley," he said. "It's just getting too nuts."

Harley laughed with an edge of anxiety that was disturbing to Owen, who had thought his brother was fearless.

T W O

AFTER MIDNIGHT, A BANK OF DENSE FOG ROLLED into the bay. When Owen snapped on the high beams, fog-caught light dazzled his eyes. Switching back to the low beams, he could see only the yellow series of reflectors along the shoulder, but at least he could follow the road.

He was worrying about the shotgun, in its case in the back of the truck, and wishing it were within reach to him now. They approached the harbor, wending their way through the warehouse district. On one street corner, under the foggy cone of a streetlight, hooded figures guarded the night. As the truck approached the intersection, one man stepped off the curb and made a hand signal. Owen swerved into the opposite lane and rolled through the red light. He heard laughter as the fog swallowed the group of men.

"A friend of yours?" Kate asked. She sat next to Owen. Constance lay curled asleep, her head upon her mother's lap. "What, you owe him money?"

"He might think so."

"So rude to run a red light to avoid an old friend," Kate said.

"Actually I think he was no friend of ours."

"Now we'll never know."

Owen attempted a shortcut through the waterfront district. They lost their way among huge warehouses. The public roads led to private ways, full of unexpected turns and one-way alleys. In the fog, they followed a one-way alley that led to a chained gate.

While they were lost, Kate said nothing. Calmly she stroked the head of her sleeping daughter. One of the aspects of their daughter's condition that they prized was her ability to tolerate, even to appreciate, a physical relationship with her parents. As Owen backed the truck past pyramids of barrels of industrial waste, he asked, "What do you think?"

"Turn left back at the intersection," Kate said quietly.

Owen made the turn. Minutes later, they came across a public road and headed for the marina.

Constance awoke, sat up, looked at the fog beyond the windshield, laughed, and lay back down to sleep.

They arrived at the marina's entrance. The guard lowered the chain. This late at night, no one was moving about, although Owen could see lights in a few live-aboard boats. Half of the marina was empty. He drove the truck to the head of the pier, close to the gate, got out and walked around to Kate's side.

"I'll help you carry the stuff," Kate said.

"Good, but stay here a moment and I'll take Constance aboard."

He scooped up his daughter and hugged her so that her head rested on his shoulder. Almost eleven now, she was heavy. Her complete relaxation made her seem heavier still. Since Constance was warm with sleep, Kate threw a small comforter over her, so the foggy night air would not chill her. Owen walked down the steps to the gate and worked the combination lock with one hand.

The *Nepenthe* was tied to the far end of the pier. The thick rain-rotted boards of the pier buckled slightly under his feet. With more than half of the lamps burned out, in the dark fog he didn't see the old woman until he was almost next to her. At first he thought she was a bundle of black rags leaning against a pylon, but then she turned her face and he realized she was a woman.

She looked up at Owen with cataract-grayed eyes. Her withered face, crisscrossed with wrinkles, contorted in a rictus of a mirthless toothless smile.

"Where are you taking the little angel?" she asked.

"To the boat," Owen said, too surprised not to answer.

"And where is the boat taking her?" the old woman asked.

"Depends," Owen said.

"On the wind and the rain and the currents in the waters," the woman said. "On the sky, on things that fall and things that rise up. Take me with you."

"No, I'm afraid—"

"Take me with you," the old woman pleaded, laying her bent, arthritic hands on Owen's arm. "Take me with you, away from the fog and the city and the great fires. I've seen the great fires and I've seen you, my lord, my strong master, rise up tall in the sky, and even the monsters could not break you. Take me with you, my lord!"

Owen pulled himself away from the old woman. He took several steps backward, but she followed, clutching at his arm. Constance woke up and looked about, paying no particular attention to the old woman.

"Stand back!" Owen finally shouted, his voice hard and harsh and full of command. As if he had struck her, the old woman fell back and cowered next to a rain-soaked pylon.

"Beware the monsters," the woman sobbed. "They want the little angel. Take me with you, my master."

Owen turned and strode toward the end of the pier. Muffled with the wet distance and the fog, the woman's voice followed him. "Who will protect me, master, if you leave me here?"

At the end of the pier, under a strong light, waited the *Nepenthe*. Forty-five feet in length, wooden-hulled, teak-decked, a substantial beam. An ocean-going boat, a cruiser. Her mainsail lay wrapped under blue tarp along the boom. Owen stepped across, boarding the boat with the surety of its master. He worked the lock on the hatchway and then carried Constance below, rolling her into her berth in the starboard cabin.

Back on deck, he locked the hatchway, with his sleeping daughter alone below. He leaped to the pier and strode briskly down its length, crossing long intervals of darkness between each pool of fog-caught light. He didn't see the old woman.

At the truck, Kate had pulled the tarp and unloaded some supplies.

"You didn't see an old woman, did you?" Owen asked.

"No. I didn't see anyone."

"There's an old crazy woman on the pier. Leave that stuff here and come back with me. You can wait on the boat. I'll carry everything."

Kate was already running toward the pier. Owen followed, but Kate quickly disappeared into the first dark stretch. He caught a glimpse of her under the next lamplight. Moments later, he stood at her side aboard the *Nepenthe*. She opened the lock and went down below.

Constance was all right; she was still asleep. "Stay with her," Owen called, then he locked the hatch with both of them below.

For the next hour, he carried the supplies to the boat. At no time did he see the old woman or any other living creature. Despite the clamminess of the night air, he was soaked in sweat before he finished filling the cockpit with the supplies. He parked and locked the truck, then returned to open the hatch.

"She's still asleep," Kate said. "Did you see that woman again?"

"No."

"I wonder where she went to."

"I don't know."

Owen handed the supplies, one by one, down to Kate, who stored them in the galley and the two-berth cabin they used for guests. When they were done, Owen stood and arched his back.

"I'm not a bit sleepy," he said.

"Why don't we just get under way?" Kate asked.

"I should leave a note in the harbormaster's—"

"Let's just go, Owen. We can radio him tomorrow."

"All right. I'll cast off."

Kate started the motor, which purred like a satisfied tiger. Owen cast off the lines, leapt into the cockpit, put the wheel over, and engaged the motor. *Nepenthe* edged away from the pier and nosed into the channel. The foolishness of getting under way at night in dense fog quickly became obvious. He could barely see the channel markers as they passed them alongside. Red and green, the channel-marker lights glowered in the fog as malevolently as the eyes of night beasts. He asked Kate to keep lookout from the bow, where she stood and called out the markers before Owen could see them. With her help, Owen pointed the *Nepenthe* down the long channel.

Streetlamps, aircraft and ship warning lights, and the headlights of slow traffic clothed the Golden Gate Bridge in swaths of red, golden, and silver fog. The swaths shifted and changed as denser and thinner patches of fog drifted past the structure. Underneath the span of the bridge, they could hear the muffled hum of road noise. Then they were past; the lights of the bridge and the fog-shrouded city were behind them.

Soon the chop of the waters took on the steady swoop of the rollers of the open Pacific. *Nepenthe* began to pitch strongly, and the mainsail was raised to steady the motion. As the boat pitched her bow into the rollers, saltwater sprayed Kate, who shouted with exhilaration as she retreated further aft. Kate was a brave sailor who loved the rough ocean.

Moments later, they emerged from the fog bank. A rich field of stars spread overhead. They could see some distant running lights of merchant ships, but otherwise the broad Pacific belonged to them. A slight breeze arose from the west. As Kate set the sails, Owen put the boat about and killed the motor in the moment that the sails caught. Now *Nepenthe* was sailing on a beam reach, shouldering aside the rollers with her port quarter. Kate came aft and laid her hand on Owen's shoulder.

"Dry sailing back here," she said.

"Go on below and get some sleep."

"Yeah, I think I can now."

She kissed his lips and descended the ladder, closing the hatch behind her. Owen clipped on his safety harness. He didn't mind sailing at night. The *Nepenthe* had an autopilot, but Owen felt safer with a pair of human eyes watching over the situation. At the last hour before dawn, his reserve of adrenaline seemed to dwindle. He felt tired and ready for sleep.

As the starlight seemed to fail, Owen suspected they had entered an area of dense ocean mist. The darkness was almost total except for the boat's own navigation lights.

A shape seemed to form in the darkness under the mainsail near the Zodiac boat. For a moment, Owen imagined that he was looking at the old woman. He thought he could even see her face. He was tired enough that his eyes could play tricks on him. Then she spoke, her voice shocking him.

"I go before you, my master," the old woman

said, then she turned and stepped into the sea. The noise of the ship's passage obscured the sound of the splash as the sea sucked her under. Instantly her black-wrapped form disappeared.

Owen shouted and put the boat about. Attempting a jibe, he put the *Nepenthe* in irons, so that she wallowed among the rollers, the sails slapping languidly. Owen screamed for Kate. He found the flashlight and swept the rough surface of the sea with its light. He threw a floating cushion overboard as a marker. When Kate didn't appear, he put the helm over. The *Nepenthe* laid over and began to sail again. Owen circled the area, searching for a sign of the old woman. After half an hour, he gave up.

Then he had a hideous thought. If the old woman had been on the boat without his knowing, then what sort of mischief or evil could she have worked below? Had she hurt Kate, or worse?

He set the wheel and scrambled down the ladder. He stumbled toward Constance's berth and threw back the curtain. Even in the darkness he could see that it was empty. Owen made a brutal sound deep in his chest, turned, and stumbled forward.

There in the forward cabin, he threw aside the curtain. Kate lay, curled fast asleep with Constance in her arms. Owen reached out and touched warm skin. Among the noises of the ship working her way through the sea, he could hear the sound of soft breathing. Amid the salt scent, he could smell the familiar odor of their living presence.

An intense emotion rolled through him. He closed the curtain, turned, walked like a drunken man through the galley, and climbed the ladder. His hand was shaking as he lay it on the wheel and set the course south-southwest. When he remembered the apparition of the old woman, it seemed so strange that he was able to tell himself that it had never happened.

Landward mountains of clouds blocked the predawn light, so that the clear western sky took light before the east. Eyes gluey with sleep, Owen grew confused. Repeatedly he checked the compass to reassure himself that he wasn't sailing north.

Then the sun itself topped the hidden horizon, illuminating ruddy flaws in the mountains of clouds. Slowly the direction of east grew more obvious. His hand on the large varnished teak wheel, Owen stood and gazed upon the strange sunrise. The hidden sun worked its rays through the clouds, turning their gray masses into lighter shades, reddened shades, rosy shades. Then it struck with force, sending through rays of clear bright sunlight. In his fatigue, Owen found it strange that the sea had turned emerald green without his noticing.

Underneath his feet, the *Nepenthe* was sliding through lazy seas with a slippery and easy motion. The mild wind was enough only to keep a headway. Not good sailing, but sailing nonetheless.

He set the wheel and went below. Constance and Kate were still asleep. Owen laid his hand on Kate's shoulder and shook her gently, then more firmly. She seemed difficult to awaken. Owen called her name.

Kate's eyes fluttered open. After a moment of disorientation, she smiled.

"What, no breakfast?"

"It was a long night."

"Anything happen?"

Owen stared at Kate for so long that she seemed unsettled. She disengaged herself from Constance and sat up in the cramped space of the bunk.

"What is it?"

"I thought I saw the old woman last night."

"What old woman?"

"The crazy old woman I saw on the pier."

Kate scooted out of the berth. Constance called out, but her mother soothed her with a touch.

"I'm not losing it," Owen said. "I think she really was on board."

"Was?"

"I think she jumped overboard."

Kate shook her head. Her hair was tangled, her eyes soft with sleep, but she seemed her old self-assured self. Her confidence bolstered Owen.

"Don't go goofy on me," Kate said. "We need you."

"All right. It was late. I was tired, and it was dark."

"That's right. Now go to sleep. I'll take a watch until noon or so."

"All right."

Kicking off his Top-siders, Owen crawled into his

own berth. Its familiar confines were comforting. He plunged into a deep sleep. What dreams may have come were not his to remember.

He awoke to find the boat bounding briskly over easy rollers. Knowing that the *Nepenthe* had found a good wind, he clambered topside. Constance sat in her customary place, in the corner of the cockpit, looking outward toward the patterns of sunlight striking the backs of waves, the brilliant scintillating ever-changing path of the sun upon the sea. Owen checked to make sure that she was harnessed in, that she was wearing her blue-blockers, and that her nose was painted.

Kate sat aft, one leg settled underneath her. The wind was streaming her hair. She was wearing her sunglasses. She grinned and shouted something to Owen, but the wind snatched her voice and carried it away.

Overhead, the mainsail was hard as a board. Kate had set the genoa, which was billowed out, full and hard. Checking the compass, Owen saw that their course was true toward the south-southwest. *Nepenthe* was making her best speed with a strong wind and easy seas. He smiled and took his place next to Kate. She left her hand on the wheel and threw her arm across his shoulders.

"Give a sailor a kiss," she cried.

Her lips were waxy with lip balm, salty from the spray. She was smiling as she kissed him, then her lips softened to a luscious circle and the soft tip of her tongue teased him. Owen pressed forward, but she withdrew her face and laughed at him.

"Nothing like a boy in rude health," Kate said.

Owen was moving closer to his wife when a

sullen thunder pealed across the cloudless sky. With a sailor's care for the weather, he looked up.

Gold sparkles danced on the top of the blue hemisphere of heaven. As tiny as flaws in his vision, the gold sparkles danced. Then, like the gentle hand of Armageddon, the golden sparkles descended, and all the Earth's atmosphere, no longer blue, turned golden.

As the goldness passed through Owen's skull, his brain chimed like a bell. He experienced transcendent clarity: of what, he didn't know, but he believed that the obscure was now revealed. He barely noticed as gold usurped the color of the sea. The *Nepenthe* plowed through gold oceans under a golden dancing sky. Owen felt a wonderful sense of completeness and harmony. *Every moment until now was dark,* he thought. *Now there is light to see.*

Kate spoke to him. Owen looked down and stared into the face of his wife, the woman he loved, his companion of eleven years, his lover, his best friend, the mother of his child. He saw her clearly; yet, staring into her eyes, Owen had absolutely no idea of the identity of this stranger, nor any firm idea that she was even human.

Kate looked into her husband's eyes, which had gone strangely vacant. It seemed as if he had disappeared, leaving behind the shell of a man. The empty gaze was too hard to bear. Averting her eyes, Kate looked out upon the blue sky and the deep blue sea. She felt a strong wave of weariness sweep through her. This surprised her, because she had slept so well the night before.

*   *   *

Next to her parents, yet far beyond their reach, Constance sat stock-still. The world was vibrating. What had been mute had found a voice. Although she did not understand the words, she sat, raptly attentive to the new gift of language.

A glorious strength was rising. An individual more ancient than the bloodline of entire species. For thirty million years, it had dreamed slow dreams, quiescent inside its immortal egg. Riding the currents of the homeworld's molten core, the egg had absorbed heat for energy and, molecule by molecule, converted the planet's hot blood into the food needed to sustain it.

It.

The Self.

The One.

Now the time of the quickening had come. Once again the homeworld was penetrating a sphere of being, where the wondrous life of the mind was possible. Now the One was able to awaken.

Strange . . .

It could sense billions of small, hyperactive creatures, their minds able to work outside a sphere of being. Fascinating and disgusting little minds, extremely powerful but miswired. Monsters. They should not be. How aggressive was life, that it sought forms in all environments, no matter how harsh! In lightless cavern pools, underneath polar caps, in the shadows of rocks bathed in volcanic steam. Such was life that it existed wherever it could, always seeking to survive, to thrive, to evolve toward something greater.

Toward something like the One, the crown of

creation. Deathless. Able to survive the thirty-million-year desert between spheres of being. What dreams the One had dreamed! Now it realized that its dreams had been disturbed by the quirky minds of these billions of impish monsters, which . . .

Auggghhh . . .

How awful. Their neocortexes simply wrapped themselves like parasites around the old brain, which maintained most of its bestial architecture. How freakish. Worse, most had only rudimentary organs for transcerebral communications. Since the creatures had evolved while the home galaxy crossed the mind-deadening desert between spheres of being, their architectures had evolved haphazardly. Just as fish in lightless cavern pools mated blindly, their descending generations devolving into hideously ugly monsters, so too had the brains of these humans devolved in the desert into something far too ugly to imagine. Accidental architectures for communication. Most couldn't even receive with clarity. Even twins could sense only the grossest events, such as the violent death of the other. As for sending! Most were unable to communicate, except for symbolic mouth noises and this bizarre adaptation they called literature. They went through life alone, only dimly aware of the minds of others. To the One, the humans were more disgusting than cannibalistic spiders.

And they were technological! How amazing! The One hadn't known that such advanced technology could arise in a mind-deadening desert. In fact, their technology was capable of destroying the One.

Death? For the One?

Yes. It was possible. Vicious creatures. The One

sensed a nuclear-powered ballistic missile subma-
rine sliding silently deep beneath the seas. How
they had developed mechanisms for wrecking one
another! Weapons were their highest art form. They
had tens of thousands of nuclear warheads, any one
of which could kill the One. How unfortunate. The
Earth was the One's garden; how it yearned to
stroll upon the surface once again after long millennia spent dreaming in its egg. But billions of these
creatures infesting the planet's surface, writhing
with their horrible weapons, would never allow the
One the peace and tranquillity it needed and
deserved. And look how they were destroying, pol-
luting, ruining, and crowding the garden. How horrible! What obnoxious pests, dangerous and so very
hideous. No, the continued existence of such creatures was absolutely unacceptable. As a matter of
self-defense and for the sake of beauty, the One
would have to exterminate them all.

Nothing like this had happened since the cycle
five ago, when the One had emerged a million
years late to find that the children had evolved
into quick, clever creatures. They had actually
challenged the One. What an epoch that had been!
A thousand years of mental battle! It . . .

Visions of power, strike and counterstrike, a war
with the children, until the One had wiped them
out . . .

The death of the children . . . murdered finally
by the One. Forget the horrible crime. Forget the
guilt. Forget . . . the poor children . . . but the traces
lingered, no matter how often the One sought to
overwrite them. Why did its many-storied mind
refuse to forget the children?

No, the One must concentrate on the present cycle. The humans were five cycles ago. It had taken the One years of battle to destroy them and their nasty weapons. Now it had to concentrate, remember the present war with the surprisingly evolved children.

But these children were all dead. The One had laid them to rest.

It . . . ah . . .

Forget.

The humans were back again. Billions of them. How had the One destroyed them the first time?

Or was it confused? Memory crowded memory. Every neuron used and reused twelve times over, dream overlapping memory overlapping memory art overlapping mental model overlapping dream. What cycle was it? How old was the One now? Three hundred million years?

Ah, yes, there was a plan. It was so difficult waking up this cycle; was it possible to be too old? No, it would feel better once it was deeper into the sphere of being. The humans were the problem now, not the children. The children had died mysteriously some cycles ago. No . . . the One was helping these humans eat themselves. Many of them wanted a paradise after death. The One was happy to raise from the hot sands of death a pleasant mirage that they could seek. And there were so many who were willing to fight and kill the others. What good tools they made!

The One would allow their desires to consume them as fire consumed the burning.

FIVE NIGHTS AFTER THE DESCENT OF THE GOLDEN
veil, the *Nepenthe* was beating southward against a
brisk southwesterly breeze. The night sea air was so
clear that the Milky Way glowed from horizon to
horizon, a broad bright path of stars, the home
galaxy as seen edge-on from one dark small planet.

Owen gazed at stars, white, yellow, blue, red,
forming the arc of the zodiac. He knew he was looking also into an infinite abyss of invisible phenomena: quasars, black-hole suns, postnova gas shells,
dark matter . . . perhaps phenomena yet stranger,
still unknown.

One star, rotating several times a second, blinked
green-white-red, green-white-red, green-white-red.
It was Sirius, the Dog Star of the Greeks, the Wasp
Star of the Maya, a malevolent star in the opinion of
both. Owen stared at it. He had always loved it,
because it pleased him to think a sun-sized object
was subject to the condition of spinning so furiously. To Owen, Sirius was a very human star.

Needle-thin streaks of greenish light, meteorites

dashed across the night sky. Having survived the destruction of the fifth planet by billions of years, the iron shards now burned to gas in the upper atmosphere over the Earth's sea, and only one man bore witness.

Owen dropped his gaze from the combusting meteorites to the gold ring on his finger. Both the iron of the meteorites and the gold of his ring had been forged in the core of a first-generation star that had exploded billions of years ago. In fact, he mused, every atom of the precious stuff of his body—every carbon atom, every oxygen atom, every magnesium and iron atom of him—had been fused in the core of a first-generation star, now long destroyed . . . yet which was in a way, existing still in this new form. He and every living creature were made from the heart of a destroyed star.

As Owen gazed upon the unmasked face of the galaxy, every star seemed like an experiment in nuclear physics, burning thousands of light-years away, thousands of years in the past, but reaching him across space and time with their effects, with the strange workings of their spectrums, this starlight. Sun-stuff had taken the form of a human mind, a mirror in which the hearts of distant stars could gaze upon one another.

Owen remembered seeing the world washed in golden sparkles. It seemed to him since that moment everything had changed. He felt as if he were seeing with new eyes, hearing with new ears, feeling with new skin. It had never occurred to him how incredibly improbable and wonderful was this world. Right now, for instance, as the *Nepenthe* swung down through a trough and cut her prow against the face of the next roller, her stern slipping slightly to the portside . . . Owen could imagine the entire ocean below him. He could sense its watery vastness and picture its lightless bottom. He was acutely aware that he was sailing a wooden-hulled boat at night with the infinite vastness of the galaxy above and the weighty vastness of the ocean below. Ordinarily he would have been concentrating on something, ignoring everything else, aware of his circumstance only at a practical level. Now he was almost overwhelmed by an acute awareness of his environment and its intense beauty and strangeness.

Beyond the noise of the wash of the water against the hull, he could hear Kate as she clanged steel pots and clattered plastic dishes down in the galley. Owen was able to picture Kate perfectly. In his mind's eye he was able to watch her as she worked, just by the cues of the sounds that she made.

In those rare moments he and Kate were able to steal, when their daughter was snug asleep in her cabin and the sailing conditions permitted the autopilot, Kate and Owen escaped to their cabin. Their lovemaking took on an overwhelming intensity. The excitement and joy, the exquisiteness of sensations, surpassed the springtimes of romance that long-term lovers experience. Here was an almost obsessive intensity. Owen had the pleasure of discovering his wife over again, his old friend, his longtime lover, made new and strange and thrilling.

Yet sometimes in moments of intimacy, as he felt himself drawing closer to her than ever before, she would disappear into some other mood. He would try to call her back with a kiss or a caress, but she would be far distant.

Long ago, their conversations had taken the strange turns of two old friends in the ten-thousandth hour of good talk. Now, sometimes Kate would say something that would mystify him entirely. He wondered whether he had ever understood how her mind worked, or whether she was changing.

As Kate emerged from the darkness of the ladder, Owen noted the time: a few minutes past midnight. She sat down next to him behind the wheel.

"Gorgeous night, huh?" Owen asked.

"Only if you like stars," Kate answered, smiling.

"We're about twenty miles out from San Cristobal," Owen said. "Do you still want to go in for a grocery run? We won't stay. I think we're safer at sea."

"Sounds fine if we can keep it short. It's not good to feed Constance out of a can for weeks on end."

"I'm going to catch a couple of hours, then, so I'm ready when we near land," Owen said. "Shout when you see the lights. The chart says there's firestacks from the refinery just north of the harbor."

"Yes, Captain."

Owen kissed her, went below, and checked Constance, who had her ear pressed against the hull, listening, fascinated with the sounds of the boat moving through the water. Owen leaned into her cabin, barely reaching to kiss her forehead. Then he retired to his cabin and fell asleep moments after kicking off his Top-siders.

Some unknowable time later, he dragged himself up from a deep sleep. A sense of foreboding would not allow him to continue to rest. Something was wrong with Kate.

Barefoot, Owen scrambled up the ladder. Kate sat in the cockpit, looking aft at black clouds that blocked the starlight. Approaching thunder rolled toward them. Slowly Owen realized that the blackness of the clouds was too absolute. A green star and a red star were too close; they were burning too brightly; they were approaching. The rolling thunder changed into the diesel motors of a huge ship. The black clouds were the hull of the ship, bearing down on them, looming now, all aft, almost overhead.

Kate was staring at the huge ship. Her hand was light upon the wheel, steering for a collision course.

Owen shouted a curse. He leaped to the wheel, grabbed it, and spun it over. The boom came swinging across the cockpit, narrowly missing the small of his back. Owen grabbed the sheet and hauled it in furiously, setting the mainsail so that it took some wind. The *Nepenthe* had come about, but only in the bow wave of the ship. The bow wave set the *Nepenthe* over and kicked it away from the ship as the huge ship's hull came into the *Nepenthe* with a hideous screech of steel against wood. Bashed in the starboard beam, the *Nepenthe* sprung away from the ship, but the ship's own hull was widening as if in pursuit, catching the *Nepenthe,* sending it scraping and groaning down its long waterline. Owen was knocked from his feet. From a position on all fours, he managed somehow to leap so that he could grab Kate by her ankles and pull her down before she could fall between the two hulls.

Nepenthe bobbed in the wake of the ship. Owen jumped up. The mast and mainsail looked untouched. He found himself on the starboard side, looking down at the hull. He had a moment of disbelief and disorientation as he realized that the hull looked sound. He turned to Kate, who was now sitting on the pilot's bench. She was gazing forward at the ship, now some distance away and growing smaller. He could see the firestacks of the refineries of San Cristobal. They were much closer than he had realized.

Owen swung down the ladder. Constance was sitting up in her cabin. Owen inspected the hull where she listened to the sea. It looked normal and felt dry to the touch.

Owen realized that he had been mouthing an incessant stream of obscenities. Only now was he calm enough to realize how much the collision had shaken him. He noticed that his hands were trembling as he went topside. Kate was still gazing at the ship.

"What the hell were you doing!" Owen shouted. "What the—"

Something beatific and wholly inappropriate in Kate's expression caused him to look forward.

The oiler had stood on straight toward the port. Now, as he watched, the oiler ran itself into the refinery terminus. Tortured metal screamed as the pipeline popped upright and twisted itself over and across the oiler. The ship drove forward, folding up the terminus in front of it, as a carpet of flaming oil spread around it as if in welcome of a king to Hell. Flames licked up the sides of the oiler, which began to crack and break up. A flash, a hard wall of air, then black oily flaming smoke towered to the stars. The ship was no longer a ship; it was a wreck, canted to one side, broken, in full flame. A kilometer away, Owen felt the heat on his face and hands. Stunned, he put the boat over and headed for the open sea. Kate stared aft at the burning port.

"What—what were you doing?" he asked.

"Watching the ship."

"Why didn't you get out of its way?"

"We . . . we were stand-on, weren't we?" Kate asked.

Owen looked incredulously at his wife. She was a good, experienced sailor, who knew that no forty-five–foot sailboat insisted on the rules of a road when the other vessel was a big ship in the channel of a port.

"What?"

"We were stand-on," Kate said. "Besides, it was so beautiful."

"What?"

"It was so beautiful," Kate said. "The closer it came, the more its shape changed. I was watching its shape."

"Its shape?"

"Yes, its shape. It was like a well of darkness that swallowed all the stars."

"Kate, we were almost killed!"

"No," Kate said, still calmly, "we were almost swallowed by the black well, down into the darkness where all the stars are drowned."

Owen stared at his wife, silhouetted by the burning port of San Cristobal. He realized that the same lunacy that had possessed Kate had possessed the crew of the oiler. They had driven their ship straight into fiery disaster. As he felt the *Nepenthe* slither down a trough, he sensed the weight of the ocean below him. Overhead the stars had dimmed, because the light of the fire had robbed his eyes of night vision.

"The shape of the ship?" he asked. "The well of stars?"

Kate nodded soberly. "I'm tired, Owen. Can you take a watch?"

"Tired? Kate, you almost killed us all."

Kate shook her head. "Constance is all right?"

"Yes, she's fine."

Kate's voice caught; then she said, "I don't know what happened to me. I was watching the ship. It was on a constant bearing and a decreasing range. And then while I was watching it, it grew more beautiful and I forgot that I was worried about it. Then these ideas about the stars seemed so important, and it was like I was seeing it but not seeing it the same way—"

Owen put his arm around Kate, who buried her face in his neck. "I don't know what happened to me," she said. She sounded weary and confused.

"Go down," he said. "Go down below and get some sleep. I'll . . . I'm going to take us further south, OK? We have enough food and water for another few days. Should we call someone?"

"I don't know, Owen. I don't know."

"Go on down and get some sleep. I'll call someone."

Heavily, Kate descended the ladder. Owen flipped open the compartment that held their UHF radio and dialed channel 16. Ordinarily, the circuit

was silent, kept open for emergencies. Now it was
jammed with overlapping hysterical voices.

"—*esperando hace seis horas*—"
"Told them that they wanted the prince—"
"Fire is spreading to the lower docks—"
"This is *Serendipity, Serendipity*—"
"—the channel, please—"
"*Ella necesita ayuda, te digo*—"
"Sam, Sam! Meet me on frequency—"
"—*matarlos antes*—"

Then he heard a long burst of screaming, followed by more voices jabbering. Owen listened
for a few minutes before turning off the radio.
Next he tried the satellite telephone. He was able
to get a dial tone, but all the emergency numbers
were busy. Finally, Owen dialed his brother,
Harley.

"Keegan," Harley answered.
"Harley, this is Owen."
"Talk to me, Owen."
"Things are starting to fall apart here—"
"Are you in trouble?"

Briefly Owen told his brother about the events of
the past hour and finished by asking, "What's going
on, Harley?"

"I can feel the whole world changing, Owen. Can
you?"

"But why would that ship—"

"Owen, planes are falling out of the sky. There's
train wrecks, hundred-car collisions, fires . . . whatever is happening is happening all over the world.
People are . . . spacing. Gapping. Has it happened
to you yet?"

"What? I—"

"Have you lost your concentration, seen anything unusual?"

"A few days ago, I thought I saw the ocean turn gold."

"Did it look like gold stardust descending?"

"Yeah."

"I see it too. It's . . . beautiful, isn't it? You're the only other person I know who sees it."

"I only saw it once."

"I see it two or three times a day."

"What the hell is going on, Harley?"

"I don't know yet, but I don't think it's all bad, Owen. It's like I look forward to seeing the gold dust. It's like waking up from a dream. It makes me feel stronger, not weaker. Is that how it feels with you?"

"Yes . . . yes, I think so. But it's dangerous—"

"You only think it's dangerous because it's strange—"

"No, I think it's dangerous because Kate almost got us killed."

"You got to take care of her, Owen. Bring the boat in, beach it if you have to. It's going to get more intense. I know it."

"How, Harley? How can you feel it?"

"I can . . . hear . . . I can feel things. I don't know how."

"All right, Harley. I wish you were here with us."

"I should've gone. I was worried about my buildings. Towers in a dream world. What crap. A boy's game."

"It was your life, Harley."

"It was somebody's life, anyway. I don't know anymore if it was mine."

"All right—" Owen said, before he realized that his brother had hung up. He stared at the telephone in his hand, then he stashed it into its compartment. Owen checked their position in the Global Positioning Satellite. They were west of Mexico, a good deal south of the latitude of Mexico City. They were too far south to consider heading back for the States. In any case, if the chaos was so general, they would be safer heading for an unpopulated beach further south. It would take at least two days of good sailing, but he believed that he and the *Nepenthe* were equal to the challenge.

Owen steered the boat on a new course toward the relatively unpopulated coastlines of the Isthmus of Tehuantepec, Chiapas, and Guatemala. Strangely, he felt as if he were still in touch with his brother. It seemed natural that they would go through this together. Although Harley was five years older, the two brothers had always been close. Owen had learned from his older brother the way to be: how to dress, how to talk to women, how to get ahead. Yet when he had fallen in love with Kate, the dynamic with his brother changed. Owen had guarded the very idea of Kate with a jealousy that quickly burst into anger. Having realized this long ago, Harley was usually circumspect.

After an hour, the breeze died down. Owen felt distracted and sleepy. Even the *Nepenthe* seemed sluggish in the water, wallowing as if weighed down by the events of the evening. Owen went below to check on his family.

At the bottom of the ladder, before his foot touched the cabin sole, it sunk in chilly saltwater. Owen stood ankle-deep in the water for a long moment before he realized that the sea had worked her way into the boat. He stepped over to Constance's cabin and swung open the door. She was asleep. Her covers felt dry. In his own cabin, he found Kate asleep. Turning back, Owen popped the cover to the engine compartment and found it completely flooded.

Owen wondered how the sea could enter his boat. Then he found himself leaning over the starboard rail and playing a painfully bright flashlight over the side. The brilliant shaft of light swept a column of illumination through the rushing seawater, surrounded by an annulus of dim, dark green water, the annulus in turn surrounded by a blackness of the sea made more absolute by the retina-aching impact of the flashlight, so that the thin shaft of light created an ocean of darkness. Specks of foam flew brilliantly white through the shaft of the illumination. Owen aimed the torch at the hull. For a moment, he believed the hull was sound . . . scraped, scarred, but sound. Then a trough passed along the waterline and he glimpsed the stove-in: two boards smashed in, one buckled out. He realized that the boat was taking in water below Constance's cabin.

The water within was mingling with the water without. It was a petty consideration. Really, it was the same water. Just that the boat was moving down among the waters. In fact, Owen mused, as he played the flashlight through the waters running alongside the boat, it was not at all a question of water. It was the air. The boat was moving down among the waters, leaving the air behind.

He looked up at the sky. From on high, the goldness had returned. Owen was not afraid. He watched as the goldness descended, the sparkles more beautiful than the Milky Way itself. The gold seemed like the internal view of each thing. Each molecule, turned inside out, reversed, shown now in true form.

With a rush of peace, he felt the goldness pass through him. He could feel it descend to the bottom of the ocean. And now for the first time, Owen heard the voices.

The voices sounded from beyond the horizon, too distant to be understood. There was a woman who was saying something over and over as if reciting a prayer. A man's voice, yet farther away, seemed to be arguing with another man or woman . . . it was too difficult to hear the voice of the second person. Owen listened attentively and heard someone say:

"—another one."

"Then we are growing," a man's voice answered.

"—one of us."

The voices seemed to come from a strange direction. He could sense that they were far away from him, two of them closer to one another, there, to the east.

"We will need the strength of him."

"He reminds me of the other."

Owen felt like telling them about the boat descending into the waters. He saw that he was aiming the flashlight toward the stars. The shaft of its light illuminated the ocean's mist, forming a finger of light pointing toward one star, Sirius. Green-white-red, green-white-red. The mainsail luffed and then cracked.

Owen realized that the *Nepenthe* was not trimmed to take the wind. The sailor within him found this deeply disturbing. He felt that the wind had moved around to the southwest. Owen stood. Their course was toward the southeast. He could set the boat on a beam reach. That might lift the stove-in above the waterline. He might be able to go over the side and make some sort of repair.

Reaching for the wheel, Owen brought the *Nepenthe* around to its new point of sail. It was a strong wind; the *Nepenthe* heeled well over. When the sheets were tight, Owen leaned over the side and inspected the stove-in, now raised above the waterline.

"Now the other is coming," a sweet, wise woman's voice said in the center of his head. Owen ran his forearm across his brow. It was hard to concentrate.

"Could you help me with this thing?" he asked.

"What is the nature of the thing?" she answered.

"The waters come together," Owen said. "The boat goes down among them. There are others with me. We must keep the boat up in the air."

"I see no others with you."

"My wife, Kate, and my daughter, Constance. They are asleep below."

"Those two? They are not of us," the woman's voice answered, no longer so sweetly. "They are . . . but this is your daughter?"

"Yes . . ."

Owen had a glimpse of Constance, awakening, still sleepy, sitting up alone in her bunk. She was staring at nothing in the darkness.

"What is wrong with her?"

"Nothing."

"She is sleeping strangely. And your wife has her face to black. She is turned to the deathway."

"No."

"She is of the deathway."

"No."

"I must tell the others." The woman's voice disappeared.

Owen found himself in the companionway. The deck was slick and canted, with the water deep to the portside. He opened the door to Constance's cabin. He was not surprised to see her sitting up, staring at nothing.

"Good morning, Angel," he said.

Constance turned her face toward him, reached out, and touched his cheek. It was one of her few gestures, one that she used only with her parents.

"Love you too," Owen said. "Go to sleep."

In the darkness, the way to Kate's cabin seemed long. He opened the door and shook Kate's shoulder.

"What?" she asked.

"You've got to work the pump."

"What? Why?"

"We're taking in water."

Owen moved aft and set up the bilge pump. He snaked its long hose down into the engine compartment and threw its short hose over the leeward side. He began to pump the seawater out of the hold and back into the ocean. He lost track of time. When his arm began to ache, he roused himself and shouted for Kate. When finally she appeared, she seemed to be avoiding his eyes. Owen set her to work.

He saw that the stove-in was still above the waterline. Harnessed in, he could go over the side and effect a repair. Owen had built the *Nepenthe* with his own hands. He always took along tools and materials to perfect his boat. He would have liked to replace the damaged boards, but that would take hours. He didn't trust the wind, or Kate, or himself to stand up that long. No, he would slap some cement and hammer a copper sheet, which would take only minutes. It would leak, but the pump could keep ahead of the leak.

Owen went below to the aft cabin, where he stored his tools and materials. He buckled on his work belt, which already held his favorite hammer and nails. He stuffed in a brush and a can of cement. He pulled a copper sheet from the bottom of the chart drawer.

"This one is a maker," an old man's voice said.

Owen tried to ignore the voice. Up in the cockpit, Kate sat, her hands idle upon her lap.

"Kate, you have to pump," Owen said gently.

She looked up at him without comprehension.

"The water is almost a foot deep. I'm going over the side to make a repair. You have to keep us on the same course, all right?"

Kate opened her mouth to speak. Owen somehow knew she was remembering a cold, snowy night, when she had been a girl in Pennsylvania. Owen remembered the night, too, as Kate remembered it. For him, however, this memory was the gateway to a flood of foreign memories. Some had the stamp of Kate, while others were unconventional: strange patterns, a delight in semantic nonsense, glimpses of meaning where there was none.

Gradually Owen realized that he was seeing the world through the mind of his daughter, Constance.

She was sitting in her favorite place. Owen reached out and hooked her harness to the running wire. He fought off the images, memories, and voices that assailed his mind.

Owen buckled on his harness, lay on his belly, and tacked the copper sheet as far down the hull as he could reach, less than a meter above the stove-in.

"The end of an age does not immediately begin a new one," a woman's voice said. "The interval is where chaos enters."

Owen connected his harness to a spare halyard. He grabbed the stays for balance, stepped over and backward, and then stood at a right angle to the hull.

"—not to be trusted with such information," a man's voice said.

Carefully Owen walked down the hull, playing out the halyard. After four steps, he stood next to the stove-in. When he squatted, a crest slapped his backside, almost causing him to lose his balance.

"—not in both realms at once," an old man was explaining. "For them, it's one or the other. If they choose one, then they are lost to the other. Only the few of—"

"Shut up!" Owen shouted.

Even though the wood around the stove-in was soaked, he grabbed the cement can, pried its lid, and swabbed cement. Done, he dropped the can into the sea. He untacked the copper sheet and slapped it over the stove-in. He nailed the leading edge, then hammered the copper to the shape of the hull. In three minutes, he had the copper sheet nailed in place.

"—the lights are a hallucination. It's the world that is changing. Not us. It's just that . . . only some of us have the eyes to see."

Owen returned to the deck and stored his tools. Back in the cockpit, Kate still sat, staring into the darkness.

"Kate?"

She neither answered nor moved.

"Kate?"

No answer. After leading her into the forward cabin, he started to work on the hand pump. He had a ton of water to put overboard. He knew that Constance should go below, too, but he felt better with her near. His daughter sat, watching Owen work the pump handle.

As the predawn light filled the sky, Owen sat, collapsed over the pump handle. Emptied of water, the *Nepenthe* sailed on. Owen's exhausted sleep was dreamless; the voices did not speak.

Constance watched the seas in the wake of the *Nepenthe*. While her father slept, she noticed that the sail was beginning to slacken. Although she had never touched the sheet before, Constance got up and pulled it taut. She looked up at the mainsail, once again stiff.

The big bright ball they called the sun rose up over the edge of the waters. Bright lights began to dance their happy dance upon the waves. None of the big people were awake to make her wear those blue eye-things. She was able to study the patterns of the happy dance. Once in a while, she thought she understood something. Then the meaning would hide from her. Then the water made a funny joke. Constance laughed.

Owen awoke at his daughter's laughter. He smiled at her, a picture of pure joy. In moments like this, he sometimes thought that he envied his daughter for her world.

F
I
V
E

THE NIGHT WAS BETTER THAN CARNIVAL, BETTER than Mardi Gras, better than Fog City's best-ever street party. Joy and a dizzying sense of power thrilled Harley. His nervous system thrummed more vibrantly than harp strings. He couldn't merely stroll down the street; he had to dance. Having glimpsed the powers of the new world, he had decided to take San Francisco as his city to rule. Before, Harley had wanted mere pieces of the city. Now he wanted it all. He knew that in the new world, he could enter other people's minds, see with their eyes and understand their thoughts; moreover, he could touch their minds, even shock them, change them, knock them out! With these powers, Harley would no longer have to play the old game according to whatever rules the rich and powerful had imposed. No, he could make the rules himself. He could take over the city, dominate all the other bad boys, and rule as king!

He was descending Grant Street, down from

Chinatown toward the Financial District. Scarlet-and-gold neon lights in the forms of dragons and Chinese ideograms blazed madly above his head. Fog swirled through the lights, diffusing swaths of gold and red. Harley had a bellyful of black pepper Kung Pao shrimp and Tsing Tao beer. The peppers had burned like a purging flame through his head; the cold silky beer had quenched the flames and slid soothingly down his throat. Harley belched; fire, spice, and malt fumed through his palate and seemingly the lower parts of his brain. So a dragon coughing flames must enjoy his meals.

In the dizzying heights of Harley's ecstasy, the city dissolved into a matrix of lights, crowded with glowing spheres of else-worldly creatures, then resolved once again into a place of wet brick and fog, people and concrete.

At two in the morning, the streets were crowded with partyers. On the third-story ledge of a bank building, a group of men and women, nude and painted blue, were throwing handfuls of money down into the street. Some people were scrambling to pick up the cash, but Harley, laughing, danced by them. Rectangles of gray and green were to Harley just the confetti of the old world.

From a darkened doorway, a woman lunged at him, giggling, trying to throw her arms around his shoulders and kiss him. Harley shrugged; the woman slid off him, and a weakness passed through her so that she slid to the ground, where she sat, dazed. Harley didn't know how he did this, but he knew he could do it again. It was one of the powers of the new age.

From across the bay, Harley had sensed that bastard MacPherson. It hadn't surprised him that MacPherson, the same man who had blocked him in four buyouts, was now one of the few growing in power. The town couldn't belong to him until he had confronted MacPherson, squelched the bastard, sent him packing so that he could rule over some lesser town. No, Fog City belonged to Harley Keegan. MacPherson could go to Salinas.

The sidewalk leveled out; he had come to the bottom of the hill. Off to his left rose the pyramidal Transamerica Insurance building. Harley glanced upwards at its peak, lost in the fog, and chuckled. Insurance was a safe world hedging its bets against disaster; Armageddon was not covered. When money itself lost its meaning, insurance policies were worth only a dark smile.

Hustling across a wide plaza, he burst upon shocking impressions of torn blouses, pathetic screams for help, tender skin exposed to the night air, brutish laughter. A gang of men was brutalizing three young women. One man was shouting nonsense as he loosened his leather belt. Like a huge wave, a peculiar, never-felt predatory lust struck Harley and washed over him. This strange perversion of normal sexual longing submerged him in a world where such brutish men were masters, all females prey. Robbed of all senses except feeling, he felt as if his genes were corroding, turning him into a perverted animal, the instincts of aggression and procreation miswiring and short-circuiting, infecting him with the rapacious mutation that had succeeded only because it succeeded, just as lampreys or Ebola had succeeded. For a moment, he felt possessed, as if he belonged in this alternative world of bestial power. He felt himself connected to a huge community of such men all across the world, now slaking their hateful lusts. It was like an army of darkness. His mind boggled as sight returned to him. The vision of the helpless young women struggling against the men found the true Harley, returned him more fully to his native self, and ignited righteous rage within him. The mix of neurotransmitters bathing his brain changed into a more volatile formula. He felt a white-hot power rising up within him.

Harley cried out as the world rang like a bell struck with an iron clapper, vibrating horizontally and shifting from mass to energy. The women became whirlpools of desperation; the men changed into flame-licked demons, shimmering creatures of ultraviolet shot with sickeningly glittering, bright white light. Somehow Harley's understanding of their wrongness translated itself into a web of connections. Without knowing how, he grounded the one to the other, allowing their own evil energy to feed back upon itself. An explosion flashed and sparks flew, leaving a stink of hot copper and scorched sulfur.

Harley felt dizzy. The darkness of Fog City returned to him. Sobbing women were crawling and scrambling away. Slowly Harley advanced across the plaza, stepping over the bodies of the brutal men, laid low and sprawled on the wet concrete. Harley didn't care whether they were dead or alive.

"I've done nothing to you, Harley."

"In which world? This one or the last one?"

"In . . . in this world."

"Maybe what you did in the last world is enough," Harley said.

"I'm sorry," MacPherson said.

Harley shook his head. He still hated MacPherson, but it occurred to him that continuing to hate him was as nonsensical as hating a figment of a dream, once the dream was over.

"What are you going to do with that trash?" Harley asked, nodding at the duffel bag.

MacPherson, a corpulent man with a tall fore-head and a cleft chin, puckered his fat lips. "I don't know," he said. "Gold is always good, I thought. People always come back to gold, no matter what troubles—"

"Gold is shit," Harley said. "No one is going to care about gold for a million years."

MacPherson sat up and took a deep breath. He seemed to think that Harley was going to let him live.

"What is good anymore, then?" he asked.

Harley shook his head. He reached out and touched MacPherson's mind. Yes, MacPherson was growing stronger, but his mind was heavily cana-lized: he could think only in terms of deals, profits, money schemes, and tax regulations. The rise of his strength would only make him a better player of a game that was over. Harley withdrew until he stood there, breathing the damp night air. He looked up into the night sky. The fog was glowing with the light of the burning city.

He was a lot like MacPherson. If he had been

five years older, he would've been too rigid. Maybe
old people were prisoners until death in their own
mental models of the world. Maybe only young
people, to whom everything was new, could accept
and bend and adapt to fundamental change.

Harley had spent his life in the old world chasing
money. For days, he had known that money was no
good, but tonight he had learned that power for its
own sake was no good, either. He didn't want to be
king of San Francisco. The mad beggar had been
right: the city was too chaotic, too large, and too
complex for any man to rule. What should he do,
then? What in the new world was worth having?

He thought about the young women he had
saved from the rapist brutes, and realized that this
rescue had been the only worthwhile thing he had
done since entering the new world. Defending
those who could not defend themselves . . .

He whiffed the harsh, chemical-poisoned smoke
of burning buildings. Down the street, he could see
the waterfront, and beyond that, the dark waters of
the bay. Into that darkness, the mad beggar had disappeared.

Yes, he would have to start over, first by following the good example of the mad beggar. He would
get the hell out of Fog City.

His midnight blue Bronco turned out to be an
excellent vehicle for the postholocaust. Jacked up
two feet clear of the road, the truck, with its over-
size tires and four-by-four traction, allowed him to
go over what he couldn't go around.

He decided to leave the city via the Golden Gate.
By the time he reached the Presidio, he knew that
he had chosen the wrong way out. The Golden

Gate was jammed, cars, trucks, and buses completely covering the bridge span. Apparently frustrated with the jam, people had abandoned their vehicles and were streaming back in the direction of San Francisco.

Harley decided that this traffic problem called for direct action. He cut through the waterfront park, running over bushes, until he arrived at the on-ramp to the great bridge. People shook their fists at him; they waved him back and shouted at him. Harley ignored them and plowed through some sand-filled fifty-five–gallon oil drums, forcing his way back onto the road.

Shifting into low gear, Harley drove the truck up the rear trunk of a Honda Accord, crushing thin Japanese steel underneath his monster tires, popping the rear windshield, rolling over the front hood, dipping and then bounding onto the next vehicle, a BMW, which provided a better surface than the Accord. Harley steered around a Dodge Caravan, because of its wall-like rear deck. The next vehicle was a Corvette, which was a shame, although it did howl gratifyingly in protest as Harley's truck crushed it. Apparently the Corvette's owner had activated the burglar alarm before abandoning it, as if he would return later to reclaim his Corvette after the police had cleared the bridge of less important vehicles. The only other car more demonstrative was an Infiniti, which, in a loud mechanical braying voice, warned Harley to stand back. Few things in life piqued Harley more than being ordered about by machines. He would no sooner accept direct orders from an imported luxury automobile than he would accept condescension from a toaster. After buckling the Infiniti once, Harley threw his truck into reverse and backed over the offensive vehicle, collapsing the roof into the leather-lined compartment. Although the Infiniti looked like a sardine can stomped under a boot heel, it still warned him in a loud voice to stand back. Harley had to admire engineering of that quality.

A third of the way across the bridge, he entered a region of darkness where the bridge's street lamps had failed. The cones of brilliant white and diffused yellow lights thrown by the Bronco's headlamps and foglamps careened wildly as the truck pitched and rolled over vehicles, spotlighting glimpses of chrome bumpers, harmonies of vertical suspension cables, vanity license plates, and open car doors. Trying to look ahead and ensure that he didn't crush any vehicle that was still occupied, Harley sensed that someone was waiting in the darkness near the center of the great bridge.

Harley didn't know how he knew this. Like all people, he had always had hunches, suspicions, and feelings of foreboding. Like most practical-minded people, Harley had discounted these feelings as mental noise. Now, however, he found himself increasingly submerged in another world, where intuitive insight and other cerebral events were more forceful than vision or sound. Harley would have preferred to trust his five familiar senses, but he recognized that he had no choice. The world was changing and he had to change with it. Meanwhile, as he drove the Bronco atop a Toyota van, he reached into the glove box for the Glock.

The headlamps and foglamps illuminated a massive automobile wreck that had choked passage across the bridge. A semitrailer pulling a stainless-steel cylinder had overturned, spilling liquid over the roadway. Cars and trucks had crashed into the overturned semitrailer.

Harley hit the brakes. The Bronco tottered atop the sturdy roof of a classic Chevy Impala. He tried to assess the situation. In the brilliance of the foglamps and headlamps, he thought he could see the Exxon corporate logo on the stainless-steel container. If it was a fuel truck, then why hadn't the wreck ignited into flames?

A fireball erupted from the wreck, swallowing the bridge in fire. Harley saw the fire rush toward him. He ducked just as the explosion hit the windshield. Crouched over, he could see flickering orange and red lights cast into the depths of the compartment, but he felt no heat and heard no noise.

Harley sat up. Calmly, he watched the burning of the midspan of the Golden Gate Bridge. Flames enveloped his own truck, but he was not roasting alive, as far as he could tell. As a matter of fact, he felt quite comfortable.

Now this was strange. Harley sniffed. He didn't smell any gasoline fumes, petrochemical smoke, burning paint, or hot metal. After a moment, Harley popped open the door and stepped down from the Bronco onto the front hood of the Impala. He stood there, hands on his hips, gazing calmly at the flames like a tourist in Hell. The person he had sensed was behind these false flames. In their chimeral lights, Harley picked his way over and around the wreck.

At the farside of the flaming semitrailer, there, in the back seat of a white stretch limousine, he saw the silhouette of a head. Harley walked up to the limousine; its passenger door swung open for him. Harley ducked inside.

The false flames ceased. A compartment light illuminated the beige leather interior of the limo. In its dim light, Harley studied the stranger who had waited for him.

A boy of nine or ten years, a thin, half-scale man with brownish hair chopped inexpertly, with a roundish head that seemed oversized for the body and thin neck. The boy had large, almondine, deep-brown-irised eyes that sparkled and gleamed. He was smiling mischievously at Harley, revealing a deep dimple in his left cheek.

"You like my fire?" the boy asked. "Made it special for you."

"Sure," Harley said. "Nice fire, but it could have used some heat, you know."

The boy crossed his eyes and blew through his lips, making a blubbering sound. "Yeah, right," he said. "You'd really have liked it if I'd made it with heat. Sure. You'd really have enjoyed burning alive."

"I don't get it," Harley said. "What was the point?"

"Bunch of losers trying to get over the bridge. Some real freaks and bad guys, too. One of 'em tried to hurt me, just 'cause I'm a kid, but he didn't know who he was fooling with. I hurt him real bad. I would'a gave him a nice monster too and chased his butt right off the bridge, but the sister taught me that it's bad to hurt people, even when they're, like, total jerks and losers. So I let him get away. What do you think? Should'a I chased him off the bridge? Like, ahhhhhh!!!!"

Suddenly the boy was screaming at the top of his lungs, his face contorted into a ludicrous mask of fear, eyes rolled up and tongue lolling out.

"Ker-splat!" the boy screamed, smacking his palms together. "Loser bites the big one, film at eleven. What d'ya think?"

Harley chuckled. "I don't know," he said. "Is this your sister or a Catholic sister?"

"No, this was the sister. Sister Josefina."

"Best to listen to her, then."

"No, not me, I'm a trouble case," the boy said. "You know who I am, yet?"

"No."

"Duh. You're Harley Keegan, right? Everyone's got to know you, you're so important and everything. And what about me, huh? Go ahead and guess."

"I don't know."

"I dunno, I dunno, I dunno," the boy said in a dopey, singsong voice. "I'm Harley Keegan, I'm so big and important, king of San Francisco, that's me! Yep, da. Da, da, da . . ."

Harley laughed as the boy scrunched one eye shut, crossed the other eye, bucked his teeth and smacked himself on the forehead as if his skull were wooden.

"Give me a clue," Harley said.

"Errrrrrr!" the boy shouted, making a noise like a buzzer. "Time's up for our loser contestant. The name's Axel."

"Axel what?"

"The sisters made up the last name, so who knows? Who cares? Just call me Axel."

"Well, what's the story, Axel? Don't you know that San Francisco is burning down, and you're keeping people from using the bridge as an escape route?"

Axel sobered as he contemplated this accusation.

"They were trying to hurt me," he said defensively.

"Why didn't you get off the bridge, anyway?" Harley asked. "Where are your parents, by the way?"

Now Axel looked withdrawn and morose. "I was waiting for you," he said accusingly. "And I don't got no parents."

"Waiting for me? Why? And when—"

"You're about the only one who's got any sense as far as I can hear," Axel said. "There's that drunk idiot, but he's got holes in his head. There's lots of bad guys, lots of wacked-out weirdos, lots of spaced-out wimps, so you're one of the few ones who isn't a total loser. I thought we could be partners and help each other out."

"When did . . . what do you mean, you don't have any parents?"

"Orphan, hello?" Axel said.

"When were you orphaned?"

"Don't want to talk about it, OK?" Axel said. "It's my business, OK? I say I'm an orphan, then you say, 'Oh, I'm sorry,' then we talk about something else. Get it?"

"All right," Harley said, realizing that Axel had been orphaned long before the present crisis. "What do you say we get off this bridge?"

"You gotta say you'll be my partner first."

"You seem to me like a lot of trouble to take on as a partner," Harley said, straight-faced.

"Yeah, I was, like, thinking the same about you."

"And what's the goal of this partnership?"

"Kick some serious booty," Axel said, mimicking a macho movie-promo voice. "Axel and Harley. They're back, and this time it's personal."

Harley considered this proposition. His first encounter with evil actors in the new world, the brutal gang of men intent on rape, had turned out successfully, as far as he was concerned: their death or mental destruction suited Harley just fine. But what about other, more powerful criminals? When he had connected with the brutal men, he had sensed a looming army of darkness. What if they attacked him? Who else was out there that he hadn't even sensed?

Although very young, this boy had demonstrated skills and powers beyond Harley's own. This proposed partnership might make sense, if he could learn from him. Beyond that, he sensed a lonely desperation in the boy. Harley felt protective of Axel. He couldn't imagine abandoning him to fend for himself.

"All right," Harley said. "But you've got to teach me that trick with fire."

"You've got to let me drive the monster truck."

"Ah, now I know why you want to be my partner."

"That's right," Axel said. "The truck. And you got to watch me when I sleep."

"Why?"

"Because when I sleep, they come."

"They who?"

"Them," Axel said sulkily. "The others. They don't like it when I sleep."

Harley stared at Axel, for the first time noticing the dark smudges under his eyes. Although he couldn't guess who these others were, he saw that a fear of them had kept the boy from sleeping for a long time, perhaps for several days.

S
I
X

Exhaustion made the broadening daylight seem surreal. Owen's thoughts had degenerated into a tangle. After he struggled through a small decision, he had trouble remembering the larger problems. Yet he knew the *Nepenthe;* he could feel the wind and the sea; he could maintain his course.

The wind continued strong from the southwest. *Nepenthe* sailed with the wind abeam, still heeled over to port. The point of sail was good, because it kept the copper out of the water, giving the cement a chance to dry.

After an hour, the morning sun felt too hot upon Owen's left side, so he set the awning and gave Constance a drink of water. Owen wished he could talk with her. He loved his daughter, but her condition was a painful burden. It was hard not to be able to communicate with her, to know her world . . . to know, in fact, who she was.

"What do you think, Princess?" he asked. In his own ears, his voice sounded hoarse and dry. "Just you and me and Mommy and the sea? Live on fishes, let the world go away?"

Constance turned her face toward her father and smiled.

"Maybe I wasn't crazy after all," Owen said. "People thought I was a weird kid. I could always see patterns that they couldn't see. So could Uncle Harley, although he tried to ignore them, while I concentrated on them. I made them the center of my life. They looked at me like I was nuts, carving bowls out of flawed wood. But Daddy knew there was beauty in flawed things. You just have to be faithful to it, flaw and all, and the beauty will surface."

Owen was pleased that his daughter seemed to be listening, so he continued, "Plus, Daddy built a fine boat to rescue his princess. Sail her over the sea far away from the bad men. So who's the crazy one now?"

Constance laughed; Owen smiled. Long ago he had taught himself not to believe that she understood more than she was able. The fantasy that she understood was too alluring. Returning to the reality of her condition could crush him. So even though Constance seemed to be listening, he closed his mouth and turned away. In that moment, he felt a wave of profound weariness sweep through him. He went below to wake Kate.

"Come on, Kate," he said. "Please come take the helm. I'm exhausted."

Kate barely stirred. When finally she opened an eyelid, her eye was rolled back into her head as if she was drugged. Owen felt her head, which was cool to the touch. He decided that she needed to

continue to rest. On his way topside, an impulse
made him snatch a chart.

Constance had moved to the rear of the cockpit.
She was staring out over the expanse of their wake.

He sat and studied the chart. Their original plan
had been to sail further south to the waters off
Costa Rica, standing safely out to sea, yet remaining
close enough to shore that they could make land-
fall, if necessary. Now given Kate's disturbing condition and the battered hull with its patchwork
repair, he should put ashore somewhere as soon as
possible. He noted their position on the chart and
then looked up to face the eastern horizon. He felt a
strong feeling of prescience, of something hugely
attractive, yet hidden and dangerous.

For a long moment, the world of light, sea, and
air dissolved into an astounding confusion of lines
of force. Owen didn't understand the meanings of
the lines of force, but he did have a strong vis-
ceral feeling that something was waiting for
him . . . there . . . an occluded vortex of indigo into
which converged many strong lines of energy, some
yellow, some white . . . further to the southeast,
subtly hidden but powerful.

Light returned to him. He could see the eastern
horizon, tropical blue sky presiding over royal blue
ocean, and still he could sense that vortex. He
shook his head and looked down at the chart.

There, in the south of Guatemala, a lake surrounded by volcanoes.

South of that lake, on the Pacific coast, there was
an odd-shaped bay called Boca del Fenix. In this
bay, two ocean currents met. It was further south
than he had thought to go, but it seemed to him that

their ultimate safety lay there. The superficial, everyday thought occurred to him that the fishing should be good there. Rivers of the sea, ocean currents were rich with life. This commonplace idea reassured him, obscured other motivations, deeper and hard to contemplate, let alone understand.

"Yes, the meeting place—"

"—stop it!" a woman's voice screamed, but softly in the distance. "Stop it! Stop it!" The voice repeated its softly screaming plea over and over.

Owen checked the GPS and set the course for Boca del Fenix. The horizons were clear. He set the alarm on his watch and stretched out with his back on the cockpit seat cushions. Constance sat watching the water. He patted her leg once before his hand went nerveless with sleep.

The insistent beeping of the alarm woke him. Owen rubbed his hand over his face and sat up. The sun was slanting down past the starboard side of the awning. He steered the *Nepenthe* throughout the afternoon, the evening, and the night. In the morning, guided by the GPS, he steered the boat northward. Slowly the mountains of Guatemala, and its distant volcanoes, as purely conical as mystic forms, rose from the ocean, towering ever higher before him.

Ahead he could see Boca del Fenix. Ochre and brown with strata of burnt orange, a dead and desiccated plateau fringed the deep, narrow bay. Overhead the sky was still broad and bright and blue. Owen studied the chart and steered toward the center of the bay.

The wind held for most of the way, but then it began to die as the southern shoulder of the plateau blocked it. Owen coaxed the *Nepenthe* toward the near shore. The boat moved strangely, because as the two currents collided, the waters swirled almost in a whirlpool. Driftwood butted up against the wood of the hull. Dead seaweed, plastic bottles, and other flotsam moved through the waters. The bay smelled richly of rot. This meeting place of the currents was the resting place of many dead things: fish, seaweed, even the corpse of a small dark whale, moving slowly through the waters.

Owen checked the chart once again. Twenty meters seaward of the breakers, some sixty meters off the sandy beach, seemed a safe anchorage. He let out the sheet and ran forward to let loose the anchor, which rattled on its chain. Owen brought down the sails and secured them.

Exhausted, he went below and roused Kate. She was so sleepy that he had to half-carry her topside. Owen set Kate down in her favorite spot, where she sat, her head nodding, her eyelids fluttering. Owen reached into the compartment, pulled out the iridium satellite telephone and dialed Harley.

"Keegan."

"Harley—"

"Yeah, I thought it was you. How's Kate?"

"She . . . she seems to be sleepy a lot."

"Like a sleeping sickness," Harley said flatly.

"Right."

"Hard to wake her. Wants to sleep all the time."

"That's right."

"People are dying of that in droves, Owen," Harley said.

During the following long pause, iridium satellites 420 miles high relayed to each brother the sound of the other's breathing. Owen watched his wife nod like a heroin addict.

"—not one of us."

"What do you mean?" Owen asked.

"I mean they go comatose and they die, Owen."

"Is there . . . is there anything I can do?"

"It seems to be a brain chemistry thing," Harley said. "Do you have any amphetamines?"

"Yes."

"What kind?"

"Let me check the first-aid kit."

Owen carried the telephone below. He searched for the first-aid kit among the jumble of supplies in the extra cabin. When he found it, he noticed that his hands were trembling as he opened it.

"—you're not strong enough for this, Owen," Harley's voice said.

Owen looked up from the kit. The telephone was where he had set it: on the table in the galley.

"I should be there," Harley's voice said. The voice was not coming from the telephone.

"Harley?" Owen said aloud.

He felt the presence of his brother as if he were aboard the *Nepenthe*. He sensed a heaviness as Harley moved among them. Owen looked around and tried to locate his brother.

"This is the way that it is," Harley's voice said. "Can you feel me there, Owen?"

When Owen replied, he did not vocalize. He thought the response.

"Yes."

"This is the way that it is. There are those of us who know. Who can move like this. And the rest . . . most of the rest are going down, Owen. Like Kate is going down."

Owen stepped over and picked up the phone.

"Harley?" he said.

Harley laughed at him.

"No, it's not the phone, Owen," his voice said. Then, over the phone, Harley said, "It's not the phone, Owen. It's the way things are now."

"What's going on, Harley?"

"Nobody knows, Owen. The world's changed. Some of us are doing better in the new world. Most people are doing worse."

Owen stood in the dimness of the belowdecks. He felt his brother moving across the boat.

"Constance is stronger," Harley's voice said.

"I think she was always strong," Owen said.

"Kate's turned the wrong way," Harley said. "I don't think that she can be turned back."

"What do you mean? What am I going to do about Kate?"

"Look at the medical kit."

The presence of his brother disappeared, leaving Owen alone in the *Nepenthe*.

"I'm . . . tired now," Harley said over the telephone; then he hung up. Static hissed in the warm confines of the belowdecks. After a minute, Owen picked up the telephone and depressed the hook button.

He wondered whether he had gone mad. The symptoms were disturbingly like madness: voices in his head, a fugue state, apparitions, and this delicious and dizzying sense of power. Even so, Owen found madness hard to accept. He knew his own mind. Harley was right: it was the world that was changing, but the changing of the world was changing everyone and everything inside the world. He was changing, and so were Kate, Harley, Constance, and everyone alive . . . he was not insane. Yet wouldn't a psychotic reassure himself with similar twisted logic?

Moving mechanically, he opened the first-aid kit and pulled out the pharmaceutical bottle full of a viscous, clear liquid: methylphenamine, a synthetic amphetamine. The doctor-scrawled prescription was wrapped around the bottle, secured by a rubber band, for the convenience of customs.

But who was he to be injecting drugs into Kate? If he *was* insane, then she was probably normal.

Owen folded shut the first-aid kit, but he tucked it under his arm. Turning to go, he noticed his bowl sculpture, *AnNautilus,* sitting on the shelf. He picked it up and took it topside. The sky was sun-filled, bright, and blue. Constance was still leaning over the running wire, staring at the beach with rapt interest.

Owen sat down behind the wheel. If nothing was real, then nothing was happening. Setting the medical kit next to him, he turned *AnNautilus* over and over. The bowl's sharp edges felt pleasingly familiar in his callused but sensitive hands. His hands made him aware of the bowl; the bowl made him aware of his hands. He gazed at the shapes he had made: the expanding upwards which turned back in on itself, creating a nautilus staircase back down to center. *AnNautilus* was an uncanny piece of work. Owen didn't know from what part of his mind it had come. He worked with the wood; the wood showed him the forms.

He looked out across the waters. Who could have imagined the bowl of the sea? The bowl of the sky?

He looked upwards to see the highest sky singing. Again, the goldness was descending to him. With a shiver of anticipation, Owen looked down into *AnNautilus*. The gold sparkles passed through him. The central spiral of the bowl's staircase grew large in his visualization. Owen felt himself as a part of this form, this small space relation that he had realized.

He looked up and saw that Kate was nodding. As his head sang, he could hear the voices over the horizon grow clearer. Now for the first time, he realized that they were not individual voices, but networks that were rising. He felt himself drawn toward one network, which seemed harmonious with him. They seemed to understand his confusion.

"—she will die."

"It is real, as real as ever."

"You have to keep her awake through the passage time."

"The brain seeks information. She is not wired for this world, but the brain will find a way, restrap itself, rewire itself, send forth dendrites to new regions, if only she can make it through the dying time. You must keep her in this world. Your love must be your strongest weapon."

He moved to Kate's side and swept her hair so that he could see her face. She seemed worse than asleep . . . unconscious, knocked out. Owen picked up the medical kit, tore the plastic off a disposable syringe, and filled it with 10 cc of the amphetamine. He swabbed Kate's arm and injected the drug into her. Kate's eyes opened wide.

"What—what was that?"

"It was a shot."

Kate's hands trembled as she ran her fingertips across her cheek.

"I feel awful," she said. "What's happening to me?"

"You're going to have to be strong," Owen said. "We're going through changes. I don't know why, but we have to be strong and make it through to the other side."

Kate drew herself closer to Owen, hugged him, and buried her face in his neck. Owen felt the force of her love. Even in normal times, he could feel her love; over the phone, in a letter, she could communicate her love. Sometimes, when he was distant, he felt her thinking of him. He would call and they would begin a conversation in its middle. But how much more so did he feel her love when they were together, close, in a lovers' embrace. Her love for him was something that enveloped him as palpably as her body heat. Now Owen could feel her love, the sensation as heady as a rush of ozone-rich, lightning-split air. He could feel his own love flow into her. They were together now. He would fight with every iota of his being to keep them together, now, for the rest of their lives, for all eternity. He and his wife were one being, one soul.

"You have to be strong," he said.

"Yes, I know."

"You have to fight."

"Oh, you know I'm going to fight," Kate said. "I'm just not sure how."

"I'll try to help."

"Don't leave me, Owen."

"No, I won't."

"Stay."

"I'll stay."

"—going down and going down," a voice said. "And down, down to blackness. Nothingness."

THE WORLD WAS DIFFERENT NOW. GOLD LIGHTS HAD fallen from the sky and risen from the sea. She could see things more clearly now. Before, it had been hard to see into Daddy's head. Now it was so easy. Mommy's head was not easy; it was too dark and too full of old things. It was like Mommy wasn't looking in the right direction.

Daddy was lost, too, but at least he was looking in the right direction. Just that he liked to listen to the silly people making the noise talk when they should be making the good talk. Silly Daddy!

That was OK. Constance had been a silly girl, too. She had listened to the water between the glasses. She had thought that the sunlights on the ocean were talking to her. Silly girl. They were stupid things. Waters and sunlights just did a happy dance. They had no brain, no mind. They could not talk.

Brain and mind. These were words. Words were what the people used because they couldn't talk the good talk. Funny how the words became a part of things, though. Before, Constance could see things naked. Now she had a word for most things. Once she could see into people's minds, their words had come flooding into her. Words had wrapped themselves around all the things. Words had a way of blinding people. They couldn't see all of the thing because they thought about the words, not about the thing. Words became part of the thing and made the thing smaller. Words were strong, though. Now when Constance had to really think, she had to work hard to shut down all those words. Noises. Talk-talk.

Good talk was much clearer. Pure . . .

Oh, Van Meers was flying across the way, arcing toward the others in his tribe. How nice! Van Meers was a clever man. Now here came that Irma woman. She was coming for Constance. She was not a nice woman. She was strong, like Mommy had been strong, but she believed in hurting people, not in healing them. Oh, she was nice to Constance, but Constance could tell that she was mean. She hurt people. She called herself a little warrior, but Constance could tell she enjoyed shooting and killing those men with the brown-and-green uniforms. Her memories of violence were so horrible, not like the TV violence most people had in their heads. Constance could smell blood in Irma's memories.

Irma was as dark and soft as the night. Tonight she smelled good. The memories of tropical flowers were so important to her that her mind was sweet and musky and mysterious. Irma made a motion as if she were going to fold herself around Constance, but Constance held her off.

You are growing very fast, Constance.

Constance answered her without words. She didn't like the noise talk, and she didn't like Irma.

You are getting strong enough to join us now.

Constance was the brave girl. She didn't have to join anyone. She was with her mother and father.

Your mother and father are going to join us. But you are going to join us first.

Constance didn't think her mother and father wanted her to go anywhere without them. They always took care of her. Irma was not her mother.

Then Irma came very close, even though Constance didn't want her to do that. Constance could see and hear and feel like Irma. She was an adult woman standing high in the mountains. The night air was cool on her skin. She could smell pine needles. Out across the big valley, the volcano was rumbling. She could feel the ground trembling underneath her feet.

It was wonderful to be an adult woman. She could go where she wanted to go, do what she wanted to do. What freedom!

Maybe Irma was not mean. Maybe Irma was clear and brave. Irma had stood up and fought the bad government. Lots of ideas, a whole dimension to life of which Constance had never dreamed: government, politics, the struggle, sacrifice, clarity, strength, the yearned-for victory.

Constance turned to her mother, but her mother was asleep. Her sleeping mind was full of junk. Constance turned to her father. He was so exhausted that just touching him made Constance feel tired.

No, better to listen to Irma. It was beautiful, really. To be a woman warrior, to fight for the freedom of the people. Her mind was glory.

Oh, and Irma had a very powerful friend. He

was hiding back there behind her, but Constance could sense him. His was different from most people's minds. Much larger and much, much older. The friend sensed her. He hid himself.

Up in the foothills, in the dank humidity of the broadleaf jungle, lower in elevation than the evergreen line, Irma stood, facing the south. Her men were resting the horses in the microenvironment of the shade of a huge centuries-old ceiba tree. Irma thrilled with power, amazed at her ability to communicate at such distances with this girl. Every day she felt her powers rising, the source of her power radiating from the core of the planet itself, flowing through her with cosmic force. Irma smiled. She loved the girl, and although she didn't understand what role she would play in the gathering war, she knew that it would be key. Later, as Irma grew in power, she would understand. Now it was enough that she knew that she had to summon the girl. Unfortunately, the girl felt such a strong attachment to her parent animals. Better to twist the explanation, so the young whelp would come to play its part in the intricate gambit.

What an interesting idea occurred to Constance! To run ahead of her parents. Not to leave them, of course, just run ahead. They would follow. Constance would show them the way. Constance was the brave girl who understood much better than most people.

She knew how to swim. Her parents had taken her to the pool since she was a baby. The beach was not that far. Constance could swim twice as far.

Take your boots, Irma said. *You'll have to walk far to meet with me here.*

* * *

Long, atmosphere-filtered, almost horizontal rays from the setting sun were playing softly on the granite face of Half-Dome and other glacier-carved mountains, turning the naked rock faces from a pinkish red to a wavering, vague violet. It was a sunset so unusual that it seemed borrowed from another world and another sun. Shadows were rising like dark mists from the valley floor, slowly swallowing the mountains from their bases. The long crimson, gold, and violet prismatic bands of atmospheric sunset, usually only seen from an airborne viewpoint, were from this great height visible across the long sweep of the western horizon. Standing there at Look-Out Point, Harley tottered in a gust of wind. A long moment of disorientation swept through him. The last that he could remember, he had been escaping the city. Driving the Bronco on the Golden Gate Bridge was the last event that he could remember.

How had he come to stand here at Look-Out Point? What was he doing here?

Harley consulted his watch. In the failing light, it was difficult to read the date, but as best as he could tell, he had lost three days of memory.

He struggled to recall anything that had happened in the past three days, but his mind was a blank. This seemed unacceptably strange. Even after one of his infrequent drinking binges, Harley had never suffered from a lapse of memory.

"Looo—hooo—sserrrr!" a boy's voice cried from afar, echoing from distant cliff faces.

Harley looked around him. Several other people were moving about the mountaintop. A young man with long hair and a brown curly beard was staring at him. Meeting his eyes, Harley had a strong impression of crowds milling about a European plaza. The woman whom he loved was selling handmade bracelets from a rust-red woolen rug spread on the cobblestones next to a fountain, where black marble cherubs beheaded snakes. The mind was full of the harsh logic of the German language.

Harley shook his head and avoided the man's gaze. Other people were moving about the mountaintop. Even avoiding their eyes, he felt the privacy of his mind violated by the intrusion of their thoughts and memories. One mind was replaying an electric guitar riff, over and over, as if this loop of auditory memory would ward away thoughts.

Ducking under a chain, Harley dodged into the forbidden area of the mountaintop. He followed a small path beaten by trespassers to a long slab of rock jutting over the precipice. He stood, the Yosemite valley floor a thousand-meter sheer drop below him. When the wind gusted, he adjusted his stance, but he did not sit down. From here he could see the massive face of El Capitan and other cliff faces, some stained gray by waterfalls since run dry.

"Looo—hoooo—ssserrrr!"

Listening to the echoes of the boy's voice, Harley felt the wind move past him. Keenly aware of the immense void below, he felt a delicious and thrilling vertigo sweep through him. He was not afraid that he would fall; he was afraid that he would jump. How much could he trust himself? For he felt as light as the breeze, as if he could step off the rock slab and float down to the distant valley floor, riding an arc of rainbow. Were not all powers given to him?

He gazed down at the valley floor, where the people looked like small dots, their arms barely visible as they swung to and fro, doing their antlike business.

An eagle swooped down from the north, soaring below him. As he looked down upon the back of the soaring eagle's brown wings, Harley's vertigo crescendoed. He tottered, one small step from committing himself to the void.

In the moment before he took the step, he hung his head back and looked up into the deep indigo sky. Starlight was beginning to pierce the atmosphere, whose claim to day was increasingly thin. A golden veil spread over the deepening starfield and descended toward him. Now he understood that the golden veil was not a hallucination, it was an extrasensory perception of a cosmic force: the light of the mind's eye. The Earth itself was moving into the golden veil. He understood that minds were reacting to the force, as the world entered a region where it grew stronger. Some minds were growing stronger in this new region. To them was given the gift of the golden veil, a golden coronation to accompany the conferment of kingly powers. More than that, Harley didn't yet understand. He didn't know what caused the force, or how it worked, or why it grew stronger. He wondered what the first humans, journeying farther north than the species had ever journeyed, must have thought when they, the first intelligent species ever to do so, had seen the northern lights. What must they have thought, seeing those immense sheets of eerie lights dancing in the night sky? How they must have thrilled with their terrible beauty! What gods did they invent to explain such otherworldly magnificence? What would they have thought, if they had been told the lights were caused by solar winds striking the planet's electromagnetic field? And who had he and his contemporaries been, to dare to presume that in their lifetime, all of nature's powers had been revealed?

Ecstasy enveloped him as the golden field coursed through his body. He could feel his entire nervous system thrill. He was not a confederation of body parts, a welded robot of brain, nervous system, muscles, and bones. His mind extended throughout his entire body, the filaments and tendrils of his brain reaching from the skull through the spinal cord and the spinal and cranial nerves, his nervous system branching out to the tips of his fingers and toes. As the entire nervous system thrummed, his awareness simultaneously spread throughout the entire valley, filling the valley as fully as air filled a bowl.

Harley's awareness connected with the thousands of people moving through the dusky air of Yosemite. Rooms within rooms, buildings within buildings, cities within cities. His native vision faded as his mind's sight rose. He found himself able to navigate through the unplanned metropolis of this accidental community of minds.

"Looo—hoooo—ssserrr!"

From nearby rooms, a cacophony of German language and electric guitar overwhelmed him. He heard German, pure nonsense to him; but by lowering his attention, he descended below the verbalization into a realm of metalanguage.

He was sick and far from home. He had left the

woman he loved alone, in a time when all the world was going mad. He should have stayed with her, protected her. . . .

. . . a burst of German, as Harley's awareness bobbed up into the verbalization . . .

. . . now evil spirits were talking to him in English, a language he had learned as a boy . . .

Harley found himself touching a region of the German's mind that networked English with German. Touching this region, he found himself beginning to understand German, absorbing not only words, but also the structures and the internal logic of the language.

Looking through the German's eyes, he saw his own back as he stood there, poised above the abyss, silhouetted against the deep purple western sky.

The German's mind was his. Harley sensed an intellect informed but not controlled by the emotions, and a confidence that was steadier than his own, based on a reliance not only on the self, but also on the community. A loner from birth, Harley felt himself rocked by the strength of a free mind that was an integral part of a strong society.

"Looo—hoooo—sssserrr!"

Grasping the gestalt of this mind, Harley felt himself strengthened by it. In a minute, he understood another way of being. In sympathy with the German youth, Harley reached out over vast distances and connected him, briefly but intensely, with the mind of the woman that he loved. The effort fatigued him, so he broke contact and returned to himself. He felt dazed but pleased with this demonstration of his growing power—he had been able to contact Owen over great distances, but never had he been able to find and connect two strangers, one of them a world away. He would need this strength if he were to join the growing communities that he could sense, but not yet join.

He became aware of a searing cascade of electric guitar, beautiful and ugly, repeating over and over. Very near, this mind was weak and filled with borrowed images, more like a tape library of popular media than an intellect. Touching here and there, Harley experienced bits of movies, television shows, rock music, and commercials. Down a level lower, though, the man was shooting an endless barrage of bullets, victims reeling in slow-motion splatters. It was an obsessive-compulsive tic, a small area of the brain given over for a lifetime to endless repetitions of murder. Below this lurked a dark region more primitive still, where a bestial aggression and bloodlust boiled. This was a junk mind, full of fragments of other people's cheap broadcast nightmares. Harley realized that this junk mind was connected with a region of his own mind, where he was forever firing the Glock. This was his self-confidence: the belief that he could kill anything that opposed him. He could be stronger than that. True power allowed one to be gentle. Harley felt himself growing.

". . . soldier of light . . ." a voice whispered.

Just two minds of the thousands that beckoned to him, but already Harley's mind was reeling. He was about to retreat into himself, when he heard once again Axel calling to him.

"Looo—hoooo—ssssserrr!"

Harley realized that until now, he had only scratched the surface. If he wanted to be a master of this new age, he would have to burrow through dozens, hundreds, thousands of minds. He would have to resist their debilitating, even evil influences, while learning from their strengths, and growing not only in mere native power, but also wisdom and . . . virtue.

Virtue? What was virtue in this world? What was good? In the old world, money had been Harley's good. Now money meant nothing. Mind to mind, soul to soul, what was good, what was virtue?

Or had he ever understood virtue? Even with such tremendous changes, was virtue something greater, something that didn't change, something so great that it could never change?

He thought of Axel, whose powers were so much further developed, but who was so alone and afraid. The boy was summoning him tauntingly, as if this were a game of hide-and-seek.

Turning his attention down to the valley floor, he felt sure that Axel was below. There he was, down at the base of the dried-up falls. Harley recognized the impish humor; the bright play of the overactive, media-saturated mind; the bravery under a loneliness that would have crushed a weaker child. Harley reached out to tag Axel, but the mind changed suddenly. It wasn't a boy at all, but rather an old man. Harley glimpsed the ruins of a great city: barrage-shattered, empty-eyed façades of buildings, streets choked with the slag of bricks and mortar, everything obscured by dark smoke and dust. He was a tottering skeleton, his self-cannibalized tissues withered and almost too weak to move his bones, starved beyond the sensation of hunger. The taste of corpse-spoiled water, drawn from a hole hacked in the river ice, would not leave his mouth, more than fifty years later. Pitr, 1945. He heard an undercurrent of Russian and a distant strain of classical music.

No, this was not Axel. The boy had been here and had left a trace of himself to fool Harley.

Why here? Was there a clue? This was a man who had cheated death five times over, who had survived the Nazi siege of Leningrad, who had fought with the Red Army to crush the Hitlerite rats and lay waste to Berlin, who had spent fifteen years fighting cold and hunger in a labor camp, who had survived cancerous pain, who was beating day-by-day an addiction to morphine. Here was a man, a survivor. Although he was anxious to trace Axel, Harley lingered in the old man's mind, absorbing a toughness far beyond the bravado of youth. This man had suffered enough for a hundred lifetimes, but he had always clung to whatever scrap of beauty, hope, or grace had been available. Even now, as his old, tough body was failing him in the middle of yet another of the world's strange convulsions, the old man was studying the trickle of white foamy water that tumbled down from the waterfall, the thin stream of water almost phosphorescent in the uncertain light of the fading sky. Here was faith and constancy, holding fast to what was good and true, whatever winds howled in a tempestuous world.

Turning from the old man's mind, Harley felt himself disembodied. He was peering through the darkness, looking for Axel. It seemed to him that he was growing stronger each time he experienced another mind. Passing through the old man's mind,

he had learned what it took to survive a lifetime of
bitter trials. It took faith, a belief in something
greater than one's self.

"Loooo—hoooo—ssssser!"

Harley's awareness leapt across the valley floor
toward El Capitan, the huge, sheer cliff face that
dominated Yosemite. The pure, dry granite seemed
to glow, reflecting the little light left in the sky,
while the greenery of the valley floor absorbed it.
He caught Axel unawares. The boy had been playing, throwing rocks as high as he could against the
massive cliff. Harley reached out to tag him, but
even as he did, he discovered that it wasn't Axel.

No, it was a young woman. Harley felt himself
uplifted by a tremendous energy and optimism.
Here was life and hope. And this young woman was
not one, but two . . . twins?

No, she was one young woman, communicating
with a cluster of twelve girls joined in a global network. They called themselves the Silver Stars. They
didn't care about the wars being fought between
evil brutes and self-righteous men. The Silver Stars
operated not at a higher plane, but in a whole different dimension, which Harley glimpsed but
couldn't understand. Then he glimpsed other ways
and other networks, a hyperdimensional universe,
each network at right angles to the next, each
barely knowable to the other. He yearned to remain
in the pure dizzying heights of the Silver Stars, but
he couldn't maintain their way of thinking. He felt
himself losing the connection and dropping down
through the dimensions of the armies of light and
darkness and returning to his own body, standing
on the outlook slab. Axel was standing next to him.

"So now maybe you get it, huh?" the boy asked.

Harley nodded. "It's not the way I thought it was."

"It's pick-up, choose sides," Axel said. "This is a team sport, no rules. No fear."

Harley looked at the boy. Although Axel was more accomplished than him, he could not have understood what he experienced, not even as well as Harley understood. He was a child, after all. The worlds that Harley had just glimpsed were far more complicated and subtle than a game of warring sides. Yet it was true that at important and basic levels, terrible wars were being fought. They would have to develop their powers to defend themselves, if nothing else.

"Who's on our side, do you think?" Axel asked.

In the middle of his head, Harley heard a voice say, "We are all soldiers in an army of light."

ALTHOUGH HE DIDN'T KNOW WHY, OWEN WAS AFRAID to sleep. He stood watch in the cockpit as long as he was able. The *Nepenthe* swung at anchor amid the swirling, crossing currents of the bay, rolled over the incoming backs of the waves. He felt content knowing that Kate and Constance were asleep below. In the middle of the night, the colors bled from the sky and dissolved into a smeared impression of blacks and grays. Owen sat down to rest his weary joints.

"Owen!" Kate shouted.

Dawn's fiery redness overspreading the sky seemed sudden. Owen sat up. Morning mist covered the deck. He coughed, feeling his lungs weak from breathing dewy air.

Kate loomed in front of him, breathing hard, her face almost unrecognizable, the muscles tensed into a mask of fear and panic.

"She's gone!"

Owen dashed below to Constance's berth and drew open the curtains. In the dimness, he could see mounds of stuffed animals. He reached out to touch the shapes and verify that his daughter was not in her berth.

Owen hustled to Kate's berth. It was empty. He began to feel the awful rising panic of a parent who can't find his child. Owen checked all the spaces belowdecks, then he ran topside and checked everywhere. Constance was not on the boat.

"What happened?" Owen shouted.

"I don't know."

Kate's chest was heaving. Her tensed face had a strange, feral look, as if she was a primitive woman ready to kill. Owen watched her as she fought an intense battle to control herself. He felt his own mind in a panic. It was the most awful moment of his life, yet Kate's struggle to control herself was so monumental that he felt awed. She stood, her hands tensed into talons, her chest heaving, her face a killer mask. Finally she seemed to breathe more easily. One tear leaked from the corner of her left eye and streaked, unnoticed by Kate, down her cheek. When she spoke, her voice was deep with controlled emotion.

"She must have gone over the side."

"She went ashore. She swam ashore," Owen said. "We have to go get her."

The more probable explanation—that Constance had gone overboard and had drowned—was too awful for words.

As he threw some supplies into a knapsack and a mesh bag, he realized that he was crying. He didn't know when he had begun to cry, but his vision was smeared with tears. Topside, he put the Zodiac into the water. He threw the supplies into the Zodiac. Kate clambered down into the powered boat. Owen fended off the *Nepenthe*. The Zodiac's engine refused to start. While Owen fiddled with the motor, Kate grabbed an oar and began to paddle toward the shore. Owen mouthed a curse, grabbed the other oar, and put his back into rowing. They crossed the break and rode the surf into the beach.

The rising tide of the Pacific had advanced waves to wipe smooth most of the beach. In the dry sand beyond the high-water mark, a single trail of small footprints climbed the beach. Kate and Owen shouted to the sky with joy too vast to be contained in words. Then they began to call Constance's name. When she didn't appear, Owen shouldered the knapsack and Kate snatched the mesh bag. They abandoned the *Nepenthe* at anchor and the Zodiac on the beach. With only some hastily grabbed supplies and the shotgun, they left the beach behind and followed the footprints up into the rocks.

Away from the water and the surf's cooling mist, the heat rose suddenly. They had walked into a wall of hot dry air that stood between the sun-heated rocks. Following the marks in the sand, Owen hustled higher up the crevice in the rocks. Soon he was climbing over boulders. When he glanced back at Kate, she shot him an angry look. She wanted him to hurry forward. Kate would keep up.

They arrived at the red and brown wall of the plateau itself. A deep vertical fissure formed a zigzagged chimney. It looked like a fast way to climb to the top of the plateau, but somehow it felt

wrong. Looking at it, Owen had the feeling that
Constance had not come this way. He looked
toward the west and saw a ghostly image of his
daughter, flitting in the heat waves rising above
sun-struck boulders. Had Constance moved west to
the distant crumbled shoulder of the plateau, or
had she climbed this chimney?

Owen had a strong feeling about the chimney.
He strapped the shotgun under the flap of the knapsack, reshouldered the knapsack, and began to
climb. Kate slung the mesh bag over her shoulder.
Carefully watching Owen's holds, she followed him
up the chimney.

It was thirty meters to the top of the plateau.
The bottom of the chimney had plenty of secure
holds. The fissure cut deep enough that the climb
was not all vertical. Toward the top of the chimney, the fissure drew closed as if healed. Smooth
of handholds, the sides of the fissure closed
together under a lip almost two meters deep. As
he climbed higher, Owen hoped he would see
some holds, but the higher he climbed, the
smoother it looked. Finally he arrived at the top,
with Kate just below him. The lip formed a roof
over his head. He could see no footholds or handholds.

"Kate, I don't see—"

Kate grunted and said, "Let me try."

She climbed up to his side. Finding a precarious
perch opposite him, she unslung the mesh bag and
handed it to him. With her back to the wall, she
braced her legs against the opposite wall and began
to walk up the last few meters. The chimney nar-
rowed toward the top, so that the angle of the join-

ing walls worked against her technique. Owen breathed heavily as he watched her climb, seemingly through the force of her will.

Precariously propped in the narrowing chimney by the strength of her legs, Kate began to sidle outwards. Underneath her was a sheer drop thirty meters down onto the rocks. Yet she seemed intent only on the edge of the lip.

With her right hand, she reached up for the edge. She could not reach. Her legs were beginning to tremble from the effort, but she continued to work her way outwards.

Kate tried for the edge again. This time, her hand reached. She felt along the edge for a good handhold. The rock was porous, chancy stuff, but one spot seemed as if it might be strong enough. Slowly she moved further out until her left hand, reaching up and over, could take hold next to the right. She took a deep breath and relaxed her legs.

Kate swung out. She could feel the inertia carry her too far; her handhold became precarious. She held onto the rock with all the might of her strong hands. Then her body swung slowly back and settled, to leave her hanging there in midair high above the rocks.

Now she had to do a chin-up from a flat hang. As she began to try, she realized that the climb had tired her arms. The muscles in her arms lacked the energy to pull her up. Kate knew that it was impossible for her to return to the chimney. Either she would climb onto the roof of the plateau, or she would fall to the rocks below.

She opened her mouth to shout, but Owen was already walking up the chimney. Wedging himself between two near-vertical faces of the chimney, he reached out and grabbed Kate's ankle.

"Now!" he shouted, as he pushed up against her ankle.

The boost unlocked Kate's arms. She chinned herself up. She could see beyond the edge onto the top of the plateau: a crack offered a possible handhold. She let go of her right hand and reached for the handhold. Adrenaline pushed her over the top. She found herself lying safe on the rocky top of the plateau. It took her several breaths to recover her senses.

Thousands of hours at his workbench had hardened Owen's muscles. He powered over the edge and onto the top of the plateau. Climbing to his feet, he freed the shotgun and shouldered the knapsack. Kate stood and slung the mesh bag over her shoulder.

"I'm sorry, Kate."

"Why? You saved my life."

"No, I was wrong. Constance didn't come this way. She must have climbed the plateau down that way." He pointed toward the west.

"How could you know that, Owen?"

He shook his head. "Everything . . . everything has a feel now. I don't understand why and I don't understand how . . . I don't know how to *read* or . . . I don't know how to feel it yet. But I think that she came up that way and she crossed over there, see? Where the ridge is over there. That's the way she went."

Kate studied her husband's face. "Are you all right, Owen?"

But Owen didn't hear her. As he stood, gazing

over the plateau and trying to divine the presence
of his daughter, the world's colors melted and its
shapes twisted. Lines of force usurped terrain, and
gravity took form. From the hard sun overhead
came streaming infinite rays, purity skewering the
earth.

God's-eye view . . .

Same as it ever was, but now he saw through the
surface of things. A feeling of glory swept through
Owen, as it sometimes had at his workbench, when
he finally visualized the shape that had been hiding
inside of the wood that he turned. Hiding from the
man who saw only with his eyes; not hiding from
the man who saw with his mind. A way that shaped
things; a shape that governed all ways. A force was
blowing through him. . . .

And there, there was Constance, an ovoid pearly
glow, drifting along an undulating line of force, far
in the distance, much further than he would have
guessed she had traveled.

"The maker is beginning to see."

"He must hurry; the soldiers of darkness are
close to his daughter."

As the world of rocks and dust returned to him,
Owen had a glimpse of someone: dark, heavy,
oppressive, evil. He whiffed a stench of rotten meat
and felt his entire body shivering as if this thing in
the shape of man had touched him. A soldier of
darkness.

Owen blinked as he stared toward the northwest.
He did not understand how, but he knew that
Constance was there, and near her were these sol-
diers of darkness.

"Owen?"

He turned and looked at Kate.

"Are you all right?" she asked.

"Come on. We have to hurry. She needs us."

The plateau was a dead, dry place. The rock underfoot was so hot that they could feel its heat through the soles of their shoes. Nothing even as succulent as cactus thrived here, only dried scrubs and weeds that had forced their way upwards from the cracks between the rocks, seeking a remorseless sun, which had granted the plants a short life before it killed them. The air smelled of dust and rock. Here, high above the surf, there was no smell of the sea.

They hiked for only an hour before they arrived at a dirt road that wended its way through a fault line in the mesa. Here the plateau softened to mounds of powdery brown dirt, baked by the relentless sun. A trail of small bootprints had marked the hillside descending into the fault line, which lay about ten meters below the roof of the plateau.

Kate and Owen descended into the fault line, half climbing down, half falling, stirring up great choking clouds of dust. At the bottom, they shared the last of their bottled water. The heat and the seeming airlessness between the walls was oppressive.

"We have to hurry," Owen said.

Kate nodded her head. Dust caked her hair and face. A drop of water running from her lips had formed a streak of mud upon her chin. Her eyes had a faraway look. She seemed to be thinking of something besides the pursuit of Constance.

Shotgun cradled in his hands, the backpack

forming an impression of hot sweat upon his back, Owen hiked up the dirt road. Kate followed him. Once, when he heard her footfalls lagging behind, he turned and offered his hand. Kate smiled and shook her head. Owen continued to reach out to her until she took his hand.

It seemed to him that his strength was flowing out through his hand into Kate. The flow came in waves: he could feel himself losing the strength as it flowed into Kate. Sometimes the sensation was so strong that he felt himself almost losing consciousness.

Owen was glad that he was able to help his wife. He wished that he had all of the strength in the world to give to her. Whenever he came close to losing consciousness, a part of him felt afraid and resentful, but he let that part of him fester in silence. Owen's idea of a husband and a father was someone who would give of himself until he was dead. A small man who resented the power he had to share was not Owen's idea of man.

Every now and then, Owen saw a small spoor left by Constance's boots. He worried when he saw her bootprints, because they looked so small and alone.

The dirt road was crossed with gullies cut by long-forgotten rainfalls and sudden desert floods. Sometimes the dirt road seemed more a path used by all-terrain vehicles. The fault line it followed cut through most of the hills, but there were still many heaves and sags of the earth, inclines and declines to climb and descend.

Owen and Kate topped a crest. From here they could glimpse the glinting sea as well as the next few winding stretches of the dirt road. Down to the left by a few hundred meters stood a zinc-roofed shack.

They descended the downslope, their horizon collapsing once again to the dirt mounds on either side of the road. As they approached the zinc-roofed shack, Owen let go of Kate's hand and clasped the shotgun in both hands.

The walls of old planks nailed horizontally were festooned with tattered, sun-bleached placards in Spanish. On the dirt ground in front of the building, two men lay sprawled.

Owen climbed the steps cut into the hill. He approached the two huge, fat Guatemalan men, lying half in shadow, half in sun. At first Owen thought they were dead, their corpses swollen by the sunlight. Then he realized that they were still breathing.

"What do you think happened?" he asked Kate.

Kate stood looking down at the two Guatemalans. She didn't seem interested.

"Do you think that they have water?" she asked.

Owen stepped inside the hut. Scattered about the packed-dirt floor were crude homemade benches, tables, and cots. He smelled something awful, the funk peculiar to the hovels of men who were both womanless and poor. Next to the raised-earth platform used for cooking, he found a stone jar. Opening the lid, he found water. Using a glazed clay cup, he and Kate drank deep of the cool clear water.

Before they left, Owen dragged the unconscious men into the shade of their hut. They continued on their way. With some cool water in

their bellies, the heat and dust seemed more toler-
able. Owen hiked, thinking of the two Guatemalans. Had they seen Constance? Were they victims of the sleeping sickness that was afflicting
Kate?

Half an hour later, they climbed a rise from
which they could see a paved highway running east
and west. A distant line of stationary shapes, inter-
spersed with brilliant reflections off glass and
chrome, suggested that the road was jammed with
traffic. Owen and Kate walked further until they
arrived at the junction of the dirt road with the
paved highway.

The traffic jam extended horizon to horizon.
Most of the vehicles were filled with people who
seemed to be suffering from the sleeping sickness.
Some cars were still moving along the soft shoulder,
occasionally pushing abandoned vehicles out of the
way.

Owen felt that they should turn and head west.
He and Kate walked along the highway. They over-
took an Indian family, the mother and father barely
five feet tall. The woman dressed in a typical Indian
fashion, while the man wore black trousers and a
faded red shirt. They carried bundles upon their
heads. A small girl and a teenaged boy, dressed as
their parents, walked behind them.

The Indians walked as if drugged. Owen handed
Kate the shotgun, and then he walked alongside
them, slightly in front so that he could see their
faces. The eyes of the parents and of the boy were
rolling as if from exhaustion. Only the girl seemed
alert. She even smiled at Owen. He tried to speak
half-forgotten high school Spanish.

"Where are you going?" he asked.

"Who knows?" the girl answered. "It seems to me a journey of fools."

"You are heading west," Owen said, for lack of a more astute comment. It surprised him how well he understood the girl's Spanish.

"The fools in the east move west, the fools in the west move east," the girl said, then smiled charmingly. "If there was a road running north and south, then fools from all corners of the world would join us here. I am happy to walk, though, because there are too many bad men near here."

"What bad men?"

"There are so many. All of the good men have gone to sleep in Hell, and all the devils have wakened to walk the earth."

"Have you seen a little blonde girl?"

"In my waking dreams, I saw a blonde girl who was walking alone near here. Without using words, she asked me for water, because she was very thirsty. Then the bad men came and scared me out of my waking dream."

"Who? Who took her away?"

"Bad men who called her a dangerous enemy, because she was talking so strongly into their heads. She made the mistake of talking the wrong way with the wrong people."

"Where did they go?"

The Indian girl pointed with her chin toward the northwest. "Out that way, toward a town called Dulce Nombre de Santa Maria."

Owen stopped walking. The Indian family continued westward. Owen searched the line of cars until he found a beat-up truck with the keys still in the ignition. A young Indian man sat slumped over the wheel. Owen hauled him out and dragged him into the rear seat of a sedan stopped behind the truck. As he started the truck's motor, Kate climbed into the passenger seat. Owen drove the truck down the slope toward the northwest, in the direction that the girl had indicated was toward the village of Dulce Nombre de Santa Maria.

N I N E

OWEN DROVE HEADLONG OVER HARD-BAKED BLACK VOLcanic sands. The old truck lurched and bucked on worn, worthless shocks over gullies and rocks. Owen's and Kate's heads banged painfully against the roof of the cab. The truck groaned like a wounded steel beast. The stuffy air in the cab reeked of volcanic dust and burning crankcase oil. Glancing down, Owen saw black powder rising through rusted cracks in the floor. In the dirty rearview mirror, he could see a huge dark cloud of dust following the truck. The west was reddening, but light still filled the sky.

"Go faster, Owen," Kate said through clenched teeth.

There was no road, only tire tracks cutting across the wasteland. A sensation of pressure in his chest made breathing painful. His fingers ached from clenching the wheel. Yet he was less aware of these details than he was of the tyranny of time. Everything was moving so frustratingly slowly that he yearned to punch through this oppressiveness that made the air thick and suffocating, that slowed the turning of the truck's wheels, that resisted his progress toward his daughter.

"—strike at them from afar," a woman's voice said.

"You need to take ownership of your own powers," a man's voice answered.

"—always tired of their condescension," the woman's voice went on. "I knew somehow that they were inferior. All my life, I knew that they were not . . . not my equals, somehow, but it is only now that I—"

"If you follow that path all the way down, you will find a mass grave," a third voice said.

Owen sucked in breath. He bit his lip and fought an urge to scream. Too much pressure, too much uncertainty. As the world was coming apart, the pieces were changing into an unrecognizable pattern. The small part of the old world he had wanted to protect—his family—was disintegrating. Constance, taken by strangers. Kate, languishing in a way he didn't understand.

Owen resisted the temptation to decide that he was mad, stop the truck, watch the sunset, and let his delusions wheel and rise and fall as they might. But no, no . . . he had to keep going. He could not surrender. Somehow he had to insist on himself, keep true to himself and his world, even if his world belonged only in his mind.

He reached over with his right hand and grabbed Kate's hand, but her hand was limp. Glancing over, he saw that Kate's head was rolling on her shoulders. Through her half-closed eyelids, the whites of her eyes showed. She looked half-dead.

He glanced through the windshield and saw dimly a paved road running north. The truck was about to ram headlong into the drainage ditch alongside the road. Owen stood on the brakes and spun the steering wheel toward the left. As the truck lurched over the ditch, his head banged against the roof cab. Owen pointed the truck up the road toward the north. He looked over and saw that Kate seemed unhurt.

He stopped the truck and tried to turn on the cab light, but it didn't work. In the growing darkness, he ran his fingertips through Kate's hair, but there were no wounds. Owen searched through the backpack, found the medical kit, filled a syringe with 10 cc of the amphetamine and jabbed it into Kate's dirty arm. She moaned in pain and then jerked as if electrified. Owen watched as she seemed to fight her way to the surface.

"Come on, Kate," he said. "Come back."

"No, I . . . want . . . I don't want to," Kate muttered. "It's too . . . beautiful."

For a moment, Owen felt the sleeping sickness that was claiming Kate and so many millions. The sleeping sickness seeped into his muscles, nerves, and fibers, all relaxing, as his joints melted to liquid wax. A delicious sensation of well-being seeped through him. All he had to do was turn inward and allow the sleeping world to become his own. . . .

This way of being felt wonderful, but it was not right. Owen forced himself to return to the dusty desert. Kate's eyes were opening. As his vision returned, he could see the returning spark of intelligence in her eyes.

"Owen."

"That's a bad place, Kate."

"No, it's beautiful," she answered. "It's like the most beautiful dream. On the other side, there's paradise. The most wonderful feeling. And there are so many of us growing close to one another, closer and closer to paradise."

"No," Owen said. "It's just dying."

"Owen, what's . . . happening?"

"It's not our world anymore," he answered. "Somehow we've lost our world."

"Why, Owen?"

Owen cranked the engine and began to drive north, in what he hoped was the direction of Dulce Nombre de Santa Maria. He turned on the headlights; a sole headlight, the left one, cast a feeble light upon the concrete texture of the road.

"I don't know," he said.

Up ahead, he could see the lights of a small town. He turned off the headlight as the truck slowly approached the outskirts of the town, passing single-story zinc-roofed block buildings of faded yellow, pink, and green. Owen pulled the truck over onto the shoulder and parked it next to a cinder block building missing its roof.

"Kate, can you stay here? Make sure that no one steals the truck?"

In the darkness, her expression pensive and sad, she gazed at him and nodded.

Owen debated whether to take the shotgun. If a large group had taken Constance, he couldn't take her back with a single firearm. He handed the shotgun to Kate and thumbed open the safety.

"Safety's off," he said.

"Yes."

"I'll go and see what I can do," he said.

"I'll wait for you here," Kate said.

"Wait for me."

"I will."

Exiting the cab, Owen stood on stiff legs and breathed deeply of the cooling desert air. Alone, unarmed, he began to walk into the town of Dulce Nombre de Santa Maria. Darkness was spreading across the desert floor. Shadows were deepening among the block buildings of the town. In front of a marketplace, an obscenely fat dog stood on its splayed and sagging legs, bared its fangs and growled. Owen crossed the street to avoid the dog. Even from the farside of the street, he could smell the stench of rotten blood. Madly protective of the meat market's scraps, the dog continued growling until Owen turned the corner. Other than the dog, the outskirts of the town were deserted, but up ahead, he could hear the hoarse shouting of a crowd.

He found himself in the shadows of the ruin of a colonial cathedral. Long poles at haphazard angles buttressed the sagging façade of the cathedral, forming almost an arch as the heavy head of the façade sought its rest upon the ground. Owen wended his way through the maze of poles, taking advantage of the deep shadow there. At the end of the ruin, he stood behind two stacked stone blocks and looked out at the public square, a concrete plaza with a derelict wooden bandstand.

The hundred people crowding the square were carrying flashlights, guns, and machetes. They were stacking wood at the base of iron lampposts.

The air was thick with smoke, fumes of alcohol, and the smell of roasting flesh. Owen heard frightened cries in Spanish invoking Jesus Christ and the Virgin Mary. As he witnessed the strange behavior of the mob, his blood began to race. He wanted to leave the darkness and seek his daughter. The crowd shifted and moved constantly. He caught a glimpse of a man tied to a lamppost across the square. His head hung down limply. The crowd had beaten him to death or unconsciousness.

Across the square, a group of people was bearing a large litter that held a statue of a black Christ. A cross on its shoulder and a crown of thorns on its head, the statue wore a purple satin robe. Gold chains swung from its neck and arms. Chanting, swaying back and forth, the people took two steps forward, one step back.

Owen watched this bizarre scene for several minutes as he tried to think what to do. Then he felt the ground below him begin a fine vibration. Golden sparkles rose from the earth, first singly, then in constellations; finally whole seas of gold sparkles rose from the ground, washing through Owen, the cathedral, the mob, and the night sky. A great cry went up: ecstatic shouts, screams of panic. The sparkles faded. A cool green fire rushed from head to head, running across the limbs and forms of the mob.

Owen felt a surge of power jolt through him. He felt as if he were the most powerful man alive. He stepped out of his hiding place and walked among the raving mob. He pushed his way through to the center of the square.

With an anguished scream, the people bearing the litter faltered and tripped over one another. The heavy litter tilted to one side and then tumbled over, spilling the statue of the black Christ and its gold jewelry onto the cement. People trapped under the litter screamed in panic and pain. A woman rushed forward and gathered the statue in her arms, raising it from the ground. A young man shouldered the cross.

Holding a flaming torch aloft, a heavyset, unshaven Guatemalan man came rushing across the plaza. He tossed his torch onto a stack of wood under a lamppost. Owen looked at the figure tied above the now-lighted fire and realized that she was a young blonde girl. His daughter. Constance.

Owen dashed forward and plunged bodily into the woodpile, kicking the flaming sticks and boards away, breaking up the pile, swatting it away with his bare hands. A heavy mass struck him from the side, knocking him onto the flaming wood. Owen wrestled with the mass as it took the form of the heavyset Guatemalan. He jammed his fist against the side of the man's head, drew back his fist to strike him again but realized that the Guatemalan had gone completely limp. Owen heaved the inert mass of the man from atop him. He leaped to his feet and grabbed a long piece of wood as a club. Eyes wild, Owen shouted and swung the club as a warning.

Two men charged him. Owen clubbed one man in the temple, stunning him, but the other rushed in, slamming into Owen and bowling him over. Then the weight of another man, and two men, and more men pressed down on Owen with such oppressiveness that he thought his ribs would crack. He tried to shout, but he had no air in his lungs. He struggled against the weight to keep his bones from snapping.

A hard object smashed against his head. Lights danced, a damp heaviness weighted the air; he felt an almost delicious descent into unconsciousness. The next he was aware, rough fiber ropes were burning around his wrists, tied together behind his back. A metal pole pressed against his back. He was standing as best he could, propped up by unfriendly hands against the lamppost. The breath of the man pushing him smelled of rum.

Beyond the man's shoulder, people were running, shouting, and gibbering. A man knelt on the cement, hands clasped together before his chest in prayer, tears streaming down his face as he stared up into the sky. A woman was tearing her clothes and screaming in an Indian tongue. Others were setting torches to piles of wood under men tied to lampposts.

He turned to look at the nearest lamppost. He was shocked when his eyes met Constance's eyes, wide-open but glazed and unseeing. Constance's muscles had tightened her face into a mask of fear. The sight of her struck Owen with the force of a blow.

A young Guatemalan man ran up and piled an armful of splintered wood under Constance. He shouted to another man bearing a flaming torch. The torchbearer began to advance on Constance. Owen tried to shout, but his throat seemed dried shut. He coughed and managed to croak, then shout hoarsely.

From the pandemonium, a priest wearing a black cassock and peasant's pants appeared. He rushed toward the torchbearer, shouting in Spanish. The priest grabbed the torchbearer by the forearm. For a moment, the two men struggled, the torchbearer's face locked in an expression of crazed terror while the priest just looked feverish. Then the torchbearer swung his free arm up into the priest's belly, doubling him over. The torchbearer pushed the priest down to the ground and then advanced on Constance.

His daughter was about to be burned alive at the stake. Owen strained against the rope. Tears sprung to his eyes, his face flushed hotly, all his muscles clenched, as he bellowed with all the might of his being.

"Stop!" Owen shouted. "No! No!"

At the height of his desperation, Owen had a strong flashing impression that his brother was present. He even thought that he saw a ghostly image of Harley, standing there behind the torchbearer, staring with hate and disgust at the man who was about to murder Constance. For a moment, Owen felt relief, because he thought that Harley was going to save his daughter, but then the ghostly image vanished.

"Owen . . ." said the voice of Harley in his mind, but then the voice, too, disappeared.

The torchbearer hesitated, turned and looked over at Owen with a stupid expression. He seemed puzzled. Whatever he thought, he began to lower the torch toward the stack of wood under Constance.

The priest struggled to his feet, advanced on the torchbearer, joined his hands into a doubled fist and then brought his doubled fist down with all his strength onto the neck of the torchbearer, felling him to his knees.

The torch landed on the wood. Immediately, flames began to lick upwards. The priest looked down at what he had done, then waded into the growing fire, kicking the wood away from Constance. As the priest was clearing away the fire, the young man who had built the pile reappeared from the crowd. Picking up a long, viciously splintered piece of wood, he shoved it through the priest's back.

Howling with pain, the priest collapsed to a heap at Constance's feet. Muttering curses, the young man and the torchbearer began to kick the wood over the priest. They shouted to an old woman, who came running with more wood. She cried out when she saw the priest, his legs convulsing from agony. The young man cuffed the old woman across the face, causing the wood to fall to the ground. Piece by piece, he picked up the wood and heaved it onto the pile. Now the torchbearer stood next to Constance, waiting for a moment before he relit the fire.

Owen strained against the ropes. He felt helpless. He could not stop the murder of his daughter.

On the far end of the square, a sudden commotion swept the crowd. For a moment, Owen thought he heard a peal of trumpets. Someone was coming. The night sky seemed to open; green lights flared to a golden brightness. A shaft of light illuminated one figure as he strode into the square.

It was a man, naked and barefoot. Translucent as the wax of a burning white candle, his white skin seemed to glow from an inner light. His long, dirty blond hair was twisted into skanky dreadlocks that fell past his shoulders. He had the sculptured physique of a paragon. As he strode fearlessly into the square, other men and women followed him, but the golden light did not illuminate them.

Machete raised high, a Guatemalan charged the man, who wheeled to face him and extended his arm with a flowing motion, palm-out. Struck with the force of a battering ram in the belly, the Guatemalan buckled to his knees and collapsed onto his side.

Gracefully, the naked man resumed his progress toward the center of the square. The crowd parted before him. A young boy was chattering something. The man raised his hand; the boy fell silent.

In the center of the square, the man knelt and spun. He swooped up and turned, palms outward, fingers stiffened and yet curved so that his hands formed the shapes of spears or jungle leaves. He danced a spinning dance, turning, his body the center of a revolving force, his gestures recognizing and influencing an invisible vortex.

A drunk shouted incoherently. The man gestured, his arm pushing outward from his abdomen toward the drunkard. A ghostly ball of white light erupted from his midsection, followed his gesture, and knocked the drunkard onto his back. The Guate-

malans nearby stepped back. Several fell to
their knees; others fell to their bellies.

With the grace of a dancing god of death, the
man flowed into other positions, still spinning,
sometimes with sweeping gestures of harmony,
other times with more linear, forceful gestures, as if
points in the vortex required direct adjustment.
Lights struck several men, laying them onto their
backs.

Now the square was silent except for the moans
of the wounded. Owen felt calmness seep through
him as he realized that everything was going to be
all right. The stranger had come to save them.
Relaxing against the lamppost, Owen became
aware that his body ached from fatigue.

Guatemalans began to sit, kneel, or lie down.
Slowly the crowd lowered itself to the ground. The
man continued the dance until the wounded had
stopped moaning.

Then he stood upright. In the most natural way,
he walked toward Owen. He had a broad face with
an unusually square jaw. His wide-set eyes were a
sun-faded celestial blue. His waxy complexion
made him seem slightly surreal. The man smiled
and said, "Hello, Owen Keegan. I'm Erik Van
Meers."

"Hello," Owen said stupidly.

Van Meers moved to the back of the lamppost
and untied Owen's wrists. Owen stepped free from
the lamppost. From across the square a woman
muttered a curse in Spanish. Absentmindedly, Van
Meers gestured; the voice fell silent.

"Let's get Constance out of this," Van Meers said.
Together they walked over to the lamppost.

While Van Meers untied Constance, Owen moved the wood off the priest, but he found that the priest was dead. The shard of wood had gone clear through his abdomen. They stood in a pool of dark blood.

"He's—"

"Yes, of course," Van Meers said gently. His accent was Nordic, a singsong that seemed charming and quaint. "There are three dead men here. Too bad about the priest. He had strength. There's a boy here who is strong. The rest of them—"

Van Meers swept his arm dismissively at the mass of prostrated people.

"There were four bad fighters here. I had to put them down. The rest of them—they are the trash of the old age. They wanted to kill your daughter because they fear what they don't understand. She must belong to the new age. We guard against the trash for a little time longer. Then they'll be gone forever. Here, take your daughter."

Van Meers handed Constance to Owen. Tenderly, Owen hugged his daughter. She was stiff with fear, but Owen did not worry: she was alive. He would make everything else better again.

Still embracing his daughter, Owen turned to thank Van Meers, but he had already walked away. Owen followed. Van Meers seemed to be surveying the crowd. He pulled one small boy to his feet.

"Vas a sequir a mi?" Van Meers asked the boy.

"Si, señor."

"Entonces, desde hoy, yo soy tu amo. Sigues a mi, y no tengas miedo de nada, ni de los hombres, ni de los

*espiritus malos, ni cualquiera criatura. Yo soy el mas
fuerte de todos.*"

Smiling, the boy rose and fell in behind Van
Meers, who turned to speak to Owen. "For you I
traveled one hundred kilometers last night. There
was a lot to do, too, and we have a long way to go
still. You'll be coming with us."

"Who are you?" Owen asked.

Van Meers smiled crookedly, as if he were exer-
cising his patience with a poorly behaved child.
"Who and what I am is a big journey to take," he
said. "You, you can begin with knowing that I am
the man that saved your life. I saved the life of your
daughter. Is this a good starting?"

"Yes," Owen said. "It's a very good start. Thank
you."

"Start. Yes. Start. Well, we begin. There are
mountains to climb."

"Where are you going?"

"We are going to the highlands."

"Why?" Owen asked.

Van Meers shook his head impatiently. He
rubbed his forehead as if pained. He beckoned to a
Hispanic man with handsome, regular features,
who hurried forward and took Owen by the arm.
Still rubbing his head, Van Meers began to wander
out of the square.

"I'll explain later," the Hispanic man said. "I'm
Hector. Erik is tired now, and please, we must get
out of here while he is still strong."

"All right."

They followed Van Meers out of the square. A
number of people were waiting for them in the

shadows beyond the tumbledown cathedral. Among them stood Kate. She rushed forward and grabbed Constance from Owen's embrace. As Kate smothered Constance's face with kisses, Owen put his arm around Kate's waist. Joined in an embrace, the Keegans followed the stranger named Erik Van Meers through the darkened streets of Dulce Nombre de Santa Maria.

ON THE DARK SIDE OF THE LAST STREETLIGHT, Erik Van Meers staggered, stopped, and stood as if listening to the darkness. Abruptly he collapsed facedown onto the muddy street. Several of his followers rushed forward and picked him up. His head swayed like a sack full of rocks. Owen watched with some concern, but Van Meers's followers didn't seem worried.

Hector shouted something in Spanish and pointed toward the distant mountains. The group of Van Meers's followers, numbering some twenty people, turned from the street and began to walk toward the mountains. After pulling clothes onto the body of their leader, Hector and several others carried Van Meers between them.

Owen stood with Kate and Constance, watching the men disappearing into the black sand desert. He couldn't think of a reason to follow this group, except for loyalty toward Van Meers, who had saved their lives. Such notions of indebtedness to strangers, though, were not strong in Owen. His first loyalty was to his family. So, hugging Constance to his chest, with one arm around Kate's waist, he headed for the old truck. Kate seemed wooden and unresponsive. A small boy came running after them.

"Hey where you going?"

"Home," Owen answered.

"No home you. The *señor* want you come us!"

"Not tonight," Owen said.

"The *señor* will mad you."

"Tell him I'm sorry," Owen answered.

As he approached the old truck, Constance began to struggle in a nightmarish way. She pitched backwards, her eyes rolled in her head, and her hands clutched Owen's shoulders as if she had the night terrors. Owen spoke to her soothingly, struggling to keep his own anxiety out of his voice.

"What's wrong, Constance?" Kate asked. "What's wrong, darling?"

Constance moaned, shivered, and went limp. Owen heard some voices from the direction of the town. He piled Constance into the old truck. Kate jumped in and scooped her daughter into her lap. Owen started the truck, turned left, and headed down the paved road away from the town. The single working headlight played dimly over the rushing surface of the road.

"That's it," Owen said. "We did it."

"I don't understand what happened," Kate said.

"I don't either. But we got Constance back."

"It was so horrible," Kate said. "She's terrified."

"That was . . . a terrifying experience."

"I don't understand. You left; then there were Van Meers and his people. He seemed so different.

They took me with them to the square. I saw Constance and you, but they held me back. Then Van Meers did that strange dance. I don't know, Owen. What's going on?"

"The world has changed somehow. Van Meers seems to belong to the new world."

"And you?"

Owen sat silently for a long time. Finally he spoke. "When the lights rose out of the ground, I felt like the most powerful man in the world, like I could do anything, but . . . I didn't know how. It was just a feeling. When I saw Van Meers come into the square, I understood somehow. He's learned how to control the power flowing through him."

"What power?"

"The power of the new world."

"And Constance?"

"This world is good for her."

"And . . . me?"

Owen looked over at Kate, whose eyes seemed sunken into her head. Even as he watched, a wave of inattention swept through her.

"This is not your world, Kate," he said finally. "Not yet."

Kate's silence had a deep, heavy feel that seemed to enlarge the space between them.

"I know," she said. "I can feel you both going away. I want to stay with you, Owen. I do. I don't want to leave you. But I don't know how to hold on."

"You have to fight, Kate."

"I have been fighting. It's the hardest I ever fought in my life, but I can feel myself draining away. The other place . . . seems so much more beautiful."

"I'll help," Owen said. "I won't leave you, Kate. Wherever you go, I'll go with you."

"No. You have to stay with Constance and take care of her."

"I won't lose you, Kate."

"No," Kate said, her voice growing dreamy. "No."

Looking back at Kate, Owen saw that her eyes were closing. For a moment, he thought it might be good for her to sleep, but then he realized that she was sinking into something far more profound than sleep. He sensed that she was dying.

"Kate!" Owen shouted.

Her eyelids barely flickered. Her hands slackened around Constance.

Owen pulled the truck off the road. He searched for the medical kit, finally finding it under trash on the floor. In the uncertain light, he filled the injection needle with 10 cc of the amphetamine. He poked the needle into Kate's arm and plunged the drug into her. Her body quivered, but her eyes remained shut.

"Kate!"

He shook her, but he was unable to wake her. He tried to wake Constance. Constance's eyes opened, but she began to whimper and thrash. Owen found himself wrestling with his daughter, trying to restrain her panic.

He felt himself panicking. He had never felt so alone and helpless. He had thought that he had saved his wife and daughter, but he had merely carried their bodies away from physical danger. They were both in a hideous danger that he didn't understand. He needed help, but he didn't know anyone who could help. Except—

Except Van Meers. He was the only master of this new world whom Owen had met.

As soon as Constance lapsed back into an uneasy sleep, Owen started the motor and turned the truck off the road and onto the desert sands. Help beckoned from the north under the distant mountains.

Here the sands were deeper and finer. Sometimes the balding tires began to slip in deeper patches of sand. Owen cursed and tugged at the wheel, trying to negotiate the truck through the deeper patches. Often, he had to reach out with his right hand and resettle Constance onto the lap of her unconscious mother.

"—false messiahs."

"It's cruel but efficient. Make them dig their own graves."

"He burned himself out, that one."

For the first time, Owen did not try to block out these voices in his head. Under the cloudy night sky, surrounded by black sands illuminated by a dim headlight, he opened his mind. He called out to the people who were speaking in his head. He felt his thoughts expanding, reaching out for the vast traces of a network. Almost immediately, he encountered another entity. He had a glimpse of dark eyes without a face, gazing at him with interest.

"That's the way," the woman said.

"Yes," Owen said in his thoughts.

"I've been waiting for you to turn to me."

"Who are you?"

"Irma."

"Where are you?"

"In the mount—"

A wave of disorientation swept over Owen. For a moment, he sat in the nighttime coolness of a long-needle pine forest. He could smell the soothing green smell of the pine. Before him stood a woman, tall and voluptuous. For a long moment, he felt himself thinking her thoughts. He felt that she needed his help in a struggle with creatures far stronger than herself. He turned his mind's eye toward those creatures, but one was hidden . . . and the other was . . . Van Meers. He felt her skills, more developed than his own, but in the reflection of her mind, he saw himself and realized that if he survived, he would grow far stronger than she. Stronger, even, than Van Meers. As he stared at her, her eyes grew in his field of vision until he was staring into the depth of her pupils, from where the black desert bloomed. He was driving the truck across the wasteland.

"—ains. Mountains."

"Can you help me?" Owen asked.

"You're very far away. It's only because we share this—" A word for a concept he didn't understand was spoken. "—that I can be with you at all. Be careful. Van Meers is a—"

Then her voice faded, like the tenuous reception of a distant radio station lost due to changes in the night's upper atmosphere.

He thought he heard another voice, sounding as if it were within the truck. Looking down, he could see that Constance was mumbling inarticulately in her sleep, which was unusual. Owen reached over and touched Kate's cheek. Her skin was cool to the touch.

Owen felt nauseated and weak. Other voices in

his head, murmuring nonsense, gradually died. The
only sound was the groaning of the truck. He
steered more toward the east. They were ahead of
him, he thought. Not too far away.

He drove for another few minutes. He was so
exhausted that he didn't notice when the truck's
motor died. He tugged at the wheel, stupidly, left
and right. The truck slowed to a stop. Owen sat in
the sudden total silence. Mechanically, he turned
the ignition key, but the motor refused to start. After
a minute, he realized that the truck was out of gas.

They were ahead of him, adding distance with
every moment as they hiked northward toward the
mountains. Owen pushed down the old door handle and swung open the creaking door. He stepped
out, walked around to the other side of the truck,
and opened the passenger door.

He couldn't carry both his wife and his daughter.
He stood staring down at them. Placing his fingertips against Kate's neck, he felt that her pulse was
slow and shallow.

Owen refused to abandon Kate. Even if they all
three died in the desert, he would not abandon her.
Owen shook Constance's shoulder.

"Wake up, sweetheart. Wake up."

His remaining strength seemed to flow through
his arm into Constance. Slowly she opened her
eyes.

"Yes, Daddy?" she asked, her voice chiming with
the innocence of a child.

Owen stood, astounded that his daughter had
spoken. Constance stared at him with a natural and
curious expression.

"Constance?" he asked.

"Yes, Daddy?" Her voice was so beautiful; it sounded as sweet and new as the voice of a baby angel.

"Are you all right?"

"Yes, Daddy. The men bad to me, but I good now."

"You . . . you can talk?"

"Constance can talk, Daddy. Siz word noises only."

Owen scooped up his daughter and hugged her to his chest. Euphoria blossomed around his head like a flower of fire. This was the moment of his repressed dreams, the happiness for which he had not dared hope. To hold her, healthy, whole, able to speak with him in his world, was a joy beyond any joy he had ever experienced. Owen gave up to the sky a great glad noise. He spoke a word older than language: the word of pure human joy.

Hugging her, he could feel the nearness of her mind. The physical distance was important, he realized. The effects of these phenomena differed over distance. He had a glimpse of bright patterns, spiraling geometric forms, an alien paradigm. It was as if the entirety of his daughter's mind was designed along lines as otherworldly as the lines of *AnNautilus*. Owen realized that his mind, his art, and his daughter were all in harmony.

"Can you walk?"

"What?"

"Can you walk?"

"Where at we going, Daddy?"

"To see a man who will help your mommy."

Constance smiled. "Smart Daddy."

"Yes."

"And the bad men, Daddy? The bad men hurt me?"

"They're gone. Daddy made them go away."

"Good."

Constance crawled out of the truck. She stood, hugging her father's waist for support.

"Mommy is sleepyhead."

"I know."

Owen scooped Kate's limp and heavy body into his arms, then turned and faced the north. He left everything else in the truck. It was difficult to walk in the sands carrying the burden of Kate's body. Beyond the illumination of the single headlight, the desert was so dark that Owen had to feel his way with his feet. Constance trudged alongside her father, her fingers curled through one of his belt loops.

"Mommy is too sleepy. Is she all right, Daddy?"

"Yes, darling," Owen said, his voice cracking. "She's just very tired."

"Me, too."

"You're a brave girl, Constance."

"No one is brave as Constance. I'm also the best girl."

"Yes," Owen said, his voice choking. "Yes, you are."

They hiked in silence for several minutes. Owen could feel his biceps begin to burn. He began to worry that even though his will was strong, his body would betray him.

After another ten minutes, he was forced to sling Kate stomach-down over his right shoulder. The relief to his arms was wonderful, but the weight of two bodies oppressed his lower back. His legs were beginning to tire, but Owen felt that he could go on, if not indefinitely, at least for a long time.

He thought that he could see a greenish glow up ahead in the darkness. For a moment, he thought it was a trick of his vision, but slowly he realized that something was out there.

"Come on, princess."

He walked forward as quickly as he could, his stride shortened because of the burden of Kate's body.

"Those are the men," Constance said.

"I hope so."

Soon the greenish glow was distinct enough that he could make out individual forms. They were moving northward, except for one, which seemed stationary, growing larger as they approached. A rent opened in the high overcast, allowing a smear of starlight to shine down on the desert. The stationary greenish glow slowly took on human form: a man, Hector, who stood waiting for them. His arms were crossed across his chest, his weight on one leg, the idle leg in front, in the stance of a man who took his rest standing.

"So you decided that you need the *señor* after all," he said.

"Yes, I did."

"One doesn't accept the help of the *señor,* show him your backside by way of thanks, then come crawling back to him, asking for further favors."

"I'm sorry."

"Don't ask me for forgiveness," Hector said. "Ask the *señor.*"

"I'll ask him."

"First let me warn you. If he forgives you, then

you will be of the tribe. You'll fight his fight. You'll belong to us, and we'll belong to you."

"What is the tribe's fight?"

"Our enemies are the enemies that Van Meers chooses."

"My wife is dying."

"I'm sorry. Many people are dying."

"Does he know how to save her?"

"Of course."

"All right, then. I'll join your tribe."

"If that is the *señor*'s desire. Come on."

Owen took a step forward, put his foot down in a depression, stumbled, and fell to one knee. He barely managed to keep Kate from falling to the earth. Hector stooped to help raise up Kate. With a twinge of misgiving, Owen allowed Hector to lift his wife from his arms.

In a matter of minutes, they caught up with the rest of the tribe, which had stopped to rest. Hector walked to Van Meers, who sat on a volcanic rock, his followers spread out at his feet.

Van Meers was glowing palely as if from his own inner light. He looked at Hector, then the woman cradled in his arms; then, his face empty of emotion, he looked at Owen and Constance. He turned away and spoke to one of his followers, who laughed. Owen stepped closer. Van Meers turned and stared, his blue eyes like pale fires.

"My wife is dying," Owen said.

"You should let her go."

"No," Owen said. "She's my wife. I won't let her go."

"Then go down with her."

"No. She has to live."

Van Meers sighed. "We need our energy to build the new world. You're asking me to waste our energy to save a scrap of the old world."

"Yes, I am."

"And why?"

"Because I love her."

"Then save her."

"I . . . I can't. I don't know how."

"Why should I save you twice in one night?"

"Because you can. For the love of humanity."

Van Meers stood and stretched. "Which humanity? You don't understand what you're asking. You're asking me to connect myself to a great, heavy mass of people, who are going down to a place that is death. I have to move up here—" Van Meers gestured, his hands flowing at a level above his shoulders. "—and you want me to reach down here." He reached below his knees and pantomimed lifting up a great weight. "Then millions of them will reach up for me like drowning men grabbing a rescuer and dragging him down with them. They'll kill me trying to take me down to their false paradise."

"All right," Owen said. "What is it that you need from me? What is the price?"

"You," Van Meers said. "And Constance."

"How so?"

"All of you. If you want this one to live, then you and your daughter must give yourselves to me."

"You're asking too much."

Van Meers shrugged, turned, and began to walk toward the mountains. The others stood and followed him. Hector walked over to Owen. "I'm sorry," he said, as he handed Kate to him.

Owen embraced his wife. As the others left them

alone in the darkness, he kissed Kate's cool lips. Owen sunk to the ground and folded Kate deeper in his embrace. Constance knelt and patted Owen's head; then she stroked her mother's face.

"Poor Mommy."

Kate's breathing was shallow. Owen looked up and watched the backs of the strangers as they disappeared into the darkness.

"Constance," he said.

"Yes, Daddy."

"Do you trust that man?"

"The Van Meers man?"

"Yes."

"He's a clever man."

"Do you trust him?"

"Trust is the love. I love you, Daddy."

"He's the only one who can save Mommy."

"Ask him, Daddy."

"I don't trust him."

"Don't worry, Daddy. I'll save you."

"You're not afraid of him?"

Constance laughed, her laughter musical with innocence. "Oh no. He's a funny man. He thinks he knows Constance. He wants to own the wind and the sun and the stars. But we are much bigger than talk-talk. Don't worry about the funny man, Daddy. He is today. Talk-talk. I'll stay with you, Daddy. Don't worry. Save the sleepy mommy."

"Van Meers!" Owen shouted, almost howling. "Van Meers!"

Owen stood, raising Kate from the ground. He stumbled after the tribe, shouting for Van Meers. Minutes later, he reached the rearguard of the tribe. Hector tried to intercept him.

"You've rejected him twice today," Hector said. "Don't go unless—"

Owen shouldered past Hector. He stumbled forward, carrying Kate through the center of the tribe. He reached Van Meers, passed him, turned, and held Kate in front of him, blocking his way.

"All right," he said. "The three of us. If you take one of us, you take us all."

Van Meers sneered at Owen. He seemed about to hit him. Finally, he shrugged and said, "More than you know."

With a whiplash motion, Van Meers struck out at Kate, his hand stopping near her face. An electric jolt coursed through Owen as Kate convulsed and her eyes shot open. Van Meers walked around them. Kate coughed and began to move in Owen's arms. Owen lowered her until she was cradled in his arms as he knelt. She wrapped her arms around his neck.

"It was so beautiful," she said. "Why did you—"

"Kate."

"Why . . ."

"Stay with me. Stay."

"I will. Help me."

Constance reached and patted her mother's head.

"Don't be so sleepy, Mommy."

"What?" Kate cried. She twisted in Owen's arms and looked at her daughter, who had been mute for ten years.

"Don't be so sleepy, Mommy," Constance said in the voice of a child angel.

"Come here, honey," Kate said, hugging Constance as she began to sob, for only the second time that Owen had known her: the first time for the anguish of losing her daughter, the second time for the joy of finding her whole. Owen's throat ached as he gathered his arms around his family. If it had been within his power to halt time, then his world would have stopped on this moment. He and his family would have remained together and safe, in this embrace, for all of eternity.

Yet the wind moved upon the desert. The Earth continued to spin under the sphere of the heavens. What humans understand as time flowed forward relentlessly.

After a long moment, the Keegans rose and began to walk together toward the looming mountains. The high mist had blown southward, revealing the hogback ridges of the dark volcanic mountains, which cut fantastic shapes against the starfield. Ahead of them, Van Meers hiked farther up the black sand wasteland. The eerie white glow that surrounded him was their uncertain beacon.

E
L
E
V
E
N

THAT NIGHT, THEIR SECOND NIGHT IN THE YOSEM-
ite valley, when a fine cold rain began to fall,
Harley learned what creatures came to Axel as he
slept. He and the boy took refuge in a tent village at
the base of a granite cliff. The rain pattered soothingly on the white canvas of the tent's roof. Sitting
down on the cot, the boy resisted sleep, until, seemingly by reflex, he laid his head down on the cot
and lost consciousness.

Watching him, Harley wondered what would happen to the boy. Although in the old world Harley had
never liked children, he cared for the little orphaned
boy who faced this strange new world with such
bravery. Harley wasn't sure whether he was taking
care of the boy, or whether the boy was taking care of
him, but for the first time in his life, Harley was experiencing a paternal instinct, the strength of which surprised him. He never had thought that he would care
about anybody more than he cared for himself.

He found himself growing sleepy. He began to nod. In the twilight between wakefulness and sleep, he found himself sharing what he thought were Axel's dreams.

At first, the creatures appeared to be benevolent. Long white spectral figures with wisps of white tendrils and pearly luminescence floated in from the darkness. Harley in the form of Axel felt warm, safe, and happy. The figures came closer and embraced Harley as Axel. They began to caress him. He felt anxious, but he didn't understand why.

Slowly the creatures took more the form of praying mantises while remaining white and wispy. Harley as Axel had a distant impression that they were feeding as they caressed him, but at first he didn't understand what they were feeding upon.

He felt himself growing weaker. His sleep, no longer restful, felt drugged or diseased. Something was happening to him that was rendering him weaker and less than what he was.

It couldn't be the visitors. They were his friends. They had come to help guard him while he slept. He should forget his worry. Everything was going to be all right.

No, it was wrong. The visitors weren't his friends. They were eating him and draining his strength. They were feeding on his brain.

It was difficult to waken, as if the creatures had fed first upon his will to survive. Harley as Axel struggled against them. At first he thought that he would drown and die in their embrace, but he was able to resist the temptation to surrender. He forced himself to continue to struggle.

Finally he fought himself free. The creatures

evaporated like mist in the midmorning light. He found himself sitting upright on a cot, staring wide-eyed at Axel as the boy tried to lift himself from his cot with movements that seemed jerky and uncoordinated. Catching his eyes, Harley was alarmed to see that Axel appeared drugged.

He sat upright, with his small hands curled and empty on his lap, his legs, crossed at the ankles, not reaching the floor. Slowly the boy's strength and alertness seemed to return.

"You saw them that time," he said in a small voice. Rain continued its quiet patter on the canvas.

"Yeah, I did."

"I don't know what they are," Axel said. "Are they monsters?"

"I don't know."

"They're always out there, waiting. They don't come until I sleep, though."

"You have to sleep," Harley said.

"I don't want to. Do I have to?"

"Yes."

"Can you hurt them for me?"

"I'll try."

"Hurt them real bad," Axel said. Then he collapsed onto the cot, exhausted.

A distant lamplight, which had provided some indirect illumination, failed. Now the darkness inside the tent was total. Harley kept his eyes open, but he might as well have been blind.

This time, Harley was on his guard. He watched over the boy, sensing nothing wrong. Using the techniques that Axel had demonstrated to him, he maintained a light contact with the boy's sleeping mind. It was restful, because he was in a very deep

dreamless sleep. Only after a long dreamless cycle
did Axel's mind rise again to the realm of dreams.

The creatures returned. At first they seemed so
real that Harley believed that they were some sort
of creature that belonged in this new world, feeding
on minds as predators feed on meat. Maintaining
more lucidity in this state than the first time, however, he was soon able to sense that these creatures
were not real. They were figments of Axel's mind.
The medium of the new age, which empowered the
boy's mind, was also empowering his nightmares.

Touching the region of Axel's mind that was man-
ufacturing the creatures, he quieted the boy. The
creatures disappeared. Axel began to dream that he
was playing in the surf of a white-sand beach.

Harley watched over Axel's mind, determined
that the child would get a good night's sleep.
Touching Axel's mind and dreaming his dreams,
Harley was still able to listen to the rain falling on
the tent roof, running in rivulets, pattering on pud-
dles. The sounds of the rainfall gave him enough
auditory clues that he was able to form a mental
picture of the land around him that was more
intense than his eye's sight. Harley stretched his
mind out between the worlds of Axel's mind and
the world of his senses. Relaxed, stretched out, he
became more receptive to mental activity. He heard
far-off voices. He glimpsed distant scenes.

Suddenly an extreme of terror enveloped him, jolting his heart from a restful rhythm to a frantic racing.
An iron post pressed against his spine. Sweat popped
from his skin. The hot atmosphere smelled of burning wood and incense. Ropes dug into his chafed
wrists, tied behind his back. A dark man raising a

torch was advancing on his daughter, Constance. He was going to burn her alive. Harley was screaming, although he was not making any sound.

But he was. He was sitting in the tent. He heard his own voice making a deep, brutal sound, ". . . huu-uuu . . . huuuuu . . ." It was a primal word, a pro-toword before language, a frightening sound meant to intimidate aggressors.

Harley was shaking so violently that the soles of his boots were clattering on the wooden floor of the tent. He had never experienced such desperate ter-ror. He hadn't known that life could be like that: to care so deeply about someone and to watch that person about to be killed. To have this horror thrust upon him, without warning, from a distance. He could feel sweat evaporating from his skin in the cold air of the tent. He felt as if he had just escaped the heat of a tropical night to find himself plunged into cold northern mountain air.

For a moment, he had been his brother Owen. He had barely had enough time to realize this before he had reverted to himself. But where was his brother?

Frantically, Harley extended himself, searching for Owen, sensing him southward and distant, but he couldn't reach him. Too much noise from too many strangers blocked him. He glimpsed dark city streets, the shine of moonlight on a wet concrete highway, a woman's face a mask of ecstasy, voices gibbering nonsense . . . no, it was too much. He couldn't reach Owen.

Harley retreated to the tent. He took several deep breaths and forced himself to think calmly. He examined the memory of the encounter with Owen.

The man holding the torch was dark, with black glossy hair, a large sloping nose, and a drooping lower lip. Staring at the man as horror had filled him, Harley had wondered who this man was.

For a split second, he had touched that mind, hearing words in a glottal, lip-popping language never heard before. He had a vision of volcanoes and of women dressed in colorful woven clothes.

Owen must have taken the *Nepenthe* into some port on the Mexican coast. Now he was probably dead. Harley had connected with him in the moment before his horrible murder.

"Harley?"

The small voice startled him, its position indicating that the boy was sitting up in the cot.

"Yeah, Axel?"

"He's not dead."

Harley listened to the rainfall as he considered this statement.

"How do you know?"

"I got somebody that's with him."

"Is . . . are you sure he's not dead?"

"Yeah. I'm sure. I'm lookin' at him now."

"Where is he? Mexico?"

"Lemme ask the boy. Huh. Yeah. He's got crappy English, but it's in this Guatemala place. That's a country next to Mexico."

"Is he OK?"

"They didn't kill him, but he's with some pretty geeky freaks. I don't like 'em. Twisted weirdos and losers. Like the kind that was trying to get me in San Francisco. We all got to pick teams, I guess, but your brother's got himself some world-class jerkoids for partners."

"Is he in danger?"

"Duh," Axel said. In the darkness, Harley couldn't see the boy, but he heard a thumping. Axel was contorting his face into a daffy grin, rolling his eyes upward, and lolling his tongue. He was thumping his bent wrist against his chest as if he were a spasming idiot. It was one of the boy's more critical gestures. "Well, gee, I guess," he concluded.

"Can I help him?" Harley asked.

"From this far away? Don't think so."

"Why not?"

"It's too far. From here, all you can do is listen," Axel said. "Like a game on a radio. You want to play, you got to get in the stadium. Get close."

Harley decided that he should join his brother in Guatemala. But how? Only a fool would fly on an airliner, even if the airlines were still flying.

"You gotta take it," Axel said.

"Take what?"

"What you want. You've got to pick up the pieces that are left and use them."

"I want to go to Guatemala and help my brother."

"Then take a plane. I mean, like, *take* a plane."

"I can't fly an airplane."

"No, but you can drive a pilot. You know, make him fly for you."

"Can you show me how?"

"Yeah, I can, but I don't want to."

"Why not?"

"Because I'm scared. There's something else down there."

Now Owen knew that he must proceed with care. To save Kate's life, he had chosen to follow Van Meers. Owen didn't need the warning of this Irma woman to know that Van Meers was a dangerous man. A seeker of beauty, Owen mistrusted anyone who sought mere power.

As a young man, Owen had chosen the way of an artist, partly because he hated supervisors. During the long years of learning his craft, even after he had married Kate, he had struggled and contented himself with simple living. When fame had brought him big money, he had spent most of it on Constance, allowing himself *Nepenthe* as his only luxury, but he had saved a lot, because he never wanted to be dependent on anyone else.

Walking in the darkness, Kate and Constance at his side, Owen regretted his decision, but he couldn't have allowed Kate to die. Now that they found themselves in the service of this stranger, Owen determined to stay on guard.

Hector moved through the tribe, encouraging the

tired and the fearful. He walked alongside Owen for a moment before speaking.

"I'm glad that you've joined the tribe," he said. "You're welcome among us."

"Thank you."

"Be careful. The *señor* is angry with you. He doesn't care to be treated the way you've treated him. Loyalty is important to him. He says that loyalty is the soul of the tribe."

"I understand that. I'm loyal to my family."

"That's right. You have this strength. The *señor* respects you for it, but he thinks that you're stupid, because you don't realize that the families of man have changed. You have to reach out and find your greater family now. There are new sacraments of marriage, new ties stronger than the ties of simple blood."

Owen was not surprised that Kate challenged this notion. "What?" she asked, her voice harsh.

"The blood is just blood," Hector said dismissively. "You don't understand most things yet," he continued, talking to Owen. "Don't judge the *señor* until you do. You may think that he's being cruel when he's only being clear. The beginning of a new age is also the end of an old age. We have many enemies, people who will kill us if they can. And there are many millions who will die simply because their dying time has come. Do not blame the *señor* because we live in hard times."

Hector nodded at Kate. "Excuse me," he said. Then he turned and walked off to another group of people walking.

"Bastard," Kate said.

"Just take it easy," he said. "We need these people."

"Why?"

"Because they know how to keep you alive, Kate," Owen said. "You were dying back there. Your pulse was about thirty beats a minute. I couldn't wake you up, not by shaking you, not with amphetamines. You were dying."

"No," Kate said, her voice surprisingly warm. "I don't think so. If that was dying, then dying is the greatest feeling in life. It was like I was losing this small shell of myself, and finding a newer, more beautiful self. It was absolutely the most wonderful thing."

"Did you see anything?"

"You mean, like a tunnel of lights?"

"Yes."

"Well, no. There was this pearly fog, but it was more like a feeling. There were dozens of people around me, but I felt their presence rather than saw them. We were connected to hundreds of people, thousands, millions. It was wonderful. I could feel myself merging into them. The barriers just didn't seem to matter anymore. It—"

"It was a typical near-death experience," Owen said. "Either it's a wonderful place we'll all go when we're done here, or it's the brain firing off all its good chemicals at once, scratch-and-sniff ecstasy, meaning nothing except you're about to be dead. In either case, there's no need to rush. Dead is dead, no matter how nice the ride is."

Kate stopped, pulled Owen closer to her, and kissed him with all her passion, love, anger, and fierce will to live. Surprised at first, Owen returned her kiss awkwardly, but then the world melted away, and he found himself near only her. He joined in the kiss with equal passion. After a moment, they heard young laughter. They realized that Constance was laughing at them.

"Mommy and Daddy! That's too much!"

They joined hands and continued the hike across the dark desert. Up ahead, one of the women began to sing a sad lovely song in Spanish. Her voice was clear and brave. Owen thought that he understood some of the song's meaning. She was singing about her first *amante*, a young man she had loved in the lost age of her youth.

Many of them wanted to stop, but Hector insisted that they cross the wastelands in the coolness of the night. He warned that if the dawn found them on the black sands, the sun would kill them. Hour after hour, he promised that the end of the wastelands was near, but their journey seemed endless.

Yet, like all journeys, theirs did end. After a night of smelling only sand and volcanic dust, they could smell the water of a river, the chlorophyll of living broadleaves, and the must of rotting vegetation. Hector led them down to the riverbank, where everyone drank despite any misgivings about the purity of the water. The river was broad and slow. Its cool waters were refreshing.

No better than migrating animals, they made their camp alongside the riverbank. The sun rose over a distant ridge of the mountain range that curved southward, far east of their position. For several minutes, Owen watched the sun rise. It was quiet, the only sound the murmuring of the flowing water. He looked down at Constance, already asleep, and over at Kate, who was watching him with a look of loving concern.

Owen smiled, satisfied with their survival. Perhaps some nameless higher power would give them some more days of life.

Soon the sun rose several diameters over the horizon. From this height, the sun punched through the coolness of the morning air and began to spill heat down upon them. Wearily, Owen lay back. He rested one hand on Constance's ankle and another on Kate's arm. In less than a minute, he fell deep into an exhausted sleep.

The One awoke from the slow roiling of a strange dream. The Hiyul had been playing an elaborate prank on the Jarred, one that had taken the energy-beings dozens of years to discover. The Jarred, that race that had taken the form of light. The Ocean-Mind, that self-designed, hyperevolved creature whose body inhabited all the oceans of its world. Too bad the Hiyul's homeworld would be departing the sphere of being so soon, in just thousands of years.

What time was it? No, this cycle had barely begun. The One's homeworld was just penetrating this sphere of being. Thoughts were weak and disorganized. It would be another ten years before the homeworld journeyed deep into this sphere of being. This sphere of being: this shell within an infinite series of shells, this crest in the wave that undulated throughout all of the universe, this stress on the interwoven fabric of space-time-matter-energy, this ripple in the laws of physics caused by the absolute violence of the moment of creation, this region of the universe where minds were able to interconnect. The One wanted to awaken after its long sleep, but here on the outskirts of a sphere of being, it seemed so hard. Better just to sleep for another ten years.

Yet there was so much annoying noise. Why were the children awakening in such great numbers? Wasn't it too early for all that? Sometimes the children *did* have to contend with desert-evolved creatures. The One had chosen a beautiful home-world, one that had developed many fascinating forms of life. Yet those dinosaurs had finally grown too annoying. A catastrophe had had to be arranged. The One was lucky to possess such a glorious planet as Earth.

Oh, it was the humans, those hideous little beasts. They . . . it had been . . . the One had developed a plan for them. What had it been? Something clever, undoubtedly. Remembering clearly was so difficult, this shallow into the sphere of being. Hundreds of millions of years of memories crowded its mind. Everything that it had done and seen, and everything that the other people had shared with it. So many millions of lifetimes, so many years.

Sometimes it seemed to the One that indefinite longevity was a heavy burden. To live forever . . . the One could remember its youth, when it had been a naive little creature, and the promise of indefinite longevity had seemed so wonderful. The One had been a sleek, sprightly little four-legged creature, frolicking in the forest. . . .

No, those were the memories of the race-dawn of the Jarred. In the second or third cycle, the One had obsessed on the memories of the Jarred, beings of light, whose thoughts had communicated so clearly and powerfully. But mathematically, they had proven that the homeworlds of the One and the Jarred would never again share the same sphere of being. The Jarred was gone forever, unreachable. . . .

As a child, the One had been . . . of a certain form. . . . Life had been new and . . . life had been . . .

The One could not remember the details. It knew that creatures were naive and joyous when they were young. For the young, all experiences were new. A young creature could thrill with the joyous beauty of a sunrise. The One could watch a sunrise and know that it was beautiful, but that particular sunrise would remind it of millions of earlier sunrises and the associated memories of the days they began, days that ranged from the horrible to the sublime. This one sunrise would remind it of joy and of sorrow; the memories would imbue its mind with sorrowful joy and joyous sorrow. Only the young had the purity to experience true joy. Perhaps there was something better than immortality: perpetual youth, the characteristic of self-perpetuating life, the way of nature. Was anything truly beautiful that was not new? Perhaps the One was not the crown of creation. Perhaps the way of nature demanded that the One cross the ever-thinner membrane into eternity. The burden of the years was becoming too heavy to carry.

Oh, this was the voice of the Hiyul envoy. The Hiyul's planet, of course, was many light-years away, so a dialogue with it took thousands of years. Yet the One so loved the Hiyul that last cycle, it had conspired with the Ocean-Mind to copy a miniature ego of the Hiyul in the One's left foremost lobe. This was beyond memory art, since the miniature ego operated and thus was alive in a sense. It was a wonderful envoy, although it did tend to jabber about the beauty of mortality and the way of nature. The One debated overwriting the Hiyul envoy, which had been too active recently, interfering with the stratagem involving the humans. Pesky thing.

No, you yourself invite this wheel within a wheel, the Hiyul envoy answered. *You yourself love the beauty of it. The art is danger.*

The One quieted the envoy, sending it to sleep. Then the One turned its attention to its meditation with the Hiyul itself, the part of its mind that communed with the Hiyul, receiving and distributing the currently arriving signal that the Hiyul had sent from its distant planet thousands of years ago. The meditation contained the usual overabundance of information about the state of the Hiyul mind itself, with the never-ending growth, maturation, and death of the brains that composed its corporate mind, as well as the thousands of other organs that allowed it to dominate its planet: the vast forests of lilylike organs that floated on the surface of most of its world's oceans, absorbing sunlight; the huge dynamos of hearts that made the planet pulse with its blood; the millions of kilometers of veins and arteries and nerve networks covering the sea bottom; the food-scoops and waterwheels and all the other organs. The One politely used the information to update its status board on his friend, then quickly and diplomatically trashed all the rest of the trivial data. The signal also contained a great deal of information about the Kaolin people, ten thousand light-years antispinward from the Hiyul. The One vectored this information to the model of the Kaolin world it had been building for the past two cycles. The Kaolin world, with its rich culture of thought poetry, was a restful place to pass some dozens of years. Making a note to visit the Kaolin model soon, the One turned its attention to the current problem.

The humans . . . the One felt a wave of depression. Usually it took the One a few years to reorganize its mind. During this transition, morbid thoughts and doubts tended to intrude. Sometimes it seemed that the voyages across the desert were becoming too difficult. The dreams were confusing its mind. The One should do what some of the other people had done. Advanced mental life outside a sphere of being was not natural. Perhaps the One should propel a world so that it rode the crest of a sphere of being forever. Yet, everybody who did that, in the space of a few hundred millennia, crossed over into eternity.

No. Eternity, the dissolution of the self, was frightening. The One maintained. It would not go down into that place.

Some of the humans were growing in strength at an alarming rate. In time, perhaps they could threaten it with techniques. Ah yes, the plan was in motion. The One's egg was streaming toward the exit point at the volcano called Atitlán.

The egg would have to blast open a few subterranean vents in order to make its way to the surface of the planet. Such blasts would probably trigger an eruption of the volcano. This was a small matter for the One, who subsisted for thousands of years within the molten core of the planet itself. In fact, to the One, a good volcanic eruption had the same natural pleasures as rainfall, lightning, and rainbows. . . . Perhaps it should really blast away and trigger a good strong shake.

Yes, a volcanic eruption and a good earthquake would be nice. Always a pleasure. Suitably dramatic. It harmonized with the One's master plan: the beautiful confrontation of two races standing on the opposite brinks of total oblivion. The One's plan embraced enough chaos that there was the merest hint, the delicious suspicion of a possibility, that it would be the humans who would survive. This was highest art.

The heat's oppression forced Owen awake. Constance was sitting up, looking around her with an expression of sleepy bewilderment. Kate was still asleep, stretched out on the grass.

The high sun was punishingly hot. Nearer the river, a stand of tall broadleaf trees cast deep cool shade. Owen moved Constance into the shade. He returned for Kate, but he couldn't wake her. He felt her pulse, very slow and fluttering.

As he stood, his joints ached. He looked around for Van Meers. Most of the tribe was asleep, but Van Meers was sitting on a rock near the river and talking with Hector. Owen walked over. Van Meers and Hector were talking in Spanish, but Owen couldn't follow their conversation. Finally Hector walked away. Van Meers turned his pale eyes toward Owen. He was so exhausted that the pale blue eyes looked unreal.

"Yes?"

"It's Kate. I don't think that she's well."

Wearily Van Meers looked over in Kate's direction.

"She's sleeping."

"Her pulse is very low."

Van Meers nodded, rose, and began to walk toward Kate, but he was so tired that he stumbled. Van Meers knelt at Kate's side. He reached over and laid his hand on her forehead. Instantly, Van Meers looked woozy. He swayed and almost passed out. When he returned to his senses, he drew back his arm and moved away from Kate.

Van Meers sat back on his haunches in a peasant's squat. He shook his head.

"She's gone," he said. "She's too far down."

"You have to help her," Owen said.

Van Meers shook his head. "I don't think so. I'm too tired."

"Please," Owen said. "Please try."

Van Meers shook his head violently, as if trying to wake himself up. He took a deep breath from the pit of his stomach and laid his right hand on Kate's head. With his left hand, he reached out and grabbed Owen's hand.

"Man . . ." he moaned, his eyes glazing.

A wave of weakness passed through Owen. He felt as if he was losing his will to live. His vision blacked out. Something heavy and dark was dragging him down. Then he sensed that Van Meers was with him, reaching deeper down for something faintly glowing. It was Kate. Van Meers reached her, gathered her to him, and began to struggle upwards.

But a multitude of spirits were dragging her down. Heavy as the earth, they claimed Kate as one of their own. Van Meers turned and struck at them, one strong blow followed by a weaker blow, but the dark spirits were rising, insisting on claiming Kate. Van Meers was losing his strength. He seemed ready to loose his grip on Kate, abandon her, and struggle to the surface alone to save himself. Owen felt a lurch of panic. He moved forward and grasped at Kate. He lent his force to Van Meers. The sapping of his strength was agonizing, the blackness so heavy. He could feel himself losing himself, his soul sucked down into this faceless mass of strangers.

But no . . . no. Kate was his. He would not let her go. The insistence of these strangers was maddening. Angrily he lashed out at them. He surprised himself with the power and focus of his anger, which struck one spirit square, blasting it, severing its needy clasping at Kate. Another spirit rose to take its place. It swelled up, formed a hold on him as if it would never let go. The fear it sparked in Owen flamed in furious energy. He blasted hate at the spirit, smashing it loose. Nearby spirits scattered in panic.

Suddenly Kate was sprung loose. Owen folded her in his embrace and began to struggle for the surface. Van Meers was ahead of him, rising as naturally as a bubble of air in water.

Vision returned. The broad daylight startled him. He realized that his eyes had been open but sightless. Now he could see Kate's eyes opening as she frowned. Owen looked over to see Van Meers staring at him, an unmistakable spark of fear in his eyes. Owen had taught Van Meers to fear him. He disentangled his hand from Owen's, lifted his other hand off Kate, stood, and looked down at Owen.

"That's the way," he said. "See if you have the strength to do it again. Wrestle with the dead if you want. I have to fight the living."

Van Meers left them alone. Kate sat up and embraced Owen.

"Oh baby," she breathed into his ear. "Why won't you let me go?"

"No."

"Don't you love me?"

"Yes, Kate," Owen said, peeved as always when Kate asked him this question. He suspected that she did it because she liked to hear the answer, but he resented the question. He told her often enough. Hadn't he just proved it? "Yes, I love you."

"Did you feel how beautiful it is?"

"No. It was awful. Horrible."

Kate looked puzzled. "You didn't feel the peace?"

"No. It just felt like death."

"If it's death," Kate said, "it's also peace. You and Van Meers were violent about the whole thing, though. About as gentle as a wrecking crew."

She stood, walked over to look at Constance, then went down to the river to cup water with her hands and drink. Owen watched her, glad to see her move, confused by what she had said. He wondered if he had ever truly known her.

By midafternoon, most of the tribe was stirring, looking about unsuccessfully for food. Hector was ready to leave, but Van Meers seemed drunk with fatigue. Finally, he yawned, his whole body shaking. He stretched himself out on the grass and slept like a dead man for less than an hour. When he awoke, Van Meers lowered himself into the river and swam to the opposite bank. One by one, the tribe followed him.

The Keegans began to cross the slow, broad river, luxuriating in its cool, refreshing waters. Halfway across the river, Owen felt something nibbling on his skin. First one, and then another, creature pecked at his flesh. He realized that small tropical river fish were testing his flesh as a food source. Constance squealed with delight as the fish nibbled her. It made Owen nervous to think that fish, perhaps cousins to piranhas, were swimming with him in these tropical waters, tasting him. What if they were just the scouts for the piranhas? But they were far north of the Amazon. Finally the Keegans arrived on the opposite bank, ending up with the others far downstream.

This late in the afternoon, the sun had grown more gentle. A well-trod path wound alongside the river, following its bends and curves. Most of the way, they walked in shade. Constance skipped alongside her parents, chattering about everything that she saw, asking for the words she did not know. Owen took Kate's hand. They walked side-by-side, talking with their daughter. They had only dreamed of such a day.

Not more than an hour's hike up the path, they came upon deserted huts, thick-milled planks roofed with corroded zinc. Foraging through the village, the tribe found some plantains, canned foods,

and a few sacks of rice and beans. The tribe took
over the schoolhouse. In a nearby hut, three people
cooked over wood fires on raised earth platforms.

As they waited in the schoolhouse, Van Meers
began to engage in a strange practice. One by one,
he sat opposite each member of the tribe and stared
into his eyes. These staring contests lasted a few
seconds or long minutes. Afterwards, the other person seemed quiet and withdrawn.

Van Meers came up to Kate.

"Look into my eyes," Van Meers said.

"Why?" Owen asked.

Van Meers glared at Owen. "Because this is the
way of the tribe."

"Why?" Owen repeated, his voice rising in challenge.

Kate cast a disapproving glance at Owen. "It's no
big thing, Owen. It's just a look."

Uncertain, Owen stood and watched while Van
Meers conducted this strange ritual with his wife. It
was over in a minute.

"Now you, you look," Van Meers said.

Owen looked at Van Meers. The pale blue eyes
seemed empty of emotion. Owen felt himself relaxing. There was nothing here, only a shamanistic ritual. Van Meers was just touching them all. If he had
the responsibility of leading them, then it was natural that he should take an interest in their state of
well-being. Owen must learn to relax and to trust
Van Meers, who had saved his life and the lives of
Kate and Constance, after all. Didn't that earn him
something?

Then, for one moment, he found himself thinking as Van Meers. The world was an arena for con-

stant struggle. Only the strong survived. He, Van Meers, was one of the strongest men alive, an adept of the new age who had been studying techniques long before the world's changes became so dramatic. This one, Owen Keegan, and his daughter, Constance, could become strong, too, if they obeyed Van Meers. No one mind was stronger than a team of minds. Owen should rejoice that he had such an opportunity to join the tribe. Together, they would forge an unbeatable alliance, a ring of minds, focused through Van Meers. What glory, when they ruled the world!

When Van Meers turned away from him, it seemed to Owen that he had gone too soon. He found himself wishing that Van Meers would linger some time longer. In that way, he would learn more about the excellence and goodness of Van Meers. After a few minutes, however, this euphoria wore off, leaving Owen with an unsettled, disturbed feeling.

The cooks were serving food nestled in broad banana leaves. No one began to eat until Van Meers was served.

"Strength to our bodies," Van Meers said. "Eat and grow strong. May our enemies go hungry."

They began to eat. Hunger made the plantains, rice, and beans taste delicious. Van Meers did not touch his food until the last of them had finished. He looked out at them and asked, "Is there anyone who is still hungry?"

"I am!" cried Constance, who had wolfed down all her food.

Several people stirred and looked away from Constance. There were gasps and even a chuckle.

Van Meers looked surprised; then he smiled. He walked over to Constance and handed her his food.

"Then eat, my little one," Van Meers said.

"Thanks," Constance said.

She began to eat. Van Meers touched her head and turned away as if food meant nothing to him.

"I'm sorry," Kate said, sparking a twinge of resentment in Owen.

Van Meers shook his head and smiled. "The child must eat. After the victory, all the food in the world will be ours."

"The victory?" Kate asked.

"Yes," Van Meers said.

"What—"

But Van Meers turned his back to Kate. With a casual wave of his hand, he strode out the door. The members of the tribe picked themselves off the floor and followed their leader.

"What victory does he mean?" Kate asked Owen.

"His," Owen answered. "His victory."

"And what does that mean?" Kate asked.

But Owen didn't know the answer to that question. He joined the line of the tribe, filing out of the abandoned town. The main street of the town joined a larger road that followed the contours of the river. Up ahead, they could see the foothills rising to the mountains. Directly ahead, the serrated mountain ridge separated in a deeply cut pass. The dirt road seemed to descend from this pass. Owen thought that the pass, flanked by twin jagged peaks, looked like a gateway to another world.

Now the sun was lowering toward the ridges guarding the west. Owen felt footsore and tired. He wanted to rest, not to continue to walk. The long day seemed a continuation of the last night's endless hike. He left Constance with Kate and advanced through the file of the tribe until he found Hector.

"What's the plan?" he asked. "Are we going to hike all night?"

Hector looked askance at Owen. "You don't feel them?" he asked.

"Feel what?"

Hector shook his head. "The others," he said. "The other tribes."

"No."

"There are two behind us," Hector said. "And one ahead of us, just south of the big pass, I think. We might be able to make some kind of alliance with the one ahead of us. Van Meers wants to meet that one first, see if he can get them to join us. If we succeed, then they will make us much stronger before we meet the two tribes who are after us."

"Excuse me," Owen said. "But would you mind very much just telling me what the Hell is going on?"

"You don't know?"

"No, I don't know."

Hector smiled at Owen indulgently, as if he were an idiot. "And Van Meers said that you were a wise man."

"How about a clue?"

Hector shook his head. "Did you know that Van Meers began to notice the change of the ages ten years ago?"

"No."

"He was one of the first to notice it. I myself didn't begin to notice it until last year. But everyone felt it without knowing it or understanding it.

They just started to react to it strangely. The slow disintegration of the old society. Millions of people stimulating their brains with dangerous drugs. Why? Only for pleasure, you think? When they were surrounded by the horrors that these drugs caused? No, because the ages were changing. They were trying to make their brains work in a new way."

"Go on," Owen said.

"Why do you think that madness became the fashion? We didn't bother to mourn the death of reason. Reason died ten years ago. Did you even notice?"

Owen looked westward at the failing light. The black mountains were silhouetted against a ruby smear of the heights of the sunrise; the disc of the setting sun was far below their high horizon.

"Everyone always thought I was crazy," Owen said. "Just because I saw things . . . shapes . . ."

"You didn't belong in the old age," Hector said. "Neither did your daughter. Your brains didn't work like theirs. Mine neither. I was a dreamer. I was a stranger in my own family. I could never understand why they acted the way they did. I laughed at the wrong things. I couldn't understand how they could ignore misery on such a huge scale. The old world was a damned strange place. I'm glad it's over."

"What happened?" Owen asked.

Hector pointed toward the sunset. Owen's eyes followed his gesture. Above the ruby smear of the sunset, a green aurora was shimmering. Some moments, the green scintillating sheen shot kilometers high.

"How often have you seen a green sunset?" Hector asked.

"Just once. Today."

"We haven't changed," Hector said, his voice hushed with awe. "It's the world, Keegan. The world has changed."

"I know," Owen said. "But I don't understand."

"Maybe no one does," Hector said, his voice low and confidential. "Maybe not even Van Meers. Why should we? We never fully understood the old world. A partial understanding turns out to be no understanding at all. Our worldviews were just simple constructs that allowed us to muddle through. We understood that food and warmth were good. Pain, bad. Sex, good. Generally speaking. Amoebas do as much. Amoebas probably are more clever at distinguishing food from poison. Now the old constructs don't work. We have to build new ones."

Owen walked alongside Hector. He found himself beginning to like the man.

"Who are you, anyway?" he asked.

"Me? How would you define me?"

"What did you do before?"

Hector sighed. "It doesn't matter."

"I was a sculptor," Owen said.

Hector smiled. "Yes, Owen, I know your work. You were good. My father had one of your pieces."

"Ah."

"That bowl you called *Jacob's Ladder*," Hector said. "He kept it on the coffee table in his apartment in Miami. He filled it with candies. Mints."

Something like a guffaw exploded out of Owen,

as if he had whiffed noxious smoke. Hector laughed.

"It drove me nuts," Hector said. "Every time I visited him there. It was an apartment he kept for one of his *queridas*, actually, so I didn't go there much. But every time I did, I'd spill the mints onto the table and I'd put your bowl up on the shelf. The next time I'd come back, there it would sit, filled to the brim with mints. He was that kind of man, my father."

"You were rich," Owen said.

"He was," Hector said. "He owned the better parts of Mexico City. I was a student."

"Of what?"

"Middle French. Bioengineering. Advanced number theory. Film. Comparative theology. It depended on my mood and the weather."

"A seeker of knowledge."

"Maybe. Maybe I just learned to trust my luck with coeds."

They were turning a bend in the road. Up ahead, Owen could see that the road was rising through the foothills and the mountain pass. The pale ribbon of the dirt road held the failing light better than the surrounding croplands.

"You didn't go to university?" Hector asked.

"No," Owen said. "It seems I spent most of my life standing in front of a lathe, breathing sawdust."

"You were an artist," Hector said. "There are worse lives."

"I did what I wanted to do."

At the head of the column, Van Meers shouted for Hector, who ran up to his leader. Owen faded back until he walked alongside Kate again. Almost word for word, in the way of longtime couples, he recounted his conversation with Hector.

"So they expect us to walk all night?" Kate asked.

"Until we meet with that other group up in the mountains, yes."

"We're going to have to carry Constance," Kate said.

"All right. I'll start first."

Owen called Constance, who obediently came to her father.

"Are you tired, princess?"

"My feet hurt."

"Do you want to ride on my back?"

"Oh yeah sure!" Constance cried, delighted with the notion. She ran around and hopped onto Owen's back. The ten-year-old weighed almost seventy pounds, but Owen was able to trudge forward under the burden.

The previous night, he had carried Kate across the black sand wastelands. Now he was carrying his daughter on his back, as they hiked up a road that ascended the foothills. Owen did not resent his wife and daughter, even when they were burdensome. He was proud that he was able to be strong for his family. Many times, in many ways far more subtle and more important, Kate had carried him. He only worried that his physical strength might fail him. Working for them, he felt the most himself.

They began to climb the first big foothill. The road did not circle along its contour line; it cut straight up the hill and continued to rise with only occasional level ground or slight dips. Every step was higher than the last.

Now that night had fallen, stars filled the sky. The Milky Way was evident, the broad shining path of the galaxy, stretching from east to west. The starlight was strong enough to cause the pale dusty road to seem to glow. Off in the cattlelands and farms, the night was a dark featureless mass.

White lights appeared at the crown of the next-highest foothill. It was the familiar glow of oncoming headlights. Van Meers barked an order. While everyone cleared the road, he stood in the center.

Grinding gears, the bus descended the foothills. It was an old school bus, gaudily repainted, rocking back and forth on destroyed shocks. Van Meers raised his hand. With a squeal of worn brakes, the bus stopped with Van Meers dead in its headlights. Watching from the shadows at the side of the road, Owen expected some sort of confrontation as Van Meers tried to commandeer the bus.

The driver leaped out of the bus and all but prostrated himself in front of Van Meers, who spoke to him softly. The driver climbed back into the bus. With a cacophony of grinding gears, he turned the bus around, backing almost a dozen times until it was headed up the hill. Van Meers waved the tribe aboard.

Moments later, they were all seated, riding northward. Van Meers, Hector, and a few others chose to ride on the roof. From the murmur of conversation in Spanish between the driver and some members of the tribe, Owen was able to gather that the driver was one of them. Van Meers must have sent him ahead to search for transportation.

The Keegans shared one bench over the left rear wheel. Constance stretched out on her parents' laps. Despite the riotous rocking of the bus, she was soon asleep. Kate seemed sleepy, too.

"I'm afraid to let you sleep," Owen said.

"I'm not afraid," Kate said. She brushed her fingers through Owen's hair.

"I can try to watch over you," he said.

"How?"

"I'm not sure. I'm afraid to try, but I'm more afraid not to. I think I may be able to do what we did this morning. Go to that place and be with you."

Kate shook her head. "That was so violent and awful."

"I can try to fight more gently."

In the darkness, Kate smiled. Her fingertips stroked Owen's cheek.

"You need to shave."

"I know."

"Don't be afraid, Owen. I know you're worried, but you shouldn't be afraid."

"I refuse to lose you."

"I need to sleep."

"Go ahead. I think I can sleep with you."

"Good night, darling."

"Good night."

Kate closed her eyes. Within moments, she was asleep. Owen gathered Kate in his arms until her head rested on his chest. He laid one hand on her temple.

It surprised him how easy it was to find her. She was a gentle spirit resting so close to him. He felt himself falling into the rhythms of her breathing. They were together in a safe warm place. He was asleep, too, he thought. Kate was sinking lower, but not too low. Owen felt his watchfulness buoying her upwards. It was altogether wonderful, he thought. Kate began to dream. They were in the old house as they had known it, but Constance was able to talk and to share the moments of the day. Rain was pattering the rooftop and pelting the windows, but the family was together inside their home, safe and warm and dry.

T
H
I
R
T
E
E
N

FROM HIS SLEEP OWEN WAS ROUSED BY DISTURBING images. Looking about, he saw that it was still night. The bus was jolting up and down, swaying back and forth. He smelled exhaust fumes. He felt disoriented and surprised that it was still dark. Footfalls pounded the metal roof. A man was shouting. Owen thought he recognized Hector's voice. The driver began to shout in Spanish. Most of the people were lurching awake. Kate's head snapped up from Owen's chest. Constance cried out in frustration at being woken.

With a squeal of worn brakes, the driver forced the bus to a stop. From the roof, Van Meers and Hector clattered down onto the hood and leaped down to the ground in front of the bus. Owen stood and mumbled something to Kate. He joined the rush of people exiting the bus.

In the headlights of the bus, Van Meers, Hector, and a few others were standing in a rough semicircle facing ahead. At first, Owen thought that they had seen a dangerous animal. He could see the outlines of something moving out there in the darkness. Then he realized that someone out there was shouting.

"—knew we'd be here," a man's voice was shouting. Groggy, at first Owen didn't recognize the voice.

"We didn't call you," Van Meers shouted.

"I'm going to come, Van Meers," the man standing in the darkness shouted. "You've got people that I care about."

"I cared enough to save their lives," Van Meers shouted. He turned to Owen. "Tell him that I helped you."

Owen looked stupidly at Van Meers. Belatedly, he identified the voice in the darkness. He turned and shouted.

"Harley!"

"Yeah, Owen! It's me. Are you OK?"

"Yes."

Owen walked forward. A hand reached out to restrain him, but he shrugged it off. In a moment, he had crossed the area of light and entered the darkness. A man and a boy were standing there. The man stepped up to him and crushed him in a bear hug: his brother, Harley.

"I found you," Harley said.

"Harley. Harley," Owen said, too surprised to say more.

"I wish you'd return my calls," Harley said. "Where are Kate and Constance?"

"On the bus."

"OK," Harley said, his voice grave. "I came for you. You know that, don't you?"

"Sure."

"Back me up, now."

"Of course."

Harley turned and spoke to the boy standing with him in the darkness. He threw his arm around Owen's shoulder. Together, the two brothers walked into the flood of light from the headlamps. Van Meers and Hector were waiting for them. Hector was holding a long-barreled pistol. Van Meers was standing tall, a haughty expression on his face.

Harley advanced on Van Meers. He didn't extend his hand. With a glance at Hector's pistol, he sneered and said, "There's no need for that. And not much use, either."

Hesitantly, Hector lowered the pistol.

"The others are gaining on you, Van Meers," Harley said.

"I know."

"I want to take my brother, his wife, and his daughter with me."

"Nothing is that simple."

"No," Harley said. "Maybe not, but I can make it that simple."

They stood, facing off with each other. Suddenly Van Meers ducked and swept up in one flowing motion, extending his hand toward Harley's midsection. Radiant light rocketed from his hand and struck Harley's middle, knocking him, heels flying, onto his back.

Van Meers spun, his hand curling. Owen felt a force strike him in the upper chest. Wind knocked out of his lungs, he stood, unable to breathe. Hector stepped forward and shoved Owen away from his brother. Van Meers loomed over Harley, making a strange gesture as if pulling a long invisible stake from Harley's abdomen. Harley's limbs quivered; then he lay still. As Owen gasped and shouted, Van Meers looked up at him and made a gesture that caused blackness to swallow Owen's soul. Van Meers began the process, for him full of sadistic pleasure, of dismembering the minds of the Keegan brothers.

In the darkness beyond the headlights, Axel stood, watching Van Meers killing his friend and his friend's brother. Axel's eyes were wide. His knees were trembling. Van Meers was much more powerful than any of the freaks that Axel had so far encountered. He was afraid. He knew that he would have to do something, but he was afraid to confront Van Meers. He thought that he would lose.

He was lightly connected with them, but Van Meers did not seem to notice. Perhaps Axel could be sly. He sunk into the Keegan brothers, covered them with a darkness. He allowed Van Meers to perceive that his work was done. Owen and Harley were dead.

Van Meers straightened. The two Americans had gone down so easily and died so quickly. He had expected more of a fight from Owen, especially. Sometimes it was that way, though, when you confronted these early adepts who had still not developed their powers. They died as easily as children.

Speaking of which, Constance Keegan was his now. And this boy, this Axel, he seemed to have some potential, too. Van Meers would take them both.

From a deathly still place, Owen's consciousness came rising. He grew aware that he was lying on the cold ground. He felt drained of energy, as if he had no desire to live. Looking upward into the night sky, he thought that the stars were sickening. They seemed to be sucking the life force from his body through the black holes of his eyes.

Yet the green lights were rising from the ground. He watched their fantastic forms as they swayed upwards. Their energy seemed to buoy him up and give him strength. After a moment, Owen sat up and looked around.

Close by on the dirt road, his brother Harley was stretched out, stirring. When their eyes met, Harley smiled, shook his head, and looked around him.

Owen noticed the bus was gone. He stood and searched horizon to horizon, seeing nothing except seas of floating green lights. They were alone on the country road that climbed the foothills.

"What happened?" Owen asked.

Harley coughed and said, "He knocked us out. He must have taken Kate and Constance and Axel too. I think that he must still be headed north for the highlands."

"What does he want with Kate and Constance?"

Harley stood. "Man I'm glad the field is thick tonight," he muttered to himself, and then he said, "Nothing with Kate, I don't think. He wants Constance. And he wanted you."

"What for?"

"His tribe. He needs soldiers. Constance could fight for him. So could you. Kate's useless to him."

"Why not leave her and take me, then?"

"Because you were challenging him. I think he decided you were too hard. The two of us together, two brothers, was too much. He probably thinks

Constance and Axel are . . . bendable. Come on, let's get moving north. We gotta follow the son of a bitch. I need some time to teach you a few things before we meet any of the other groups."

Harley and Owen began to hike north. The motion of walking comforted Owen. It gave him strength to be walking in company with his brother. He didn't feel afraid; he felt angry and determined.

"What the hell is going on, Harley? And how did you get down here?"

"Shut up, Owen," Harley said. "Why do you insist on talking?"

—*Get a clue*, Harley's voice said within Owen's head. *It's like you insist on playing checkers, and the game is chess. Things have changed. Why don't you change? Are you stupid?*

—*It's my world*, Owen heard his inner voice answering. *I won't give it up without a fight. Nobody can take it away—*

—*Nobody is taking it away, you idiot. The world just changed. It doesn't have a damn thing to do with you except that you're in it. Now deal with it, won't you?*

—*I am dealing with it.*

Harley's communication with Owen took on a more profound force. It went beyond words. Owen sensed Harley's fury. He was bitterly angry, not at Owen, but at what he thought was the weakness in Owen. For the first time, Owen began to understand his brother's attitude. Harley was a much more elemental man than he was. Harley had always been a beast of survival. He understood life as a contest for survival. The strong would supplant the weak. The only inheritance of the weak was death and oblivion. Owen, with his dreams, his art, and his ideals, was indulging in weakness, but the time for weakness was past.

He had to learn a new attitude. He also had to learn a number of new skills. It was competition at a new level with new rules, but it was a very old struggle. It was the struggle for survival. The strong would prove themselves. The weak would die, not because they deserved to die, but merely because they were weak.

A mind could attack another mind. It was something that minds had always done. Ideas had always contended, bodies had always fought, yes, but minds themselves had always been involved in a secret struggle of their own. A mind was a phenomenon of a brain. This phenomenon existed because of the brain, yet it also existed in and of itself, in a unique realm. It was a phenomenon that had its own properties. One of the properties was the generation of subtle and powerful forces. Through these forces, a mind could connect with another mind, near or afar. It could support that other mind and make it stronger: harmony. It could degrade that other mind and confuse it: dissonance.

In day-to-day life, in the great busy collision of minds, this is something that everyone had always known. Everyone had experienced the effects of these subtle and powerful forces every moment of every day. Every moment spent with other people, they had felt the disturbances caused by the other minds. They had met people and immediately either liked them or disliked them. Why? Because of the complex interactions between minds. There were people who made others feel well and others who sickened and scared them.

—And that was in the days when the effect was weak, Harley thought. *Now it's growing stronger. The world is shrinking to the size of a synaptic gap. All minds are now next to all other minds.*

Then Harley began to show his brother how to control the forces of the mind. It began with the realization that his thoughts had power. They mattered. Then he had to learn how to listen to the minds of others. In fleeting moments, in exquisitely subtle shades of thought, appeared momentary openings, places of leverage where he could enter and influence another person's world.

So they walked in the night, higher and higher into the foothills. The country around them grew wooded, the sky overhead more dark. The two brothers walked side-by-side up the increasingly mountainous road. Owen grew more adept by the minute.

In the hour before dawn, he found that he knew things that he could teach his brother. At first, Harley resisted, rejecting the notion that Owen could be stronger than him. Blow by blow, however, Owen showed Harley that he had learned everything that Harley knew, but he had learned it more profoundly. Owen showed his brother that he was not weak. In fact, Harley realized finally that he had mistaken his brother's strength for weakness. Owen's determination, his strength of will, and his confidence in himself were in fact far greater than Harley's. They also discovered that Owen's brain was better adapted to this new world than Harley's; his skills, once learned, were much more subtle and strong. By the time they reached the first foothill from which they could

see the black expanse of the ocean, the two brothers realized that they would never be the same.
Owen, the younger brother, was now the stronger.
Harley had to admit that from now on, he would
follow his brother. It was strange for Harley to feel
lesser than his younger brother, but he tamed his
pride and found comfort in walking in his
brother's shadow, as he remembered the darkness
that Van Meers had seeped into his soul.

Just south of the pass, the bus ran out of gas.
They had scavenged as much gasoline as possible
from vehicles abandoned by the roadside, but now
the fuel was gone. Van Meers ordered the tribe to
continue the march. He was worried that they had
made only thirty kilometers since they had killed
the Keegan brothers. Irma and her tribe were still in
pursuit. She was such a powerful threat.

The medium was thick tonight, however. Van
Meers felt very strong, perhaps stronger than he had
ever felt. As far as he knew, he was the most powerful man on Earth. Why should he worry about Irma
or any other adept? When life held such joys?

Like the pantomime with Owen's widow and
orphan. Having assaulted and probed Owen's
mind, Van Meers knew its feel and reach. He also
understood Kate and much of Constance. It was not
too difficult for him to assume Owen's aspect.

Van Meers walked up to Kate. He put his arm
around her waist. "Are you OK, honey?" he asked.

Kate looked up into Van Meers's face. Instead of
seeing the ghostly skin and the pale eyes, she saw
Owen's dark handsome features.

"A little tired," she answered.

"Do you want a shot of energy?" Van Meers asked.

"Yes."

Van Meers penetrated deeper into Kate's mind. He allowed some of his energy to bleed into her. As soon as she had risen enough in her energy level, he retreated. Van Meers hated to waste his energy on this woman. It had its uses, though. There were some branches of possibilities involving Kate.

"Feel better?"

"Yes, thanks, Owen."

"Let me go check on Constance," Van Meers said.

He walked further up among the tribe. Half an hour before the sunrise, the eastern sky held enough light that the hogback shapes of the mountain ridges stood out more clearly. Van Meers admired their twisted features, the curls and spires and ridges. He felt as if he were entering the realm where he was king.

Van Meers walked up to Constance and said, "How are you, princess?"

Constance glanced at Van Meers and smiled. "I'm OK, Daddy. My feet are getting sore, though."

"We'll be stopping soon," Van Meers said. "Then they can rest."

"Good!" Constance cried. "Why did you fight with the Van Meers man back there, Daddy?"

Van Meers was surprised. He had thought that he had blanked out Constance's perception of the struggle. The child's mind was so strange, though. Perhaps that explained why he had gotten it wrong somehow.

"We weren't fighting, princess," he said. "Van Meers and I were just talking something over."

"Why did he hit you, then? And what happened to Uncle Harley?"

Van Meers assaulted Constance's mind. Her childish defenses were not a threat to him. He brushed them aside. Van Meers savaged her memories of the fight with the Keegan brothers. He obliterated many hours of her most recent memories. Then he withdrew to the point where he was merely influencing her current perceptions.

"Give Daddy a kiss," Van Meers said.

He placed his arm around Constance's narrow shoulders. He drew her closer to him. Dutifully the girl raised her face to the man she thought was her father. Van Meers bent down and with his waxy cold lips he kissed the sweet and soft lips of the girl.

His face close to her face, slowly, he smiled.

The other tribe caught up with the Keegan brothers in the moments before dawn. The sky full of light, the grasses and leaves had taken on their full green, but the sun had not yet topped the eastern arm of the mountains. Birds were singing energetically as they flew from their secretive night perches to their morning places, where they would gather food and water. The air was cool and fresh. High in the western sky, a long, thin strand of gray cloud was warming in the first rays of sunlight and expanding into pinkish white fluff.

Horse hooves pounded the dust of the dirt road. Owen turned and saw a group of a dozen horsemen riding hard toward them. Harley grabbed Owen's elbow and said, "Here they come."

The horsemen were dark-skinned Indians. Most wore the rough clothes of an Indian peasant: sandals, black trousers, a thick wool poncho secured with a wide leather belt, and a wide-brimmed straw hat. Some wore jeans and cowboy shirts. They all carried pistols or rifles.

Their horses were mostly scrawny, small creatures. The mounts included cheap saddles and impromptu burlap saddlebags. Winded after their gallop, the horses were lathered, their flanks heaving, their eyes rolling with fatigue.

The horsemen surrounded Owen and Harley. Most of them pointed their weapons casually at the brothers, but gave no other indication that they intended to shoot.

Mounted on the largest, most powerful horse, a *mestiza* woman with long black hair called out in Spanish and then in an Indian dialect. The others lowered their weapons. Owen looked at the woman. She was taller than many of the men. Her skin was sunburned a dark copper. Her coal-black eyes shined intensely. She had a heart-shaped face and prominent cheekbones. When her eyes met Owen's, she grinned, revealing bright even teeth and a carnivorous glee. She swung down from her horse and walked up to him.

Standing close to him, the woman put her hand on Owen's shoulder and stared into his face, studying him closely. Without a word, she turned and studied Harley. Then she turned to Owen and communicated. Owen heard a subsurface rumbling of words in Spanish, but he understood her as clearly as if she were speaking English.

—*I am Irma.*

—*Owen.*

—*Yes, I know. What I don't understand is why you*

left your wife and your daughter in the care of Van Meers.

—I had no choice.

—Maybe you chose not to choose. There was a killing time. Why didn't you kill him? In this moment . . .

Irma excited Owen's memories of the moment Van Meers looked up at him. He had a strong memory of the pale look of those eyes. He could remember now anticipating that Van Meers would make a move toward him. Now the memory played out so slowly that he could see all the details. Irma's awareness was nearby, helping him see how it had happened. Van Meers had looked at him. He could sense the menace behind that pale look. He knew that he was in danger, but he preferred to doubt that there was anything that he could do about it. Earlier, Van Meers had touched him there, somehow, so that now he was afraid and dull. He had frozen for one second. Van Meers had begun to move toward him.

There, deep in his mind, where thoughts did not take the form of words, was the knowledge that he had to move *this way* and turn his energy toward Van Meers. But he had done nothing. Van Meers finished his movement. Owen found himself staring into the memory of the power failure sweeping across his brain, the memory of a black pool of unconsciousness.

—You chose not to choose, Irma told him.

—Maybe not, Owen answered. *Maybe he sabotaged me earlier. Maybe you're sabotaging me now.*

—He needs you to be weaker than he is. I need you to be stronger than I am.

"Do you understand?" Irma asked. Her voice was

low and musical. She spoke English with a trace of a southern Spanish accent.

"No," Owen said.

"There will be time to understand," Irma said. She turned and shouted to the others, who dismounted from their horses.

"We almost killed the horses catching up with you," Irma said. "We'll have to walk slowly, but we'll walk."

She swept her hand in front of her, inviting Harley and Owen to precede her on the way, the pale ribbon of dirt road that climbed toward the pass in the hogback mountains.

Harley glanced at Owen. They began to hike northward, every step higher than the last as they climbed toward the mountains.

"Who are you?" Owen asked.

"Do you really want to know?"

"Yes."

"I am a fighter," Irma said. *"Una guerrillera.* There were three thousand of us in the mountains. We were strong and growing stronger every day. The army feared us. We controlled the roads. The people, the poor, supported us. There were men who marched with us with empty hands. When one of us fell, one of these brave men would pick up his rifle. And then the world changed."

Irma fell silent for a moment.

"So many died. After so much death in the fight, and then this . . ."

Her bright eyes welled with tears. She blinked. Large round tears cascaded, marking trails in the film of road dust that covered her cheeks.

"So many good people, so many wonderful peo-

ple, so brave," she said. "And they just laid down
and died."

Irma turned her tear-stained, sunburned face
toward Owen. Strangely, she smiled through her
mask of tear-stained dust.

"I had a comrade," she said. "Like me, he was
from the city. From the upper class. University-
educated. He was a physicist. And do you know
what changed about the world? Do you know what
happened?"

"No," Owen said. "What? Tell me."

"The density of reversed neutrinos increased ten
percent."

"What? What does that mean?"

"Quién sabe?" Irma said. "Only a few people ever
pretended to understand subatomic physics, and
reversed neutrinos. Who knew? Pablo said that we
could only infer their existence by watching the
reactions of atoms exploding after they rammed
into each other at almost the speed of light. The
mathematical proof of the increase in their density
was fifty pages long. Fifty pages, and the only sym-
bol I could recognize was the equal sign. Pablo was
a very deep brother."

"He died?"

"Yes, with most of the others."

"Why?"

"Not because he was stupid. He was a genius.
He began to stare off into space and he went
somewhere . . . somewhere else. Then his body
withered and he died."

"You loved him," Owen said. It seemed obvious.

"Yes," Irma said. "Almost as much as you love
your Kate."

"You know too much about me," Owen said.

Irma turned her face toward him. As if she were using his eyes as a mirror, she began to dab at her face with a clean, folded red paisley bandanna. She succeeded in cleaning the tracks of her tears from her face, leaving only slight smudges.

"I'll be glad when we come to the stream up ahead," she said. "We need water."

It was now midmorning. The sun had risen high enough that it was radiating heat like the open door of a blast furnace. The blue tropical sky seemed not to filter the sun's heat, but rather to focus it. Sunlight struck the exposed skin like a hostile cosmic force. The radiated flesh began to bead and run with sweat and then to burn. Exhausted, the horses were beginning to drag their hooves in the dust. When they arrived at a stretch of the road protected by shade, most of the horses stopped and refused to continue.

"We'll rest here," Irma said. One of the Indian men spoke in his dialect to her. Owen was able to understand that if they stopped here, the horses would not move any more that day. Irma answered that the horses would move after ten minutes' rest.

Irma, Harley, and Owen sat down in the shade. Owen was anxious to continue, but he told himself they would travel more quickly once the horses were rested. Sitting in the shade, he realized how tired he felt. When a breeze moved past them, at first it felt cool as it wicked away their sweat, but then they were able to feel that the air itself was hot. Owen had never felt such a hot breeze. He watched with thirst as Irma's men cupped their hands and watered the horses with what was left in their canteens.

"Why are you after Van Meers?" Harley asked. His voice was raspy.

"He is the most terrible man alive today," Irma said. Especially in contrast to Harley's voice, hers was still musical and sweet. Owen had an insight into her strength. She had struggled under the burden of hardship for so long that it had toughened her. "We have to kill him before he grows any stronger. It is the same revolution. Only the dictator has changed his mask."

"No, I really don't think so," Harley said. "I think you and Van Meers are in a race. Something is going on up in the highlands. You've seen it, I know."

Irma smiled gently. "Yes," she said. "It's there—"

Owen had a vision of the distant highlands. He sensed the shapes of conical volcanoes under the blackness of a night sky. A huge energy was erupting, boiling . . . something, a great mass, an alien energy, clouded or obscured somehow. A heaving mass dotted with millions of pinpricks of light.

—*This is the place,* Irma said. *Look away. Someone is watching us. They know—*

"—too much about us already," she finished, speaking. Despite the heat, the sun on the green fields looked rich. Owen found comfort in the company of his brother and this beautiful stranger. "You, Owen, you've been about as subtle as Chernobyl. You've been flaming across the sky. People in Egypt know you. You have to learn to move without being seen. And either Harley or I are going to have to go into you and undo what Van Meers has done."

Harley said, "I'm not so sure Van Meers did anything to him."

"Oh yes," Irma said. "He has." Then she laid back on the grassy ground. She closed her eyes, and within a moment, she was snoring softly. She slept with her mouth closed. Her lips were full, chapped from the sunburn. Her nose had a slight point to it, her pinched nostrils vibrating slightly in harmony with her snoring. In sleep, her eyes, with their long curly black eyelashes, had an exotic beauty that no makeup could match.

As she lay pitched back there on the grass between the two brothers, her back was arched. Her full breasts pressed against her green cotton shirt. Owen found himself studying their round shape. When he looked up, his eyes met Harley's. His brother smiled knowingly.

Before noon, the Van Meers tribe arrived at the pass. The dirt road had degenerated into a path, cut with deep gullies, especially at the switchbacks, which had grown more numerous the higher they climbed into the mountains. Second-growth trees, weedy deciduous upstarts, crowded both sides of the path. Sometimes their leafy canopy blocked out the view of the mountains. With all the switchbacks in the path as it wound its way left and right under the canopy, it became difficult to maintain bearings. South became tangled with north, yet their way was always upwards. Not hesitating, Van Meers continued to march with his best speed. The tribe had to struggle to keep up with him. Boulders, some as huge as houses, choked the pass. The tribe began to climb over them.

For hours, Kate had been struggling. She felt exhausted. It was difficult for her to remember who

she was, where she was going, what mattered at all.
Kate felt an increasingly strong urge just to stop.
She wanted to lay down and lose consciousness. A
few times she was on the verge of collapsing, but
when she glimpsed her daughter, climbing like a
mountain goat, she remembered who she was. She
could not leave her child alone with Van Meers.

Kate worried that Van Meers had killed Owen.
Hector and other members of the tribe had assured
her that Van Meers had left him with Harley, but
Kate wasn't convinced. It distressed her that she
couldn't consult her own memory. The night on the
bus was like a blackened smudge. She could only
remember falling asleep, her head resting on her
husband's chest. Her next memory was walking in
today's sunlight with Constance traipsing alongside.

Under her hands, the boulders felt so rough and
heartless. She climbed, waves of inattention sweeping through her brain, so that sometimes she hung
there, coming back to find herself hanging there,
trying to remember where she was going.

She was the only straggler. All the rest had
gone ahead. Kate was afraid to sit down, because
she felt as if she would pass out, here, alone, with
the western and eastern peaks that rose above the
pass as the only witnesses.

Finally, Kate climbed the last boulder. A fero-
cious wind blew past her face and streamed back
her hair. The roar of the wind filled her ears. It
seemed that storms ripping through the pass had
cleared it of any weak deciduous trees, leaving only
small scrubby pines, their trunks twisted, hugging
the earth and crevices of the boulders as if they
were consciously avoiding the ferocity of the wind.

Kate looked for the others. Down below, where the path descended into green, lush, dark woods, Constance was straining against the gripping hands and blocking arms of men, as they pulled her along with them. Constance's mouth was open, but the wind was roaring so loudly that Kate couldn't hear her cry. Kate tried to shout out, but it seemed that she couldn't remember any language. Words seemed strange. She felt confused.

She knew she had to descend the boulders, but their northern faces were slick with mosses and fungus. The way down looked steep, slick, and dangerous. Perhaps she would just sit a moment and gather her strength. She sought shelter from the wind down in a man-sized crevice. Kate lowered herself into the crevice. Here the sound of the wind was a low moan. She sat down and tried to remember who the men had been who had been trying to . . .

That girl . . . the young girl with blonde hair. Kate knew her somehow. She was very important, somehow.

She reminded her of that man, the one with the dark eyes that looked at her so seriously.

Oh, she was tired. Kate closed her eyes. Immediately she began to descend into blackness.

It never occurred to her that she had been left behind to die.

FOURTEEN

A VOICE CALLING HIM STARTLED OWEN FROM AN UN-expected sleep. As he rose to consciousness, he sensed something desperately wrong. He turned toward one presence, but it wasn't the person calling him. Then Constance's presence overwhelmed him, as if his daughter were rushing through him. Louder than a shout in his ear, he heard her voice: *Daddy!*

—*Yes, Constance! I'm here!*

—*Save Mommy! Save her! The men are bad men*—

Strong men were hauling him down into dark woods, overpowering him with their bulk and strength. Then he realized that he was sharing Constance's experience. Up there, in those rocks, he could see the pale smudge of Kate's face. Giant peaks towered above masses of boulders, a cloud scudding past the more distant peak.

Owen searched for Kate, but he couldn't find her, the search causing him to lose contact with Constance. Sensing a strong presence come rushing toward him, he turned to meet it.

Van Meers struck him, hard as hate. Owen felt his mind boggling under the unexpected onslaught. Van Meers shocked the primitive regions of his brain, triggering an almost absolute fear and numbing his mind. Hallucinations of scarlet-and-gold explosions jammed his vision.

Two powerful entities stood up. Although Van Meers was stronger than both of them, they were closer to Owen, the closeness augmenting their strength. Harley and Irma knocked Van Meers back. As Harley confronted Van Meers, fending off a flurry of reattacks, Irma seeped into Owen's mind and calmed him. Slowly Owen regained self-control.

He returned to the noonday sun pouring intense heat onto the fields. Harley was standing, his body tense, facing the mountains. Irma was bending over and studying Owen's eyes.

"Owen?" she asked.

"Yes."

"It's over now."

Shakily, Owen rose to his feet. Most of the Indians were asleep. The strong smell of horses comforted him. He reached over and put his hand on his brother's shoulder. Slowly Harley relaxed, turned around, and scowled at Owen.

"You've got to stay down," he said. "No fights to the death without a warning bell."

—*Constance called for help. She and Kate are in trouble. We have to save them.*

—*Kate is dying,* Irma said. *They've left her alone to die. They've taken your daughter with them.*

Owen stood, staring up at the mountain pass, judging its distance: it looked about fifteen kilometers away. He turned to the others.

"Harley, you, and me, on the best horses," Owen said. "We can get there in time if we hurry."

Irma looked uncertain, but she nodded. "We can try," she said. "It's important for you that we try."

She turned and shouted in the Indian dialect. Instantly the camp burst into activity. An Indian brought Irma's mount to her. She grabbed the saddle horn, swung up swiftly into the saddle, stood up on the stirrups, and shouted again. Her men led two of the larger horses to Owen and Harley, who mounted. As Owen was wrapping the cracked leather reins around his right hand, an old Indian fighter ran up to him and offered up a vintage Colt .45 caliber pistol. Owen shook his head. The old Indian man turned and offered the pistol to Harley, who grunted, took it, checked the safety, and tucked the pistol through his belt.

Owen kicked his mount in the flanks. With a snort, the horse took off at a full gallop. Surprised by the suddenness of the acceleration, Owen felt himself falling backwards. Unless checked, his inertia would carry him head over heels over the back of the horse. He grabbed onto the saddle horn and pulled himself forward. Now he had the horse under him. It had been ten years since he had ridden, but he and Harley had learned to ride as boys in their uncle's farm in the Laurel mountains. He kicked the horse again. He knew that he couldn't force the horse to gallop ten kilometers uphill, but his anxiety would not let him go any slower.

Behind him, Irma was shouting something about reins. Quickly, her men rigged long reins for two other horses. She tethered them to her saddle and then kicked her mount. Together, she and Harley

chased after Owen. The two riderless horses gal-
loped after Irma.

—*Slow down, man,* Owen heard Harley's voice
say.

Ignoring his brother's plea, Owen continued to
urge the horse forward. The hill peaked and then
the road descended gently toward a valley. A large
village of peasant huts lined both sides of the road.
Hundreds of motionless people were sitting or lying
about, some in shadows, some in the sunshine. As
they passed the first group nearby to their right,
Owen's horse spooked, reared, and threw him. He
fell far and landed hard on the middle of his back.
Despite having the wind knocked out of his lungs,
Owen forced himself to stand. Unbreathing, he
stumbled forward and grabbed at the reins, but, its
eyes rolling, the dancing and kicking horse stamped
Owen's foot. His agonized gasp gulped air into his
lungs, restarting his breathing. Irma and Harley
rode up. Expertly, Irma dismounted and blocked
Owen's horse from running off. Owen reached and
grabbed his horse's reins.

"Calm down!" he shouted.

A scarlet light licked from his head to the
horse's head. The horse's eyes dulled, and slowly
it gentled. Owen coughed and spat onto the dust.
He glared at Harley and Irma and muttered a
curse.

Looking over at the peasants, he saw that they
had remained motionless. Owen walked over to a
group of them sitting under a pitted red round
Coca-Cola sign that hung outside a rustic grocery
store. The peasants were sunburned as brown as
the shells of Brazil nuts. They looked emaciated, the

skin of their faces stretched tight over protruding cheekbones. Even their gums and teeth bulged against their hollow cheeks. Their open staring eyes had the weird gleam of the starving.

One of them moved his head so that he was look-ing at Owen. He opened his mouth, but made no sound. His arm began to raise, in increments, jerk-ily, as if muscle reflex no longer worked normally. He raised his palm to Owen.

Owen wanted to reach out to help him. An instinctive feeling warned him, however, that if he were to touch this man, his mind would be drained from his body. He sensed that these people were as heavy as a black-hole sun that captured even light in its gravitational pull. This was the deathway.

"This is how they are," Irma said.

Muttering to himself, an old white priest in a dirty cassock emerged from the stone chapel across the street. In his hands, he carried a plastic gallon milk jug filled with water. The old priest bustled up to the peasant with the outstretched hand and raised the water jug to the man's lips. Greedily he drank.

"Without someone to help them, they die," Irma said.

The priest looked over at Owen as if he was see-ing him for the first time. He muttered something. Owen understood only a phrase: "the end of time."

"Come on," Owen said. He tugged on the reins and walked the horse through the village. On both sides of the street, the peasants stared at them unseeing. It was like walking through a gauntlet of zombies.

He limped from the pain in his right foot. Irma

walked her horses alongside Owen. "We might make it on a trot, but not a gallop," she said.

At the farside of the village, he turned his face up toward the mountain pass, where clouds were covering the peaks. It was another ten kilometers, at least.

Owen reached out and searched for Kate. Gently, carefully, he sought her. For the first time, his perception was fine enough that he sensed the presence of animals: nameless, shapeless, some mere cravings of predatory hunger, others a scurrying locus of fear, moving up there in the mountains. Focusing on these primitive minds, slowly he realized that Kate was there, high and alone in the rocks, surrounded by an emptiness, small and sinking down into darkness. Owen reached out to her and made contact.

—*Kate.*

She didn't answer. Her mind felt inhuman, her thoughts disorganized. The verbal layer of consciousness was missing. Just touching her sapped energy from Owen. At this great distance, the draining of energy threatened to break the connection between them, but he fought to maintain it. As much as he could over this great distance, he tried to pour energy into her. At first she didn't respond, the energy wasted, like blood poured onto the floor. Then, slowly, she turned to him, and he sensed the glimmering of recognition.

—*Owen.*

He felt himself blacking out. It was too difficult over this great distance, but he insisted as long as he could. As the connection wavered and failed, he heard her think, *Come.*

He returned to himself limping before the horse at the outskirts of the town. Irma and Harley were already mounted. Owen swung up into the saddle.

Without any physical prodding, the horse began to trot. The three of them were soon climbing the road, which, after a minute, took a sharp turn eastward, following the contour line of the mountain. As if merciful, the gathering clouds passed overhead, providing instant relief from the heat of the sun. Already lathered with sweat, the horses breathed more easily now that they trotted in the shadow of the clouds.

As the road switched back westward and climbed more steeply, the horse slowed to a walk, but Owen shouted and dug his heels into its flank. With an awkward lurch, the horse broke into a trot. Owen glanced at the other mounts: Irma's looked tired but strong, but Harley's was clearly in trouble, foam dripping from its mouth, skinny flanks heaving.

He was surprised when his eyes met Irma's to see a welling of sympathy for him.

—I tried also, she thought. *I tried as much as you're trying, but he went away despite anything I could do.*

—I won't let her go.

—I hope you can save her. Maybe you're strong enough.

The connection with Irma was so clear that it frightened Owen. He needed to focus on Kate, not Irma.

Overhead, the clouds were darkening as they poured southward out of the mountain pass. That the storm was coming from the mountains seemed strange to Owen. He thought that the weather should come from the south, the direction of the sea. Despite his preconceptions, the storm clouds were blowing southward out of the heights of the mountain pass.

His horse's breathing was growing labored, its lungs rattling with mucus. Exhausted, it stumbled, put a bad hoof down, managed to recover, but broke stride to a walk. Equally exhausted, the other horses also slowed to a walk. Owen jabbed his heels into the horse's hide, but it ignored him. He smacked its neck and shouted at it, but the horse refused to change its gait.

When he grabbed its mane and shook it angrily, red energy rocketed down his arm into the horse's head. It snorted and broke into a labored trot. Owen left the other riders behind.

Again, the road switched back toward the east. The horse tried to slow to a walk, but, determined, Owen forced it to maintain its pace.

After a kilometer, the horse began to falter. Owen finally allowed it to slow to a walk. The road had deteriorated into a path that climbed into the forest.

Nearer now, he reached out to Kate. Knowing where to look for her, he was able to find her more easily. Since he had last contacted her, she had languished so deeply that she felt barely there. It sickened him to connect with her. Her nearness to death was like a black-hole sun, sucking all the life from him. The others surrounded her now, the strange spirits that seemed fair to her and foul to him. Several of them attached themselves to him, murmuring sweet promises of rest and harmony. It was suffocating. All the energy he tried to pour into her seemed only to weigh her down more.

Suddenly he felt himself catapulted out of this perception and back to his natural self. He was on his hands and knees. Behind him, he could hear a hideous wheezing. Owen stood and turned to see the horse, lying on its side, its prominent ribs heaving. The horse's eyes were rolled back in its head so that it seemed to be staring at him with ghoulish white eyes. Its tongue lolled out of its mouth, the froth forming a pool of mud in the road dust. With a great wheeze, the ribs heaved one more time and then the body of the horse was still. Owen had ridden the animal to death. He felt sorry that he had killed the horse. It had not deserved such a death.

Neither did Kate deserve to die alone in the mountain pass. He turned and began to hike up the path. His right foot was so swollen and painful that he wondered whether the horse had broken a bone. Owen shunted the pain away as best he could and forced himself to jog.

In ever-greater pain, Owen managed to climb a kilometer into the mountains before Irma caught up with him. He noticed that she was riding a different animal, one of the two that she had tethered.

"Where's Harley?"

"The other horses are worthless," she said. "Take this one. Go ahead."

Irma dismounted. Owen climbed slowly into the saddle. He looked down into Irma's face, which gazed at him with an expression of sympathy.

"We'll catch up with you as soon as we can," she said.

Owen willed the horse forward. It began to

climb the path. They came to a switchback, after which the path was smooth and level, cleared by generations of Indians' feet. When Owen kicked the horse's ribs, it reluctantly broke into a trot. They rushed through the long clearing, slowed for a switchback, and then, valiantly, the horse began to trot up the next climb. Riding as well as he could, Owen urged the horse forward. They managed to climb several kilometers before the path became so steep and rocky that a man could proceed faster than a horse.

Owen dismounted and wrapped the reins around a tree limb. He began to climb the steep path alone. Storm clouds had darkened the sky so that it seemed like evening, the air heavy and soundless. Intense pain blurred Owen's vision, yet he pressed forward.

He reached out to Kate. The spirits had surrounded her so deeply that he sensed them rather than his wife. Despite the distance, Owen tried to fight them off. He focused his energy, hitting one and then the other, peeling them back like lanced parasites.

Finally he found Kate. She was still alive, but reclining, her mind slow. Connecting to her was like reaching through a portal into another world. He sensed millions of other entities.

Gently, Owen touched what was left of Kate's consciousness, and with all his love he poured himself into her. Dimly he was aware that he had reached the pass. He was climbing steep boulders.

Selflessly, with all the dedication of love, Owen Keegan gave himself to his wife. She was now on the other side of death. Connecting with her and offering up his energy was as absolutely painful as staring into the sun. He could feel himself beginning to dissolve. An impression of his own death struck him, yet Owen ignored his fear. With every scrap of his will, he was determined that she would not die.

—*And if I cannot bring you back, then I will go with you.*

Sheets of heavy tropical rain began to fall, in an instant soaking his body. Owen felt a strange duality, watching his hands climbing the boulder, the visual image nothing but a ghost against the overpowering experience of connecting with his wife through the portal of death.

Here was her face, pale and lifeless. He drew her to him and kissed her cool lips. There in the other world, they were gathering him up too. He was too fixated on Kate to notice these other creatures.

He gave and he gave some more. He would give everything he had. Something she had become was taking the energy now. She was turning to him.

—*Owen.*

—*Yes, Kate.*

—*Stay. Save Constance.*

—*No.*

They were joined now, sinking down together toward the deepness, a dissolution of the self. Owen was no longer aware of his body. Crossing the threshold into the realm of death, as he died, he gave.

No TUNNEL OF LIGHT, NO ETERNAL BLISS, NO CHOIR of angels, no reunion with departed loved ones, no encounter with the supreme being . . . Owen discovered that death was a highly overrated destination. The near-death experience, as reported by people who had died clinically, turned out to be a story that the brain told itself as it went to sleep. This was a natural reaction for any organ that had searched for gratification all its service-filled life. Why waste perfectly fine neurotransmitters? Why not throw an endorphin party for itself? Like sneezing, dying felt good, but not for any good reason. The simple truth was that sneezing and dying, being inevitable, might as well feel good, at least in the brain's considered opinion.

At the end of the endorphin party, though, Owen entered into the state of death, which was completely different from what any religion, story, myth, or popular science article had led him to expect. Death was not like anything that Owen had ever experienced. Worse, death wasn't even like nothing.

It *was* nothing.

Not blackness. Not a strange sensation of an absence of body, like the itching of an amputated limb. Not some remnant or form of being observing nothing, not from the inside, nor from the outside, nor from the farside, nor from any which side.

Nothing.

Game over. End of story. End of transmission. Dead.

As it turned out, life after death was an oxymoron, because life was a body-based experience. Specifically, life, as humans knew it, required a central nervous system. Without the brain, the spinal cord, and the nerves, life was over. As humans had discovered, it was possible to muck along without a lung, a kidney, or even a heart, but without a brain. . . . No, once the brain closed down operations and the wetware chilled, the phenomenon of the mind ceased to exist.

Owen ceased to exist. After he died, he was dead.

This self-sacrificing death thrilled the One. In truth, it had known its victory would be sure, but it hadn't known that the Owen animal would die so soon, days before and miles away from the rendezvous. A primitive mating instinct had doomed it to a premature death. Certainly this demonstrated the weakness of the human species and their unfitness for survival.

Yet the Hiyul envoy was speaking to it.

You surprise and disappoint me, my friend, the Hiyul envoy said. *We were anticipating a masterpiece of art, an exquisite and ultimate confrontation between races representing fundamentally different ways of being. This is simple genocide. Do you feel that this is worthy of your mastery?*

These remarks stung the One, but they proved once again the value of the Hiyul envoy. If a mere model of the Hiyul's mind reacted in this manner, how would the One bear the criticism of the Hiyul itself, when it witnessed these events in a few thousand years? What shame!

I am only beginning, the One answered, dissembling. *Death is a theme of the peace, is it not?*

Yes, truly: death and the way of nature.

Death is a way of nature for those who cling to their natures as animals. Simple mating imperatives, paternal instincts, base appetites . . . randomly evolved primitive blood and flesh, not truly of the mind.

Nothing is random about evolutionary selection, my friend. Why will you never concede that there are ideal forms that shape our ends? You have such a blind spot when it comes to such matters. For example, have you not seen this line of possibility? the Hiyul envoy asked, indicating a long, thin, but vibrant curve along the n-energy sense.

The One forced itself to contemplate this curve. It frightened him, because of all the possibilities, this was the one that most probably led to its own destruction. Yet the One had to admit that it had an almost seductive beauty.

Do you really think the humans are capable of such art? the One asked.

Why don't we find out if they are? the Hiyul envoy answered. *Surely you're a match for such creatures, even if we strengthen the hands of their heroes?*

I am not afraid of these pests.

Then allow me, my friend, to take this one by the hand and give him just a little help.

The One considered denying the Hiyul envoy, even just rewriting over the lobe that generated it, but then what would the real Hiyul think? Surely that the One was a coward and a weakling. No, it would have to allow the Hiyul envoy to raise the stakes.

Why do you think that I have brought us to this juncture? the One asked. *Do as you will, because all that you'll do, I have foreseen. I am the One. I maintain. I am everlasting.*

The Hiyul envoy intruded into Owen's quiescent brain. Resuscitation of the inert organ was possible because the tissues had not yet begun to rot from a lack of oxygen. Stimulation of the appropriate nerve centers jump-started his heart and lungs. Oxygen-rich blood began to flow once again into the 1.4-kilogram bundle of neurons that was Owen Keegan. Then, the Hiyul envoy removed Owen's mind from the One's observation, hiding it in secret memory arts where the One never ventured, hidden below traces of the memories of the death of the children.

Owen rose to consciousness in a great darkness. Owen looked around him and saw a blackness so absolute that he thought that he was blind. He floated weightlessly, staring into the darkness. He felt himself totally alone.

After a long while, he caused himself to turn. He thought that he could see a smudge of grayish light. Staring at it, he wondered whether it was a flaw in his vision or whether it was some sort of ghostly light. Slowly the smudge of light darkened, leaving Owen alone in a black universe.

He was just moving his eyes away from the spot where the smudge had been when—

A power swept through him. Beyond sight or feeling, a fundamental change to nature itself swept through him. It was a shock wave, an ever-expanding stress sphere in the fabric of time-space. A second wave flowed through him, then a third. These were spheres of being, waves thrown out by the violence of the big bang. Inside these spheres of being, as they passed through him, Owen felt himself to be utterly alone. No one else existed. The universe was empty of life.

Then he floated in blackness. As of yet, light itself, a form of energy, had not reached him.

Then it blossomed, a hideous flower of painful absolute light. Although it was almost perfectly spherical, it seemed to strike Owen with a malicious exactness, as if a ray of light had speared through his eyes.

The stuff of one hundred billion galaxies, each of one hundred billion suns, had been collapsed into a volume smaller than what would become the Earth. Darker and more dense than a black hole: a state before the universe, before the shining of the first light. Singularities of a black-hole cosmos, a state without place, where the newborn laws of physics had been tortured, where pressure, density, and heat had approached so closely to the absolute that time itself almost did not begin.

If the black-hole cosmos had been perfect, it might have maintained a steady state. Time might never have begun. But the black-hole cosmos contained the germ of a flaw, a wrinkle between masses too dense to imagine. This flaw was the

seed of the new universe. In a nanosecond, the
black-hole cosmos had rotated around a wildly
careening axis, yinshape and yangshape seeking
each other, then—

Absolute violence.

A sphere of nascent galaxies flung away at nearly
the speed of light. The laws of physics changed
eight times in the first second of the new life of the
universe, then mostly settled down into what
would seem to some immutable and eternal
laws . . . yet the absolute violence had launched ripples through that which held space, gave form to
energy, structured mass, and defined time. Ripples,
stress lines, waves, ever-expanding spheres.

Another sphere of being flowed through Owen.
Something was trying to connect with him.

He was floating in a globe of light above the
cloud forests. Hundreds of his fellows were harrow-
ing the survivors of another battle in the canopy.
Hyperevolved descendants of the devolved, the carbon-based creatures had taken to war again. Owen
felt himself settle over the nervous system of a
dying creature. He captured its pattern, set it to
spinning inside of himself, popped a new plasma,
and then released it into the sphere of being.

He felt weakened, but his mates surrounded
him, lending him their energy until he was vibrating at the proper frequency. He touched the newly
liberated creature. It chimed with a dulcet tone.
This was the joy of the Jarred, transcorporeal creatures, living balls of lightning.

Something—

Six billion years in the future, on the opposite
wall of the slowly contracting universe, in a place

where humans would never arrive, he felt himself leaving himself, because—

—was trying to contact him.

He was standing in the marketplace. Carbon-based once again, he felt the solid pleasure of breathing the rich air of the Queen's market, where the spice merchants were so wealthy that they allowed free samples of their wares to perfume the air. What could compare to the opulence of the Queen's market, where one lungful of air was worth a week's wages in the provincial mines? Farguey beans and orchid perfumes, the incense of rallisonde bark, hundreds of other scents, and the most precious aroma of all—the fermented nectar of the Walli, which flowered only once in one hundred years. His fellow merchants, tall creatures, silvery-leathered, with long, three-nailed hands and lustrous black eyes, emitted a pure musk of happiness and brotherhood that bonded all the other scents together. It was the most delightful place in the world of Ag'nsteer.

—calling him.

Huddled over a planning table, pointing with a chopstick at the red-lines-on-black display, Owen found himself explaining yet again why they needed to order another desalination plant from the Axtrax Folk, vice repair the old native machine that kept breaking down. The population of their city under the sea was now over ten million. The two native desalination plants had such-and-such capacity . . . blah . . . blah . . . blah . . .

He tired of explaining it to the proud fools, but he tried to maintain his calm. Marwan was looking at him. She had studded her shoulder plates with artificial emeralds again, which made her look rather old-fashioned, but fetching. Owen found himself losing his train of thought as Marwan flexed her mandibles, allowing the subdued light to gleam off a gold stud through the carapace. That was rather naughty of her, and it made it even more difficult to concentrate on the municipal freshwater situation.

"Owen?"

The black-ringed ones were not holding still. Under the sky of ice, the cold air was flowing slowly. The fifth and third moons were flying; it was the time of holding still. Red-dot and tube-trunked people were sleeping. Why did the black-ringed ones insist on moving? The cold air was rich with food. Now was not the time to move. What if the suns were to rise and the evil swimmers found them without a safe anchor? Red-dots did not understand the black-ringed people.

"Can you hear me?"

The morning air was pure and cool in his young lungs. Sunlight glowed greenly through a canopy of deciduous leaves. Owen was standing in front of the outdoor sink, brushing his teeth. He remembered: he was a ten-year-old boy in summer camp. Raising his hand toward his mouth, he thought himself lucky that he was able to live so vividly in one of his memories. Then he saw that long brown fur covered his arm. Instead of a toothbrush, his hand was holding a twig. With his powerful molars, he chewed the end of the twig, flattening it into a fan of fibers. Not thinking much about anything, Owen began to use the twig to brush his teeth. Overhead, the canopy of the forest was one hundred meters high. Later, unless he was lucky enough to find a breadfruit tree inside of the tribe's territory, he would have to grub.

Owen realized that he was not a victim who was unstuck in time. He was a superhuman with the godlike power of direct access to all time and space. Time had ceased to be linear. He was eternal, outside of time. He could reach out and touch it anywhere, anywhen, and he would join with the creatures there.

But where was his body?

Where was Kate?

Why should he care? He was the king of space and time. He had only to choose where and when he wanted to be, and there and then he would find himself. A king—

Atop the highest pyramid, with the black granite temple towering behind him, he stood, gazing down into the far-below plaza. Three hundred thousand of his subjects crowded the square. From this height, their forms were radically foreshortened; he could see their upturned faces, their shoulders, and their top arms. In the middle of the crowd, fifty thousand prisoners stood in five formations of one hundred by one hundred. Ropes joined them, neck to neck. They stood, waiting for the victorious king to decide their fate: liberation, slavery, indentureship, ritual death, or soul death. Owen's head priests, generals, and ghouls stood, ranked by precedence to his right (Red-Sunside; life-side) and to his left (Yellow-Sunside; death-side). For two days, Owen had fasted and let his blood. Both suns poured their heat down onto his skull. The Red Sun was rising; the Yellow Sun was sinking. In just a moment, they would balance: the moment of decision would intersect, the king the focus of their divine energies. He felt dizzy and gods-ridden. He was weary of the wars that had claimed his father, grandfather, and great-grandfather and that one day would claim him, but the rains demanded his obedience and the sacrifice of the blood of the faithful. Otherwise who could guarantee that the summers would rise and the winters fall?

For a moment, he felt so dizzy that he might topple and fall, end over end, down the long steps of the pyramid. Perhaps the Yellow Sun demanded more blood from the king. Then he felt his strength return. He glanced to his left; the death-side priests seemed content. To his right, the life-side priests seemed anxious.

The suns cast equal shadows down into the center of the great plaza. The moment of decision was upon him. Owen raised all four of his arms above his head. Into the total silence, down into the hushed crowd, Owen shouted.

"Liberation!" he cried.

Fifty thousand throats roared with joyous surprise. No king had ever captured such a host of prisoners; no one had expected liberation, least of all the prisoners. Among his own people, some widows dared to ululate, while the rest stood in stunned silence.

Soren, the power-hungry, forever-conspiring priest of the Old Way, broke from his ritualistic stance and dared to approach the king, there on the pyramid-top as the entire nation watched.

"You are ridden by a foreign demon," Soren hissed into his ear. "It is he, not you, that outrages the sacred in this foul manner. The portents clearly call for the sacrifice of blood."

Owen smiled at Soren. "You are right," he said.

Swiftly Owen spun and grabbed Soren, top-arms to bottom-arms, bottom-arms to legs. In one smooth movement, Owen hoisted the bony body of the obnoxious old priest above his head and threw him headlong down from the pyramid. The first bounce was on the steps some twenty meters down, far enough that Soren's bones snapped and shattered. If he was not dead by the second or third bounce, he was certainly dead before the body reached the plaza.

Screams of panic, fear, and sudden revolt tore the air. The shocking assassination of Soren was an unmistakable signal for revolution. Owen turned his back to his people and faced the oligarchs flanked in front of the temple, daring them to attack him. Battle cries sounded; knives and swords rang as priests and generals of both the Old Way and the New Ways unsheathed their weapons. Three Old Way assassins rushed him, but his generals flanked them. Owen laughed as the religious and military leadership of the nation, dressed in full ritual regalia, converged and swept and danced before him, killing each other and dying sloppy deaths on polished marble. In less than a minute, the fight was over; all the followers of the Old Way had been pitched down the blood-slickened face of the pyramid.

In the plaza, the people, witnessing the almost perfect coup against the Old Way, began to storm the western temples. The temple guards and the junior priests of the Old Way attempted to defend

themselves, but the mob swept up the wide stair-
ways with the undeniable force of a two-sun tide.
Minutes later, the mob had forced its way into sacro-
sanct temples within temples, murdering the
acolytes and pillaging the treasures that had been
guarded there for dozens of generations.

Alfran, the king's closest friend and most trusted
ally, approached, bearing a bloodied chest plate of
an Old Way general. He lay the trophy at Owen's
feet. Standing, he raised his eyes to the king's and
said, "Who knew that the blue skies hold lightning?"

"The lightning-struck," Owen said.

"He lost his rights when he dared to approach
you with the suns in balance. This was the most
brilliant revolution in history. Your name will never
be lost."

"Who am I?" Owen asked.

"You are Rangnon, king of kings."

"Keegan, actually," Owen said.

Alfran's face wrinkled in puzzlement and slowly
faded. Owen had wished for a more peaceful place.
He found himself standing in an alpine meadow.
Spring flowers, brilliant yellow and white, flourished from deep green, flood-watered plants. Crusts
of snow clung to winter in the shadows of crevices.
The air was thin, crystalline clear and pure,
smelling of the distant glacial ice from which the
winds descended. A stream of clear, cold water bur-
bled and tumbled down the middle of the meadow.
The morning sun was bright upon the snowy face
of the mountains that loomed above this high
meadow.

All of space and time. He could be a hero not

only for one people in one time, but for all peoples in all times. He could choose his moments of heroic intervention, appear and disappear at will, redirecting the histories of entire planets by a subtle touch in the perfect, pivotal moment. He could strangle Hitler in his crib—

A baby was crying. Owen was standing in the dimness of a candlelit, humble cottage. Except for the squalling baby, he was alone. He looked around him, noting the wood-burning cast-iron stove, the damp cloth diapers hung to dry from string, the chipped-paint furniture. The air was fetid, close, and far too warm. He took a hesitant step toward the hand-hewn wooden crib.

The baby's face was flush. Its little button nose was reddened and running with a smear of mucus. The baby's eyes were open, staring at him with coal-black, burning, feverish intensity. Apparently the mother or nurse had deserted the cottage for a short while, perhaps to seek medicine. Surely she would return any moment.

Owen stood, alone with the baby that would one day become the master of Germany, the man who would cut short the lives of tens of millions of innocents. He had only to palm that little face to snuff the most evil man who had ever lived.

What was the difference between a human baby and an old four-armed alien priest? Dizzy with bloodletting, fasting, and double-sunstroke, he had not hesitated to kill the old priest. Why should he hesitate now?

Yet he did hesitate. He was himself now, wasn't he? Not some hybrid of himself and an alien king. Owen raised his hand so that he could see it and convince himself of his own reality. He was shocked to see that his hand was a woman's hand, white, plump, and rough with housework. He realized that he had not projected himself into the empty air of this cottage; he had projected himself into the body of the woman who was caring for the sick baby.

A woman who did not know the fate of Hitler. A woman who had hopes that her child would survive this fever and grow up true and strong and good.

"Stop it! You're making me dizzy!" a voice said.

Owen turned to see a boy standing there. He looked like a half-scale man with an oversized head. His long straight brown hair was untamed, unruly, trimmed inexpertly in flights and steps. He had large almondine eyes that sparkled. His white skin glowed with an undertone of Asiatic gold.

"What?"

"You have to learn to control yourself, man. You're making me dizzy with all these jumps."

"Who are you?"

"Axel. Orphan, loser, geek, now with amazing superhero powers."

"No, I mean, who are you? You're the boy who taught Harley how to do things, aren't you?"

"Yeah, I taught him a few moves. Harley's my partner. Man, he'd die to save you, you know that? I wish I had a brother like him. I reached out to him; Van Meers is busy. I got him, but he said to try to find you, because he couldn't follow you so far down, and so I went down, and then I was lost, but then somehow I found you, but it's like some sort of weird level, this place. Something bogus is going on, that's all I know for sure."

"Are you still with Van Meers?"

"Yeah. The guy they had watching me was afraid to follow me here. I can't see your daughter, but I think she's OK. I don't know. I wish I was somewhere else. You ain't going to hurt that little kid, are you?"

Owen thought that he couldn't kill any baby, but Hitler as an adult . . .

The cottage disappeared, to be replaced by the shore of a vast gray lake under overcast skies. Small waves lapped upon a pebbly shore. Overhead hung wet black branches of bare winter trees. Minutes after sunset, the dusk light was failing. He turned up toward the road. Through a thicket of bare winter branches, he could see Adolf Hitler, alone, in full uniform, walking toward him and the lake shore.

—There is no time. Time does not exist, a woman's voice said in the center of Owen's head. *Think about it. Time is a lie. What you see, is not.*

Owen looked out over the water and tried to think. How could he exist in the past? Were the past and the future places that he could inhabit? What was time, after all? Was time truly a dimension like space, or was it just a way of thinking about things? A useful conceit that had no real grounding in reality? Matter and energy could be perceived and manipulated, but perhaps time and space were just ways of thinking about things.

The lakeshore dissolved into a woven fabric of gold and green lights. His companion, Axel, became a spheroid of glowing pearly light. Owen ignored this latest metamorphosis. He had to think.

If matter equaled energy divided by some very large constant, then matter was just a form, an instantiation, a condensation of energy. Everything was energy, then. He and Axel, and everyone and everything that he had once considered solid, were dense packets of energy, whirlpools of energy that stood for a while, then dissipated into nothingness. Perhaps they were and had always been creatures of light.

He had seen, heard, and felt a world, but seeing, hearing, and feeling were psychological phenomena. The world of the senses was all in the mind. The world he had lived in had been a world model in his own mind. The outside world, which he had considered solid and massy, perhaps was instead highly intricate and dense patterns of energy, formed along designs, following laws and working toward purposes that he was by his very nature unable to understand. The outside world existed, but was it possible that it had a form and substance radically different from what he had believed it to be?

Who was this Axel, anyway? Owen turned his attention to the boy, this glowing spheroid of pearly light. He felt immediately that under his manic boyish energy was a crawling fear and anxiety. All his life, the boy had been alone, abandoned by his parents. He didn't even know why they had abandoned him. He needed to reach out to others, but he didn't know how, and he was afraid they would betray him. In this new world, he was running toward people and running away from them. He was afraid that any embrace would be a preamble to betrayal.

—*The lie that is time is your clue,* the woman's voice said. *Follow it, if you want to escape.*

Time, then, time . . .

Time was merely an idea. It was impossible to travel into the past, because the past was merely a concept. He had never stood on the temple-top, never killed the priest of the Old Way, never waited by a German lakeside for a dictator fifty years dead.

If these things were lies, then who was the liar? Where was Owen, and how were these things being shown to him? And why?

Where was he? Where was Kate?

He had to search, then, for himself. He had to make his way through this unknown world until he found himself. Then he would have to seek out Kate and travel back with her to the real world, whatever its true nature might be. Then together they would find Constance.

—*Heal the boy. He will show you the way,* said the woman's voice.

Owen looked around for the woman. Now he could see that the world of lights was full of people, although they were distant from him. Small egglike shapes of lights, skittering near the horizon of his vision.

"Is this the way things really are?" he asked.

"This is just a view," the woman's voice said. "Just one way of understanding the way things are."

"Who are you?"

"I am the Hiyul," the woman said.

"What's the Hiyul?"

"We are the Ocean-Mind."

"I don't understand."

"You are within the mind of our old confused friend, our present enemy. Heal the boy. The boy will show you the way."

"I don't understand."

"The sphere of being should be a realm of great harmony. All should give praise to the glory of creation. Yet there are those among us who confuse their own magnificence with the glory of creation. Such confused creatures are fantastically dangerous. You are within the mind of such a creature, our old friend, the One, our present enemy. To escape, you must heal the boy and follow him. He will show you the way."

Owen concentrated on the Hiyul. He sensed an intelligence unlike any he had ever encountered. A multiplicity of awarenesses focused on him, like slightly varying reflections of himself in a dozen dark mirrors, each of them true, but different from one another. The Hiyul felt so distant and complex that it seemed more like the ghost of a world than a person.

"Are you one person? Or a group of people?" Owen asked.

"I am the Hiyul; we are the Ocean-Mind. Postnatural, self-designed, a complex mind now made up of 12,783 mature and 439 nascent brains all neurally interconnected. These brains and the million other parts of our body are spread throughout the oceans of my homeworld. I am the soul of my planet. You are singular and natural. The One, who has taken your world as its own, is singular but postnatural and self-designed. Its way is no good. It is impossible to maintain a single brain indefinitely. The One degenerated into madness late last cycle. I allow my old brains to die and my new brains to carry forward only the best-chosen memories. Therefore we are the master of the past and not its slave. I allow the past to die. It is the present that concerns us now and tomorrow."

Owen tried to digest these startling statements. "Where are you?"

"My homeworld is twelve hundred light-years distant."

"How can you communicate with me from such a distance?"

"I cannot, not at this speed. There is nothing faster than light. Even inside a sphere of being, at this distance, it is impossible to communicate as it seems that we are doing. You would need a lifetime of tens of thousands of years to connect with us in the way that does the One, the Jarred, or the Phoenix. Our friends communicate across a sphere of being in the way that your blue whales bellow across hundreds of kilometers of ocean depths, both speaking at once, thinking about what the other said long ago, until we fall into a harmony of understanding. This communication is not truly with me. It is with a small model of me that, for fifty thousand years, I grew in the mind of the One. My homeworld is now three-fourths of its way through this sphere of being, far deeper than your Earth. The One does not yet suspect the work I did on this model of my mind, hosted in its own brain, in the past two of your years. Right now, it can't even detect that my model is communicating with you. This is mastery of an order higher than the One can imagine, but we are the Hiyul, I am the Ocean-Mind, whereas it is merely a very old, insane animal."

"Then I am communicating with this One?"

"At this moment, you are in fact completely contained in the mind of the One."

"How so?"

"The One allowed us to revive you after you descended too deeply into the deathway. We have a purpose for you. You must help to kill the One. You should be aware that its mind is divided against itself. Some of it yearns for death, but most of it will fight never to die. Strengthen its death wish, because that is your point of leverage."

"What are these worlds I've seen?"

"These visions of the birth of the universe and the offworld societies are mental models contained in the mind of the One, which I am using as a place for you to learn and to strengthen your powers."

"Are you this One?"

"No . . . I am a shadow of the Hiyul, cast upon the mind of the One. An illusion, a dream. Believe me when I tell you, however, that the One intends to kill you and all of humanity. It is your greatest evil. You must cleanse your mind, build your powers, and oppose it. The boy is real. Follow the boy and he will lead you to where you need to go."

The woman's voice disappeared. Owen sensed a tremendous loss, as if the pressure had equalized in his inner ear, as if a great symphony had ended, as if he had lost in death a good friend. He turned his attention to Axel, a glowing spheroid of pearly light hovering close to him.

Why would he have to heal the boy? What was wrong with him?

His attention turned to Axel, Owen felt himself extending his consciousness to him. In a flash like an electric glitch, he felt his awareness connecting with Axel's awareness. The ovoid light was rotating as frantically as the star Sirius, the extreme centrifugal force throwing him off. Axel did not want anyone to know his mind. He wanted to remain alone and safe.

Yet Owen had sensed that this was a defensive reaction and that the boy truly yearned for friendship. Owen relaxed himself and thought that he would not impose on the boy's privacy. He would allow Axel to communicate with him, if he wanted.

Moments passed. Owen's relaxation increased until he found himself in meditative state. He could feel himself generating waves of well-being and peace. Axel calmed down; the spinning slowed.

"Hello?" Owen heard the boy's voice say.

"Yes, hello."

"You're like your brother, but you're different, too. You don't have much of a sense of humor."

"I know."

"But you are real intense. I'm glad you're on our side. Why do you want to be my friend?"

"I need your help."

"I'm just a kid."

"In many ways, you're smarter than me."

"Yeah, I know," Axel said, his voice regaining confidence. "I grew up in this world. For you it's strange, but I always—"

In the heightened state of communication with Owen, Axel's mind was accelerated. Thinking about the history of his mental life, Axel triggered a complex of repressed memories, which cascaded in a painful revelation. Communicating with him, Owen shared the moment. Even as a baby, when the world had just begun to enter the sphere of being, Axel had experienced this mental life. He had seen with the eyes of others. He had known the ideas of adults. His mother . . .

Owen saw Axel's mother as clearly as if she were standing before him. A young pale woman with shining blue eyes and curly reddish hair, gazing down at him with the look of motherly adoration. Then her eyebrows knitted and her eyes sharpened with alarm. The baby was reaching out to her, thinking in her own mind. She loved him, but what strange spirit was moving through him? Was it witchcraft?

A dozen other memories. He was looking through his mother's eyes as she was driving the car, gazing out the kitchen window as she washed the dishes. Axel found it more and more easy to connect with his beloved mother, reaching out to her with a baby's instinctive need for a mother's love, but she was reacting with increasing fear. The baby was diabolic, a thing of the beast that one should not name. Her baby was cursed.

A priest, sprinkling water on his brow. Glimpses of spire-bristling cathedrals, sunlight trapped in stained glass windows, the stench of incense and the waxy smoke of burning candles, masses of people singing indistinctly.

She could not free the baby from this creature. She had to abandon him with the sisters.

"That's it!" Axel screamed. "That's it! I remember now. She hated me because I'm bad. I'm a bad thing, a freak, I'm—"

"No," Owen shouted. "No!"

In this pivotal moment, Owen intervened. He allowed Axel to see himself through Owen's eyes. If Axel was a freak, then so were Owen, Harley, and

Constance. They were people who were born with
the abilities they shared. Axel had not meant to
harm his mother. He had no more been able to control his babyish thoughts than he could have controlled his thirst, hunger, or need to sleep. His
mother was not a cruel mother; she had been inca-
pable of understanding. In those days, no one could
understand. Only now was it possible to see that
the world was changing. Axel and Owen and people
like them were stronger in this new world. It was
not Axel's fault. He was a good boy, worthy of
respect and love.

"My own mother hated me. . . ."

"Your mother did not understand."

"I'm alone. Nobody loves me."

In this moment, Owen understood the boy. He
knew him in his totality: his brilliance, his vulnera-
bility, and his heroic strength under a crushing burden of loneliness. In fact, he was a lot like Owen,
who had grown up in a world where he had never
felt particularly welcome. A powerful wave of sympathy and understanding rose through him. Owen
allowed the boy to feel how he felt. Axel was a good
boy, brave and strong.

Connecting with Owen, seeing himself for what
he was, not ugly and evil, but good, strong, and
true, Axel felt a tremendous upsurge in self-esteem.
Harley had been too new in his powers to address
Axel as an equal; in him, Axel had not found a reaf-
firming authority. Now Owen showed him that he
was all right. The relief from a lifetime of self-doubt
brought him a rush of joy.

The intensity of joy was so extreme that the
world of lights disintegrated. For a moment, Owen

was kneeling on wet rock. A gusty mountain wind blew sheets of rain against his face. His eyes were fixed on the western horizon, where the leaden belly of the clouds was letting fall a dark gray slanting veil of rain. To his left, in the corner of his eye, he could see Kate, sitting like a statue atop the rock. To his right, he could see Harley frozen in his steps, just emerging from the shadowy forest at the base of the rocks.

Then a power moved through him. He found himself back in the world of lights. Axel was glowing more bright and more pure. Rather than spinning furiously, the ovoid sphere of light was rotating slowly and steadily. Owen sensed that the boy was stronger and more stable.

Owen turned to Axel. "Are you all right?"

"Yeah. I'm OK, now. Thanks."

"Are you ready to go?"

"Yeah. You bet."

"Where do we go?"

"It's not so much where, it's who," Axel said. "I got here because I was looking for you. We have to want—"

"We need to find Kate, my wife."

"Then what's she like?"

Owen thought about Kate, remembering the way she had been: he saw her entering through the kitchen door after working a double shift, her feet dragging from exhaustion, but still, she smiled at him. He remembered the delicate sensitive touch as she ran her fingertips across his forearm.

He remembered the night that he had stood at his lathe, three hours past midnight, his shoulder muscles knotted from long hours of frustration. At his feet, ruined fragments of bowls littered the saw-dust-choked floor. He could see the form in his mind, but he couldn't find it in the spalted wood. A spalt, a black flaw in the wood. Who would be so stupid to spend a lifetime trying to make beauty out of flawed wood?

Kate had carried in his long-forgotten dinner, wordlessly guiding him to sit and feeding him with her own hand, taking care of him for love, as she took care of patients for duty. Then her strong fingers began to work his knotted shoulder muscles. As his muscles regained their flexibility, Owen realized that he had to have faith in the wood. He was trying to impose a shape on the thing; he had to find the shape hidden in the thing. He had returned to work and begun the bowl that became *AnNautilus*.

Kate's caring nature struck a responsive chord in the boy. He was curious; he wanted to know more. For a moment, they shared a common appreciation of Kate as Owen touched dozens of other memories of her. Axel came to understand Kate: her toughness, her wry intelligence, her tremendous capacity to nurture and support.

"I think I know her now," Axel said. "She's not like anyone I ever knew. Let me try to find her."

Axel turned and cast his attention far afield. Owen followed him as best he could. He saw that he had to focus his thoughts, concentrate on his idea of Kate, and block out the interference from hundreds of thousands of mental events. Once, he thought they had contacted her, but it was another woman. After a few minutes, Axel's attention began to waver.

"Something is strange," Axel said. "Things don't work in this level like they do usually. Something is wrong."

"Listen to what the Hiyul said."

Owen allowed Axel to listen to his memories of his conversation with the Hiyul. Axel listened, hooting when the Hiyul told Owen to follow the boy. He became alert when he heard that the Hiyul had said that they were completely contained in the mind of the One.

"This whole level is bogus," Axel said. "Nothing here is real. It's real good, though. I can usually tell a fake level right away, when some loser tries to run a game on me. This One is much better than anyone else. We're going to have to break on through."

"How?"

"It's hard. You've got to concentrate for a long time on one thing. Then the bogus level disappears."

"All right. Go ahead."

Axel redoubled his efforts to focus on the idea of Kate. The horizon in the world of lights was a thin white line. As Axel focused, the line seemed to broaden and then grow indistinct. Suddenly, it inverted, running now upwards and downwards, as if direction had lost its meaning.

"It's not real," Axel said.

Slowly the line grew larger until it enveloped both Axel and Owen. It seemed to disintegrate and grow more and more fuzzy.

"Now reach out for Kate," Axel said.

Owen turned his attention outwards, seeking Kate. Like a wave, a disturbance rose in him, crested, and subsided.

In the undertow of the retreating disturbance, the scene before his eyes changed, brilliant point by point, until he found himself falling toward a mansion of a million rooms, a house bigger than one hundred cities, a violent frozen collision of every architectural type and design theory that had ever existed, with thousands of towers, tunnels, buttresses, and roof gardens.

He and Axel landed together on top of a large roof garden. Palm trees, lianas, and orchids in flower crowded the garden. A mossy stone wall was partially ruined and half-tumbled by the patient insinuation of veiny roots. Strangely, the gaps in the stone wall opened up into a well-lit white room, a dining table set with golden plateware and fine china.

"Weird," Axel said.

Owen looked down at the boy, who stood there, his shoulders squared and feet spread, the stance of a brave half-scale man. Axel squatted down and scooped up a handful of the garden's dirt.

"Is it real?" Owen asked.

"No," Axel said. "It's bogus, but it's good. This is memory-stuff."

"What?"

Axel stood and looked up at Owen. "I call it memory-stuff. This woman explained it to me once, about three months ago, when things started to get interesting. It's like dream-stuff, but better. You get it when the links among a group of people start to get real strong. They start to share each other's memories and bit by bit they build a place."

Axel swept his small hand across the horizon, indicating the riot of towers, buildings, plazas, and rooms.

"This is a big shared space," he said. "Look, it doesn't shake at all. Spaces made of dream-stuff don't hold still. This place is as solid as . . . well, geez, it's as solid as something real."

"How do you know it's not real?"

Axel treated Owen to one of his faces: one eye shut, other eye rolled up into his head, mouth agape in a goofy smile, and tongue stuck out to the left at its maximum extension.

"Duh," he said.

Owen laughed. "I get your point."

"I dunno," Axel said. "Looks real to me. Yep, yep. Just another city made up of a gazillion crazy rooms. Uh huh. See 'em all the time."

A woman's voice, the voice of the Hiyul, echoed in Owen's head. "You healed the boy; he has led you from the One's mind. Now you have entered a human consensual hallucination; this is a place hosted by some of the millions of minds that are rising in your world. Follow . . . and grow stronger."

The boy brushed aside a brake of ferns and pushed his way through to the ruined wall. Following him, Owen stepped down into the formal dining room.

In the pure white light cast by a crystal chandelier, the dining room sparkled. Surveying the room, Owen saw that the wall through which they had entered was a rich amber stucco, cracked in openings that corresponded to the openings in the garden's ruined stone wall. Axel glanced about, then bustled toward the far doorway. Owen followed.

No hallway, but a wrought-iron spiral staircase that descended halfway down a huge concrete well.

"Sheez, this place is weird-city," Axel muttered, as he climbed down the staircase. At the second turn, they came upon a landing that led to a mezzanine carpeted in a foot-worn floral pattern. Axel hustled across it until he arrived at the far end, where a Moongate doorway stood without any walls to justify it.

They crossed through the doorway. The new room was a colossal darkened cavern with an irregular floor. Screams of pain and shouts of brutish joy were echoing. Axel spun and fled from the room.

"Watch out!" he shouted. "Freak alert!"

Owen hesitated a moment, but as he turned to follow Axel back out of the cavern, he heard a man shout after him. Owen shook his head and shouldered through the Moongate door, following the boy as he ran across the mezzanine.

A group of men were chasing them. He could hear their brutal shouts and their running footsteps growing louder.

"Bad news!" Axel shouted. He waited at the foot of the spiral staircase. Owen reached his side, but Axel, his expression twisted between fear and determination, was turning to face the crowd of pursuers.

Owen turned in time to see the men: six large, hairy, muscular, bestial men, almost Neanderthal in appearance. Their hands were empty, but their eyes had a glassy feral look. Although humanform, they did not look human.

"Look out for me!" Axel shouted, each word louder until he was screaming "me" at the top of his lungs.

From Axel's midsection, a flaming light erupted

and blasted the men, knocking them backwards. Screaming obscenities, Axel bathed the men in flames. When he finished, they lay there, limbs twitching.

Axel coughed a few more obscenities, ending with, "—and that's what happens when you mess with Axel, you butt-munch losers."

Owen walked over to the sprawling forms. He toed one man's leg, which already seemed stiff with rigor mortis.

"Are these guys real?" he asked.

"Yeah, they're real," Axel said. "Come on."

As they climbed down the spiral staircase, Owen shouted, "How did you do that?"

In response, Axel connected with Owen and replayed the memories of his attack, emphasizing the technique of throwing his will and his hate against the men. It was like learning kung fu not by watching the movements of a master, but by reliving the master's own muscle memory.

"Them kind of freaks think they're so bad," Axel said, as he swung off the spiral staircase into a long low studio-lit gallery. "They got only one or two moves, but they bust some heads, and they think they're all that. Don't know who they're messing with."

The gallery was hung with paintings. Owen paused to study the brushstrokes of a van Gogh. The person whose memories had built this gallery had understood the way that van Gogh had laid down the paint, each dab of oil referring simultaneously to the paint, the brush, the act of seeing, the mind of the seer, and the object itself. The next painting was Alex Gray's *Kissing*, a god's-eye view through the skins of a man and woman, all nerves and blood vessels and infinity loops of holy fire joining their hearts and their brains.

"Come on, Owen!" Axel called.

From the direction they had come, Owen heard a noise. He turned in time to see three men swinging down from the staircase. Two of them held knives; the third held a fiery torch. Seeing Owen, they hooted and ran for him. Axel shouted something that Owen didn't understand. Squaring himself toward the men, Owen shouted and connected with them.

They were strong, bent on growing stronger. They wanted to enslave Owen and the boy and harvest their powers. The men were part of a large tribe, which Owen could sense connected to them, lending them strength. They took what they wanted and destroyed everything else.

Behind them flowed the force of all history. They and their kind had pillaged, raped, stolen, tortured. They had been the strong men. The weak had died by their hands. Now, in this new world, some of them had powers. Their army of darkness would rule the world.

But Owen had powers, and Owen was not of their tribe. As his forces began to coil for the strike, Owen felt himself touched by a tribe at least as strong. They had been watching him. In this critical moment, they lent him their force, as pure as silver and true to the light. They would stand between what was good and brutes such as these.

An ecstasy of worldwide focus centered in Owen's skull as he shouted and power rushed out, branching like lightning and striking the brutes.

Hate for what was hateful, the mirror-image of love of the good, a righteous hatred that crackled and burned and purged.

Then the ecstasy passed. The brutes were laid low. Dizzy for a moment, Owen stood, trying to remember where he was or what he was doing.

"Good one, Owen!" Axel shouted from the far end of the gallery. "Now come on, let's go."

But Owen was not ready to go. Although he had burned down these three men, he still sensed the lingering existence of the larger tribe. A fiery force was still singing through him. He was not afraid. He reached out toward them and connected forcefully with the entire brutal tribe, the army of darkness.

They were spread throughout the entire world. A strong network of men and a few bent women, constantly preying on those weaker than themselves, physically and mentally. The naked stench of aggression, acts of rape and mental murder, violence against the gentle and the weak.

Owen launched into one, killing him. He spun and attacked the next nearest, in turn burning him down. Soon he was embroiled in a bloody fight, as if he stood in a grassy valley, a broadsword of fire in his hands, fighting the fight of holy zeal, a berserker strength inflaming his brain, his blood a rush of red fire, accelerating the power of his muscles until he was the hero of his people, the strength of his nation, unstoppable, invincible. He killed one after the other. Some stood before him, some attacked him, others ran; but Owen struck them, gutted them, smashed their minds.

The battle lasted one hour that seemed a lifetime. Sometimes Owen was blind to his eyes' sight; sometimes he could see rooms, passageways, and vistas of the sprawling house of the memories of mankind. The more he fought, the stronger he became. He was a creature of flame, burning the blood of his people, purging malignancy.

Yet even a berserk strength had limits; Owen felt his forces begin to fail. His sword arm became leaden, hard to lift above his shoulder. In that moment, he wished for help.

From across a vast expanse a soldier of light came flying. He arrived like a rush of hot wind, furious and ready to fight on Owen's behalf. Immediately, the soldiers of darkness that had stood before Owen fell at his hand.

Owen turned to the soldier of light, seeing him not in the flesh, but as a fiery angel with hot eyes and glints of painfully bright sunlight in the folds of his clothes. The soldier was wielding a sword of flame. Behind him were arrayed a hundred figures of flame and fire. Owen understood that the soldier was a centurion, leader of one hundred soldiers of light.

—*Who are you?* Owen asked.

—*I am Rashid; these are my warriors.*

Rashid shot Owen a message explaining the origin of his tribe. Rashid himself had been a Saudi mechanical engineer who had worked in the oil fields of the Kuwaiti desert. When he had sensed the world changing, two years previously, he had embarked on a pilgrimage to Islamic holy sites and, eventually, to most sacred places around the world. As he had traveled and his powers had grown, he had formed a network of like-minded men: sharp, zealous, intolerant of evil. Now that the battle was rising, they formed a battalion in the army of light. Rashid offered Owen a place in his command.

—*What is the army of light?* Owen asked.

Rashid explained that no one could agree on the definition of the army of light; his was one of the more organized and disciplined units, but most units continuously reorganized with kaleidoscopic complexity. Moreover, there were units of the army of darkness that masqueraded as units of the army of light. Rashid kept his definition simple: anyone who preyed on the weak, who violated the dignity of women, or who spoiled the innocence of children belonged to the army of darkness and deserved the sword.

—*Join us,* Rashid said.

—*No, but I will fight alongside you,* Owen answered, *as your enemies are my enemies.*

—*We are proud to have a man as powerful as yourself fighting with us,* Rashid answered.

Rashid dipped his sword to Owen. Then he turned and sought the enemy, which also was rising in organization. Now they encountered fewer bands of three or four; now, instead, groups and phalanxes as large as five hundred. The assault of the army of light was forcing the army of darkness to organize. Other forces joined Owen and Rashid, and so the battalions began to wheel and maneuver. Small clashes were escalating to general war.

Then the moment came when the enemy grew afraid of them, and in their fear, they practiced stratagems and wiles. Owen found himself fighting men who weren't the men he thought they were: he attacked and killed people who were not the enemy. The blood of innocents stained his hands.

In a dungeon deep below the earth, he found himself with the body of such a victim. The brutal men had masked over the mind of the victim; striking at them, Owen had struck instead at one of their victims.

Who am I now? he asked himself. *What is the difference between my enemy and me?*

His self-doubt infected Rashid's one hundred. For a moment, the battle paused.

Then a gentle voice of a woman, the Hiyul, said, "That is enough for now. The true fight is an unending war, not a battle to be won in one hour of one day. If you accept this paradigm, this construct of memory-stuff, this consensual hallucination that is the world for so many people, then you accept its terms and its limitations. There is a higher way, a higher love, a truer enemy. You must learn to see with higher eyes."

The arena of war dissolved before his eyes, like the sparkles of failing vision from a blood-rushed brain. Owen found himself standing in the gallery, Axel by his side, looking up at him with large wondering eyes.

"That was intense, Owen," he said. "You're a fast learner."

"I have a lot to learn."

At the far end of the gallery, Axel pushed open a door of hammered copper and led the way into the next room, a book-lined library three stories high, the ceiling a high dome of dark glass, the pale face of the sun haloed by millions of fine scratches.

A man was reclined on a lounge of stainless steel and black leather, reading by the light of ten tall candles. A large leather-bound book lay open atop an embroidered throw pillow on his lap. The man looked up and studied Axel and Owen. He had white wiry hair brushed straight back, a tall forehead, a prominent hooked nose, and full lips. The eyes with which he studied them were pale blue and deeply knowing.

"What are you looking for?" he asked. His voice was deep, mellow, and self-assured.

"I'm looking for my wife, Kate," Owen said.

"Then why have you wasted your time wrestling with pigs?" the man asked.

Without warning, he connected with Owen and explored his mind to a profound depth. Just as quickly, he withdrew.

"The woman you are seeking no longer exists," he said. "You are going to have to accept that."

"But I don't."

"She no longer exists. She's not yet dead, but she's dying. Even if you find her and bring her back into the world, she won't be the woman that you remember. She'll be fundamentally different. Just as you are different from the man you used to be. The old world is dead and everything that was in it has gone. Can you understand that?"

"Yes."

"Can you accept that?"

"No."

"You'll have to learn to accept that, but if you like, I'll show you where you can find her."

"Yes, please."

"Through that door over there," the man said. "Under the bust of Frankl."

Owen and Axel walked across the library, through an inner room made of a book-lined marble canopy, and through the door with a small marble bust over the lintel.

They entered an airport terminal, crowded with people who seemed comatose. Hundreds of zombielike people sprawled on the vinyl sling chairs and on the granite floors.

"Losers," Axel muttered.

Owen sensed a deep depression and a lack of spirit. The airport terminal full of zombielike people saddened him. He reached out and touched them, discovering to his surprise that underneath their sullenness was a great well of communal joy. These people had given up their individual lives to form a community that joyfully celebrated their descent toward death and the promise of a paradise.

"Careful," Axel said. "These losers are going down. They'll take you with them—"

"Hey, Kate is with them," Owen said.

"Sorry," Axel said, stopping in his tracks and turning toward Owen. "Then . . . well . . . let's go for it."

Axel joined with Owen and tapped into the crowd of the zombielike people. It was as if they were sucked down a long black whirlpool into the highly pressurized depths of an alien ocean. Millions of people were with them, interconnected strongly, but quiescent and sinking lower.

Then it hit Owen with the same beautiful revelatory clarity of the first time a new drug showed its particular fashion of ersatz ecstasy. Life was too hard, too complex, too finite. It was better just to sink down into death and pass through eternity into the paradise beyond. The only true forgiveness was the oblivion of death.

For a long moment, Owen luxuriated in the false bliss. It was wonderful. Death was like a shoreless dark sea that waited eternally on the other side of life. So vast, peaceful, and inevitable. Why struggle? Why muddy himself in the world, where truth mated with falsehood and gave birth to a hideous beauty with the lifespan of a gnat?

Death, a warm dark ocean . . .

"Don't believe it, man," Axel said.

There, almost at the bottom of the network of the tribe of the false bliss, was Kate. Owen sunk lower, down into depths where the changes were so profound that he was no longer truly himself. He sloughed off himself, he accepted these strange dimensionalities, so that he could reach her. Finally he was able to stretch down and touch her.

"Kate," Owen said.

But she was no longer Kate. She had embraced the memories of a million strangers; she had allowed their common yearning for peace to flow through her. They had accepted her as one of them. Now she was just shy of the threshold of death. Owen to her was as dim as an ancestral memory.

"Come back, Kate," he begged.

But Owen was foolish not to understand. She was in love now with something far more easeful than life. The distant din of the struggles of the living was only so much annoyance. She was almost home now: the black vacuum of space, the compost of consciousness. Nothingness. And beyond that, a paradise of union.

"I need you," Owen pleaded.

But Owen was just a man, one of billions of men who had needed women, just as billions of ants had needed their queens, just as billions of other creatures had needed . . .

"Constance needs you," Owen said.

He had touched her in the one place that was still human enough that he could grab hold. Constance was her daughter. She was in danger. If it had been possible, Kate might have returned, but what good would it do? She was weak and evil to her daughter. . . .

"No, you aren't. You're a good mother."

Then the aspect of Kate's character that had never occurred to Owen, a self-absorbed artist who had never suspected the central fact that defined his wife's way of being: she was guilty. It was her fault. The doctors had said that it wasn't, but she knew, when her poor girl was born deaf to the world, that it was her fault. She had hidden this guilt from Owen all these years because it was a knowledge too horrible to share. She had kept it even from herself, but it was the pain that constantly twisted in her guts, the source of all her sorrow. Easier now, to descend with her brothers and sisters into the final passage.

"No," Owen said. "It's not your fault. Constance was born that way because of me. Harley and me, we're different, we have these brains that . . . Constance was born to live in a world that didn't exist. Now it does. She is home now in the new world. You have to come back and help me find her."

Owen detected a glimmer of hope in Kate. She began to move slowly, twisting, her surface glimmering as it fought against the pull of the others. Her face achieved almost a humanform.

"How sweet it would be," she said. "If that were true. If I weren't guilty. If it wasn't my fault."

"It is true. You aren't guilty. It isn't your fault."

"It's too late. I can't—"

"Let me take you up."

"No, it's too late."

"Just ask. I'll try."

Kate turned her face one last time toward the darkness, the easeful death, the false bliss. She thought about her daughter, alone in the strange world. What if it were true? Was it possible that life could be so sweet?

"All right," she said. "Help me."

Owen embraced his wife and looked upwards toward the surface, impossibly high. It seemed that they could never return from such a great depth.

Looking up, he saw that Axel was part of the way up toward the surface, and above him, he could see Harley, and beyond Harley, as if in the light-filled sky beyond the surface of the water, he could see elements of the army of light. Kate, Owen, Axel, and Harley were all connected, and through them, the deathway network was connected to the army of light. All their power focused on him, as he gathered his arms around his wife and began to try to pull her toward the surface.

The deathway dreamers clung to Kate, but he pulled strongly, and so they stretched up with her, and in the moment of greatest tension, the dwindling life forces of tens of thousands of people flowed into Kate. Simultaneously, power arced down from the elements of the army of light, through Owen and into Kate.

A lightninglike discharge of power, coursing and

branching through her nervous system, firing every neuron simultaneously, recanalizing her entire brain. In a split second, the tens of thousands of deathway dreamers fired their memories into Kate's brain. Suddenly desperate to live in the moment of their death, they poured themselves into her mind. They attempted to enter Owen's mind, too, but he refused them. He tried to keep them away from Kate, but he failed. Only the power of the army of light allowed him to continue to hold onto Kate as she metamorphosed into something strange and different.

In one moment, Kate lived tens of thousands of lifetimes. She understood; she knew; she saw.

Tens of thousands of wills, tens of thousands of powers . . . Owen felt Kate grow strangely stronger. In these weird dimensionalities, he felt her being bequeathed the life force of ten thousand people, who sunk down and passed into the realm of death.

The gap that these ten thousand people made in the community healed almost instantly. The millions of other people who were sinking blissfully toward death flowed inward and renetworked as smoothly as if the ten thousand had never existed.

Now the battalions of the army of light began to ascend. Their power pulsed through the embracing Keegans. Owen continued to climb with Kate toward the surface, hoping against hope that it would be possible that they would breathe once again the air of the world. . . .

S I X T E E N

DARKNESS SURRENDERED TO BRILLIANCE AS LIGHT WENT flying from them, fading slowly to a gray world under storm clouds. Owen found himself kneeling on rock. He had thought that he was embracing Kate, but his arms were empty. He could see only a rain-darkened crevice of rock.

He turned and looked up toward the sky. Long streaks of rain were falling from the leaden gray clouds, pelting his head, shoulders, and arms. His soaked clothes hung heavy, cold, and clammy against his skin.

On the ledge above him sat Kate, her head flickering with a pearly fire shot with small lightnings of an electric silver. She was staring out toward the north. Slowly she turned her head and looked down on him. Her skin was as translucent as that of Van Meers, her eyes glowing with a gentle pale fire. Staring at him with her otherworldly eyes, slowly Kate smiled.

—*You loved me,* she said.

—*Yes.*

—What you loved is lost.

With a great deliberateness, moving limb by limb as if only through the force of will, she lowered herself from the ledge to stand next to Owen. Gazing into her eyes was a new experience now. His peripheral vision blackened, his field of vision narrowing until he could see nothing except her eyes . . . mesmerizing eyes without a face, not mirrors into her soul but portals into some unfathomable deepness.

—What happened? Owen asked.

—Love without limits has led you to a place that you did not know.

Kate turned and gazed down the southern side of the pass.

—They're coming.

Owen looked down and saw Harley and Irma climbing the southern face of the boulder-choked pass. Within minutes, they joined Owen and Kate at the top.

Harley's expression was aghast as he stared at Kate and Owen. He circled around them, keeping his distance.

"What the hell? You're like Van Meers," Harley said. "Both of you!"

Surprised, Owen looked down at his own arm. His skin was pale, almost translucent. If he looked deeply enough, he could see his veins and even the lines of his muscles and the runs of his nerves. He looked up at his brother. Looking at him, he had a visual flash of his own appearance. Pale. Ghostly. Eyes that seemed to glow from within, irradiating an unearthly light.

"I . . ."

"Christ, Owen, what have you done?"

Irma interjected, near to gibbering with fear: *Van Meers has come from that place. You have become what he is.*

Looking out at the land, Owen could see where the medium was weak, where it was strong, where living minds disturbed it. The more distant, the dimmer. Next to him, Irma, Kate, and Harley stood like pillars of fire. Seeing them in this way made his eyes grow dim and stupid, as if his mind's sight blinded his natural vision.

"No," he said.

He turned to Kate and forced himself to see. Her aurora flickered and flamed. The dark pools of her eyes robbed his concentration. He didn't know who or what she had become, but his faith in himself was strong.

"No," he said. "I'm not like Van Meers. He might have gone down to that place too, but he wasn't like me when he went down, and he wasn't like me when he came back."

When Owen stepped close to his brother, Harley flinched, telling Owen that indeed the world had changed. He reached up to his big brother and placed his hand on his shoulder.

"Harley," he said.

Harley's face contorted, overcome with conflicting emotions. Abruptly he embraced his brother. "Man," Harley said. In the embrace, each found comfort in the solid presence of the other. Since boyhood, they had been a team. Where Harley was, Owen did not know fear.

"Always together," Owen said. "Always together."

"That's right."

They separated. Owen turned to Kate and reached out to her.

"Kate," he said, speaking to her for the first time since she had gone down to the place of death. "Let's go get Constance."

Kate smiled and shook her head.

—*Constance cannot use me. I am not.*

"Come on," Owen said. "Let's go."

Kate shook her head again. Turning inward on herself, she darkened and became difficult for Owen to see.

"Kate!" he called. He had meant to be commanding, but his voice sounded plaintive even to his own ears.

Slowly she seemed to return to them. She regarded Owen's outstretched hand as if it were some alien object, but then she reached and took his hand. Their auroras merged fiercely, an energy sweeping from Owen and jolting Kate. She had been turned in some strange direction that he didn't understand. Part of his will surged forth and shocked her, trying to reorient her to him.

"Owen," Kate gasped.

"Yes. I'm here, Kate."

"Constance? Where is she?"

"We have to go get her."

He turned and looked toward the north. In the multilayered, interwoven fabric of forces, he sensed that Constance was *there*, not more than fifteen kilometers ahead.

The rain was slowing to a light drizzle. On the opposite hill, clouds like gray smoke drifted through the canopy in the forest.

"Let's go," Owen said.

Kate pointed at Irma.

—*She can't come with us,* Kate said. *She loves you only for your power. If she comes with us, she won't rest until I'm gone.*

—*No that's not true,* Irma said. *I don't know what you are but I don't want to hurt you. I just want to stop Van Meers.*

—*What's a Van Meers?* Kate asked. *He's just a phenomenon. It's Owen you're with. It's Owen that you're after.*

—*Stop,* Owen said.

He interposed between them. He believed that they could not communicate unless they came through him. In this, he thought he would be more buffer than medium.

He began to descend from the pass. The north faces of the boulders were thick with green moss, making the descent more treacherous than the ascent. As Harley followed, and then Irma, Kate stood watching. For a moment, Owen thought that he'd have to return for her, but then she too began to descend.

As they reached the path, the sounds of the drizzle pattered lightly on the leaves. They began to hike down the path as it gradually wound down toward the central valley. Even though the rain had soaked the land, the path was still hard. Generations of barefoot Indians had worn the path to a smooth-packed surface that allowed the rainwater to drain to lower elevations.

In this central valley, where the weather swept up from the east, the forest was much more lush than the forest of the southern slopes of the mountains. Here the forest might be mistaken for jungle, but the jungle was dead. For hundreds of thousands of years, primeval jungle had flourished in this valley. Giant trees of mahogany, chicle, and zapote, hundreds of years old, had reached a hundred meters high, their foliage forming the sun-seeking canopy. Billions of creatures had lived in this jungle. Then, three generations previously, in one month, loggers had eradicated an ecosystem that had endured for hundreds of thousands of years.

Now the soil was too poor to support a rebirth of the original forest. Instead, lesser, weedy trees had sprouted, forming a canopy only twenty meters high. In the triple-canopy jungle, the floor of the forest would have been dim, still, and open. They would have been able to see a long distance in some directions, since the vegetation on the floor would have been low, mild growth such as ferns and mosses. In this forest, sunlight broke through the patchy canopy at odd intervals, causing a riot of weeds, vines, and upstart trees. In this new ecosystem, only one in a hundred of the jungle's species survived. Yet life struggled forward, surviving somehow one more uncounted holocaust.

After zigzagging down toward the floor of the valley, the path began to follow a contour line, curving westward for the north. Owen limped along as best he could for the first hour, but it became increasingly apparent that he couldn't go further in such pain. He stopped and stared at his foot, which had swollen inside his boot. He held up his hand for the others to stop. He could sense that the medium was growing stronger.

Then it seemed so simple. The pain was more

than a mechanism to keep him from stressing damaged tissue. It was a signal that helped him to focus. He was aware not merely of his right foot, not merely of the second and third metatarsus bones. He was aware of fibers of living bone, a long crack and several smaller fissures, ruptured blood vessels, inflamed soft tissues.

As he wished that the wounds would heal, blood flowed to the damaged tissue and nervous signals fired in new patterns. Swollen tissues shrank; damaged tissues pressed against each other. Metabolic heat burned in his right foot. When he was done, the pain had vanished.

His awareness began to rise toward the normal plane of the senses, but as it did, Owen became aware that his body was riddled with imperfections: lumpy scar tissue, arterial plaque, fissures in his bones, tears in tendons, unevenness between spinal disks. Owen felt as if he had been sleepwalking every moment of his life, only dimly aware of his own body. How strange! What was more clear and immediate than his own body? He had only to focus, to stand up straight, to let the power of his body flow as it should through the most minuscule tissues, to allow the heat to rise.

He didn't need to be imperfect. These flaws were avoidable. He only had to allow himself to correct them.

One by one, tissue by tissue . . .

It was a pleasant purging heat. It burned through him, strengthening everything it touched. The stronger he became, the stronger he was able to become. Soon it was easy. He didn't have to think about it.

His natural vision returned to him. He saw
green leaves dripping, slick with rainwater. The
beads, sheets, and rivulets flickered with an illumination like reflected lightning, yet there was no
thunder. The strong light illuminated the forest
around him.

Owen turned and looked at his companions.
Irma and Harley were difficult to see. He looked at
Kate, who was smiling at him, her aurora brighten-
ing. He reached out to her, not with his hand, but
with his thoughts. As she joined with him, their
auroras joined and flared.

Through her, he saw that he was shining ten
times more brightly than before. His aurora was
bright white fire, a hot sheen that shimmered with
every color. Like the corona of the sun, it extended
far from him.

Owen coughed fire. An amazing energy coursed
through him; euphoria fired his mind. He had
never felt so good. His body was perfect. His mind
was a hundred times more active. Whole regions of
his brain that had flickered feebly, now blazed. He
was burning with life.

Nothing could stop the invincible man. Injury
was a mere inconvenience; death, only a veil, easily
brushed aside. Then, just as his arrogance was lim-
itless, Constance screamed to him.

Help me, Daddy!

Constance was brave, but she hadn't known that
men could be so evil. Only days before, Van Meers
had seemed a simple creature, but as Constance
had grown wiser, she had realized that he was
more than a fool hungry for power, like a moth in

love with flame. He had teamed with monsters beyond her understanding. She had realized it almost too late, only moments before he took her mind.

Now she could not stop him, nor even scream. He was moving her legs and arms, forcing her to climb with the others higher up the mountain, toward the monster that waited in the highlands. Constance's throat was tight. With every breath, her chest heaved painfully. She wanted to throw herself onto the mud, grab a root and cling to it until they left her, but he was inside her mind, controlling the movements of her muscles.

Constance was a good, strong girl, but Van Meers was big and powerful. She didn't know how to stop him. Most of him was moving outwards to other people. Only a part of his mind was concentrating on her, but that part did not understand mercy.

Yet Constance was clever. She was able to hide her true self from Van Meers. She showed him a small scared girl, but she kept secret within herself all her true memories and thoughts. Occasionally, when Van Meers would try to overwrite some of her memories, Constance would allow him, but when his attention was turned away, she wrote her own memories back. Constance was a good girl; she would never allow this Van Meers to see her true self. The Silver Stars were a big help, but she wanted her Mommy and Daddy. They shouldn't have left her with Van Meers. Daddy had said he would protect her. Why had Daddy left her alone?

Van Meers hesitated, surprised that anyone would consider him evil. Taking advantage of the hesitation, with all her mind, in the voice of the scared little girl, Constance screamed.

"Daddy!" she screamed. *"Daddy!"*

Constance's torment struck Owen with the force of a physical blow, revealing the futility of his pride. He only cared about protecting his daughter; he had failed her.

From close by, he sensed a horrifying power rising. As he turned to face this unexpected power, he felt it continue to rise, a coiling wrath gathering force like a tidal wave cresting on the shore. Owen expected the power to strike him, but it rocketed outwards toward Constance.

No!—he shouted.

But Constance was not the target. The power was flowing from his wife, striking Van Meers. From this distance, Kate focused savage force on Van Meers, who withdrew from Constance's mind and doubled up to save himself.

The realization that Kate could summon such power shocked Owen, but then he remembered Constance's torment and joined the attack on Van Meers. He sought the weakest point in Van Meers's mind, but the distance was too great. As the power flowing through Kate ebbed, the connection with Van Meers and Constance failed.

Returning to natural sight, he saw Kate standing in front of him. Behind her towered a thick stand of yellow bamboo, the sharp shapes of green shoots cutting through the sheen of her waning halo. Her downturned face looked angry and exhausted. Her eyes gleamed normally, her irises dark and sad. She looked more like the Kate that he knew and loved. Owen stretched out his hand, but he mistook the distance between them, so his hand didn't reach her.

—*Kate.*

Too exhausted to cry, she looked up and met his eyes.

"That was the most awful . . . the most awful thing I . . . how? How did we allow this to happen to Constance?"

Owen realized that he was guilty. Back on the black sand desert, he should have listened to Kate and allowed her to die. He should have saved Constance, taken her far away from Van Meers. Until now, he had never imagined that life held horrors worse than death.

"I'm sorry, Kate."

She shook her head. "You should've let me die back there on the desert, Owen."

"I couldn't. I could not."

Shaking her head again, Kate glanced at Irma and Harley, who stood further up the path.

"Let's go get closer to him," Kate said. "Then we can kill him."

Shaken, Van Meers clutched the ground and pressed his face into the dirt. The phenomenal long-distance strike had savaged him so excruciatingly. When the Keegans had attacked him, Van Meers almost wished that they had killed him, the pain was so intense.

Van Meers looked up at his tribe gathered around him. Only those to whom he had been connected had felt the attack.

They were atop the summit of a mountain. Standing, Van Meers could see southward to the

Pacific. To the north loomed a volcanic mountain range with towering peaks much higher still.

In the confusion of the attack, Constance had tried to run away, but Hector and others had grabbed her. His men stood, staring at him, waiting for instructions. Constance struggled pathetically against their restraining arms. His wrists tied behind his back, the boy, Axel, stood looking at them with a deceptively empty expression.

Something touched Van Meers, giving him an upswing in mood and energy. Everything was going to be all right. All power waited for him in the highlands. There his mighty ally would strengthen him so much that he would never have to worry about humans again.

Van Meers considered whether he should kill the girl. He doubted that sparing her would win him any mercy from her parents, if they ever got hold of him, yet he knew that killing her would erase any possibility of mercy. He would have to take the battle to them and hope that he was able to kill them first.

"Hector," he said.

Hector came to his side.

"Take Carl and Gerry with you, go back down the path, find a place, and ambush this Keegan man and his party. Kill them."

Hector nodded.

"With skills, *señor?*"

Van Meers shook his head.

"No. Use your skills as a shield only. Harden your mind. Be still and empty. Do what you need to, but get close enough to them and shoot them."

"Yes, *señor.*"

"Don't come back to me until they're dead," Van Meers said.

Hector nodded, but Van Meers thought he detected a shifty gleam in his eye. Van Meers believed that he understood the mind of his lieutenant, but now, for some reason, he was unable to read his thoughts. Such resistance was strange and worrisome.

S
E
V
E
N
T
E
E
N

HAVING ABANDONED THE PATH, OWEN, KATE, HARLEY, and Irma were descending a slippery and treacherous slope. The path had followed the contour line, curving around far to the west before turning back to the east; the Indians who had made the path had known that sometimes the surest way was the longest. Desperate to overtake their enemies, Owen, Kate, Harley, and Irma had headed straight north, up over the summit of the lesser mountain. Now they were struggling to keep their footing as they scrabbled down the muddy northern slope.

Looking up, Owen could sense that Constance was still ahead, yet the way between them felt uncertain. He had the uneasy feeling that he was making a mistake. His foot slipped. Reaching out for support, he grabbed the trunk of a small tree. Needles pierced his palm. Owen grunted with pain and snapped his hand open. Black-tipped needles, a defensive mechanism, furred the trunk.

Kate appeared by his side. Her eyes were beginning to glow with their eerie light. She took his hand and studied the wounds.

—*Ignore the poisons, Owen. They are for more common animals, not for the likes of you.*

—*I'm just a man.*

—*No. You were a man.*

—*If I'm not a man now, then what am I?*

—*Who am I to say?*

Kate released his hand. She continued to descend the mountainside. Watching her, Owen's misgivings intensified. Who was she? In fact, what had any of them become? Was it even possible that he could save his family? Perhaps they had changed so much that they could never return to the old way.

Harley's hand clapped his shoulder. Owen looked over and met his brother's eyes. Harley's expression was one of watchful concern, a look of care, a look worth ten thousand smiles.

"I used to know a boy," Harley said. "He was a happy boy. A lot of fun. When he grew up, he turned into a stranger. A man who kept to himself, who didn't talk much, who was serious, who built things I didn't understand. I loved the boy. It took me years to get to know the man. He was always my brother. I loved him if only for that, but when I learned who the man was, I loved him for who he was, and I realized that I had never known the boy. Not really. Not in the way I knew the man."

"People change, Harley," Owen said, defensively.

"Yes, they do. But maybe the core of who we are remains the same. Maybe we just have to learn to know somebody over again in their new form. That's Kate ahead of us. And we *are* going to find Constance."

"All right."

Together the two brothers and the two women continued to descend the mountain. They were entering a steep valley, far wetter and greener than the forest on the southern slope. The canopy overhead was growing thicker, blocking out the sunlight. Under thunderclouds and the thickening canopy, the midday was growing as dark as late dusk. Here the slope of the valley had been too steep for the lumberjacks to bring their machines. In this narrow fold of the mountains, the native jungle still survived. Descending into its depths was like traveling backwards in time hundreds of thousands of years.

Owen sensed Kate reaching out toward Irma, investigating her mind. As if stung by the contact, Irma flinched and coiled her mind into a defensive position.

—*She's hiding something*, Kate said.

—*Leave me alone*, Irma said.

Owen interposed himself between Kate and Irma. Kate's reaction was surprisingly violent.

—*Who do you trust?* she asked. *Do you trust her or me? She is hiding something, I tell you.*

—*Leave her alone*, Owen said.

—*As you command, O lord of light*, Kate said.

For a moment, Owen turned his attention to Irma, who stood, holding onto a swoop of a descending vine for support. Her svelte form was silhouetted against the greenery of the jungle.

"Are you all right?" Owen asked.

"I don't know why she hates me," Irma said.

Owen turned and looked for Kate, but she had gone far ahead and disappeared beyond a thick brake of giant ferns. The others thrashed through the vegetation, emerging to find a riot of vines swooping down from the canopy. Here the whir of insects, the bleating of frogs, and the rumbling of the storm clouds sounded wet and muffled. Purple, pink, and scarlet orchids clung to the forked limbs of giant hardwood trees. Underfoot, the floor of the jungle, thick with the compost of the season's dead leaves, felt padded and soft. Kate was nowhere to be seen.

—*Kate!* Owen called.

She had gone missing, from both his natural and his mind's sight. Owen concentrated until his natural sight dissolved and he could see only the disturbances in the medium. Irma and Harley were as evident as burning flames. He could sense the animals, even down to the pinpricks of the insects. Nowhere was Kate. Owen expanded his awareness, looking further and further away, until he touched carefully on the tribe, there, up higher and to the north.

Someone was moving off there, to the northwest, but their minds were strangely transparent. They were difficult to read. Perhaps they didn't exist at all.

Kate had disappeared. Had she died? Was it possible that within the last minute, Kate had died?

His natural vision snapped back into focus. Owen cried aloud and rushed forward, calling, "Kate! Kate!"

In that moment, the belly of the sky opened. Rain deluged the forest. High overhead, the rain tattered on the broad leaves of the canopy. Yet here below, the rain did not feel as intense as it sounded; most of the water, splashing on the canopy leaves, cascaded down the limbs and vines. The jungle was drinking deeply of its mother rain.

"Kate!" His voice sounded hollow against the roar of the rainfall.

Owen ran, searching for his wife. Half-expecting to find her pitched face-forward on the ground, he looked in the niches of the high arching roots of a banyan tree; he looked under the canopy of a tangle of creepers climbing a network of thick black vines. Harley and Irma also searched for Kate, but she was nowhere to be seen.

"She must have gone forward, Owen," Harley said.

"Let's go!"

They scrambled forward, deeper into the jungle, descending an ever-steeper slope.

Hector had been walking quietly along the path ahead of the other two tribesmen, when suddenly he had felt Owen's mind touch him. Hector tried to keep his mind still and transparent, yet he could feel Owen sensing him. The other two men were even less successful in evading detection.

Then the connection terminated. Hector signaled to the other two to be silent. Gingerly, Hector extended his awareness toward the southeast. Yes, it was true. There were strong disturbances down there, off the path, down in the valley between the two mountains.

"They've left the path," Hector said.

Hoisting his rifle and tilting his head, Hector tried to think. Something was teasing the borders of his consciousness.

The vision was given to him: in the center of the

valley, where the river ran, was a crossing where they would meet.

"Follow me," Hector said.

He stepped off the path and began to hike southeast, down into the valley, down toward the place where something had told him that he would meet Owen. He wondered whether he would be able to kill the man. More disturbingly, he wondered whether he wanted him dead.

Owen and Harley were struggling through a thicket of four-meter-tall grasses, horribly thick and interwoven, solid as a wall. Owen was swinging the one machete they had, Irma's machete. His arms and shoulders ached, his breath came in gasps, and his skin rolled with sweat, as he fought to part the grasses. A break in the grass wall had seemed to indicate that a creature, perhaps Kate, had penetrated its barrier, but now, deep into it, Owen found it difficult to believe that any animal could ever have stood in this spot on Earth. It was frustrating and horrible, struggling through the wall of grasses.

As they approached the farside of the grasses, the sound of rushing water began to double: the rain still battered the canopy, but now a muted roar of water was rushing ahead of them. Owen broke through the farside of the grasses. He could see the dark gray underbelly of the storm clouds; thick drops of rain were streaking downward. Looking out, he saw that he stood on the brink of a chasm. Under his boots was a small precipice of rain-darkened rocks, and beyond that was a long drop down the chasm, at the dim bottom of which rushed the whitish waters of a rain-swollen river.

Owen reached back and grabbed onto a handful of the thick grasses. "Stop!" he shouted to Harley and Irma, who were jostling him in their desperation to escape the grasses.

"Damn!" Harley shouted, when he saw the chasm and the river that had cut it.

Irma studied the terrain. To the east, the land fell away steeply, following the river as it descended. To the west, the land looked more gentle. From brink to brink, the chasm was almost ten meters wide.

"I was afraid of this," Irma said. "We'll have to go upstream, try to find a crossing. Either that, or go back."

"If we go back, we'll lose Van Meers. We'll never catch up," Owen said.

"Let's go upstream, see what it looks like," Harley said.

The way was extremely dangerous. Seeking the direct sunlight that poured down through this break in the canopy, weeds and grasses crowded them to their left. Underfoot, the precipice was treacherous with slimy mold and crumbly volcanic rock. Owen led the way. As they climbed westward, the hillside to their left gradually was steepening into a cliff. At one point, they came across a tree that hung from the steep hillside. Head-high to Owen, half-exposed roots clung to the rocky soil. The tree struck out at a sharp angle, seeking the light of the center of the chasm. Its strategy had allowed it to grow to an impressive height, but, there, alone in the middle of the chasm, storm winds had torn it, almost uprooting it. Now it clung precariously with half its roots.

Owen used its exposed roots for handholds, as he continued to climb toward the west. Quickly it became obvious that the cliff face was steepening, both above and below where they were climbing. After a couple of slips and near-falls, Owen stopped.

He felt trapped. Desperate to move ahead, he was opposed at all sides by natural and seemingly supernatural forces. For a long moment, he hated this new world. He wanted only the safety of his family. Why was the entire cosmos conspiring against him? He trembled with frustration. For a moment, it almost seemed better just to throw himself down the chasm and be done with it.

Softly Irma's hand touched his shoulder. He looked around to see her beautiful face softened in a caring expression.

"Follow me," she said. "I thought of a way."

They backtracked to the tree that hung over the chasm. Irma climbed up the hillside, using the exposed roots for holds. With difficulty, she found a place to stand that was higher than the tree. She called for the machete.

Expertly, she wielded the dulled but sturdy blade, chipping V-shaped cuts into the tough exposed roots. She was able to sever two smaller roots before her arm grew tired. Harley climbed and took over the machete. He cut several of the roots before giving up the machete to Owen, who finished cutting all the top roots before the tree groaned as if mortally wounded. Its foliage shivered.

Owen, Irma, and Harley hung onto the steep hillside, watching the tree slowly fall. Around their feet, roots tore from the earth. Leaves rustled and shook, branches snapped, larger limbs broke, as the top of the tree crashed down on the farside of the chasm. For a moment, it seemed that the tree might fall top-first down into the river, but then it quieted. Its rain-wetted trunk now formed a bridge across the chasm.

Irma laughed, shook her hair, and climbed around the severed roots. With her head held high, she began to walk across the trunk.

"Magnificent," Harley breathed.

Irma walked with grace. Her boot heels trod surely on the tree trunk, which was less than a meter thick. When she reached halfway across the chasm, the tree shivered. Limbs snapped as the tree settled. Irma quickened her pace. She grabbed a vertical limb, swung swiftly around it, and then climbed through the broken and tangled crown to safety. She stood and waved at the two men.

"I'll go next," Harley said.

"No need to walk," Owen said. "Just crawl across."

Harley looked down at his younger brother and smiled crookedly.

"No fears," he said.

He began to walk across the tree with his characteristic confidence, as if the rain-slicked tree over the chasm was only a prop for a demonstration of his competence. Owen resisted the temptation to call out to him to be careful.

An eastern wind sprung up from the chasm, thrashing the canopy of the forest, buffeting Harley as he walked in the center of the tree. He swung his arms wildly, struggling to maintain his balance. He overcompensated to the left; his center of gravity remorselessly moved toward the left. He struggled to regain his balance, but the moment came when there was nothing more he could do. He was going to fall.

So as not to fall over backwards, flailing ridiculously, as his feet began to leave the tree, Harley made a little hop to the left. He did it gracefully, as if he were a gymnast hopping down from a balance beam. As if he would not be penalized so heavily, if at least he fell with grace.

Gravity took hold of him. Silently, without a scream or a curse, Harley plummeted down toward the rocky bottom of the chasm. No time at all seemed to pass before he crashed onto the rocks. The sound was one of many snapping bones, simultaneous with a solid, heavy thud as his body was destroyed against the rocks.

Then all was silence, except for a low moan of the wind, which tumbled rainwater from the broad leaves of the jungle, the rainwater pattering on the lower leaves as if the wind had brought fresh rain.

Shocked, Owen stared down into the chasm at the body of his brother. He knew it would be no good to call out to him. It would be no use to do anything, as a matter of fact. He was unaware that long minutes passed before Irma called to him, "Owen!"

He looked up.

She waved him onward.

Owen looked at her. It occurred to him that he would have to cross the tree. Slowly he stood, pulling himself through the roots until he arrived at the base of the trunk. He knew he should lower himself until he straddled the trunk, and then, hands on the trunk in front of him, shimmy himself across, but he could not do that. In his shock, he thought that he owed it to his brother to walk across, to balance life and death, step by step, above the fall.

He began to walk. The wind was gentle upon his cheek. He felt himself balanced above the void. The space on all sides around him felt immense. Gently, the tree thrummed with the energy of the wind. Almost halfway across, Owen stopped and stared down at the mangled body. The first emotion that penetrated the shock was a swell of resentment. Harley had abandoned him. He had said he would stay with him, but he had escaped into the absoluteness of death. He had left Owen alone.

Again, the wind rose. Owen crouched, dropping his center of gravity lower. The wind caused the trunk to vibrate under his feet. He could feel limbs snap at the far end. He waited for the wind to intensify. If the wind rose, he would throw himself down on the trunk and hug it.

Slowly the wind calmed. Owen took a deep breath and recommenced walking. Within a minute, he arrived at the vertical limb. Grabbing it, he swung around the limb and began to climb through the ruined crown toward safety.

Then the ground was firm under his feet. He wondered what he should do next. Where was Kate?

Irma reached out and touched his cheek. Her touch caused Owen to realize that tears had leaked from his eyes. He wiped at his eyes with his biceps.

"I'm sorry," Irma said.

"That was the way he was," Owen said.

"It's my fault."

"No. It's not. It's not mine, either. Maybe it's not even his fault. Not his fault."

With no more words over his brother's death place, Owen turned and began to climb the steep hillside, still toward the north. And Constance. And whatever was left of his world.

Down in the chasm, where Owen had last seen the body of his brother, wet rocks gleamed next to the gushing whitish water. Wet-blackened rocks, whitish water, and nothing more.

Holding on to the vertical limb, Harley stood, gazing with horror down at the shattered body of Owen. Why had he insisted on walking across the tree trunk? Why hadn't he crawled across, as Harley had done?

Harley shook his head as if nauseated. He had been a stranger to grief. Now grief overwhelmed him, teaching him bitter truths about life that he thought he had known before; but his awareness of the poignancy of mortality had been academic, a boy's shallow perception. Now Harley realized that the one person whom he had loved in all the world had been his brother, Owen, and now Owen was dead.

Suddenly the rain recommenced, now intensified, falling in thick sheets that blocked out almost all the light. The depths of the chasm grew so dark that Harley could barely discern the form of Owen's body. He looked up, searching for Irma, taking long moments to realize that she was gone. Like Kate, she had disappeared.

Harley was alone. For a minute, he didn't know what to do, but then he remembered Constance.

Although Owen was dead, his niece was still alive. She needed him.

Running his forearm across his eyes, Harley turned and recommenced the hike northward.

Hector and the two other men had made good progress toward the rendezvous place. The rain provided good sound cover, so they moved quickly. They were descending down a wide area clear of cover, heading southeast. Carefully, Hector was sensing for Owen and the others. The woman, Kate, had disappeared. Hector imagined that she had finally died. When the other one, the brother, disappeared, Hector began to worry that it was a trick, but he was able to catch a flash of Owen's reactions to the death.

It was convenient, really. Hector had been worried about attacking four of them. Now there were only two.

Huge mahogany trees towered around them. Since Hector was devoting only a fraction of his attention to his natural sight, at first he didn't understand when Kate stepped out from the cover of a rain-darkened trunk. His mind's sight told him no one was there; his eyes were registering a woman who glowed from within with an eerie light.

—*Stop*, Kate said.

Hector and the two others halted. They raised their rifles to point them at Kate.

—*No*, she said.

Suddenly it seemed to Hector that he was on a fool's mission. Van Meers had sent him to kill a man. Why? Why did he follow Van Meers? Long

ago, he had respected him, even worshipped him.
But now he realized that he resented and detested
the monomaniac. What had been wrong with him?
Why had he allowed himself to become the slave of
such a man?

It was the woman, pointing out gently that Van
Meers had forged manacles in his mind. He had
taught him to believe certain things, to see certain
things, while turning a blind eye to others. With a
touch, the woman freed them of these manacles.

Now they were independent. They did not have
to follow her, although she was going to the north to
bring their former slavemaster to justice, lay him
low, destroy him.

"We'll follow you," Hector said.

—*Yes. Yes, I know.*

"And your husband?"

—*My husband is doom.*

WHAT IS DARKNESS, OTHER THAN THE ABSENCE OF light?

What is death, other than the absence of life?

The One had gone for a long stroll through its mental model of the Kaolin world, where it spent many pleasant hours reviewing its favorite thought poems. This poem, though, was somewhat jarring. It had a whiff of the Hiyul envoy to it, which was strange, since the envoy should have no access rights to the Kaolin model. In any case, the thought poem was dreary, and it reminded the One of all the problems it was experiencing with the latest reentry into a sphere of being. Its attention diverted, the One realized that the processes monitoring the humans had been alarming now for almost an hour. It would have to leave the pleasant Kaolin world and attend to the problems.

Strange . . . strange . . .

The army of light was growing so rapidly; some elements were not so easily manipulated. How startling! The One would have to consider that the humans' potential was greater than it had believed. Perhaps it should allow some of them to live: they would make good pets.

A wave of fatigue washed through the mind of the One. So shallow into the sphere of being, it was hard to concentrate on this problematic present. To muse upon the glories of the past was a great temptation.

No, the humans were a threat, both physical and, as it now appeared, mental. The One must deal with them. Besides, there was glory in the art of their destruction. The One had its two thralls helping it, but one of them was too independent for the One's taste. Those two siblings named Keegan . . . it was good that the One had separated them. And so cleverly! What a pleasure to witness their mirrored delusions of the death of the other.

But this animal named Owen had progressed so dramatically. Who had taught him so much? It was almost frightening. The One would have to treat him with care.

The disappearance of his former mate was strange. How did that play into the One's master plan? No, the One had not even foreseen this possibility. Where was the creature named Kate? Who were these Silver Stars who clustered around the female offspring?

Slowly a feeling of foreboding, such as the One hadn't experienced in many millennia, began to surge through its massive and many-layered mind. The humans were far more complex and dangerous than it had realized. This art was too risky; the One should abandon it and unleash genocidal techniques even more deadly and fast-acting than the deathway. The master plan with all its prettiness should be incinerated in a lake of fire! Killing the humans as quickly as possible, individually and as a species, was the only reasonable course of action.

Yet . . . how lovely was this fear. The One thrilled with the primordial urgency of this death fear. Where was the art, if there was no risk? The elements were coming together. Its master plan had always embraced some chaos, and what to the mighty One were a few twists and turns?

No, bring it on. The One welcomed the challenge. It would strengthen the male thrall, and perhaps cut back an element or two on the humans' side, but the confrontation itself would occur.

What a beautiful fear . . .

In the highlands of southern Guatemala, three huge conic volcanoes loomed above the shores of Lago de Atitlán. One of these volcanoes, Volcan de Atitlán, was erupting, throwing a pillar of magma fifty meters high. A huge cloud of volcanic ash was bellowing upwards, mixing with the lowering thunderclouds, precipitating a sooty rainstorm hundreds of kilometers wide. On the volcano's northern slope, a vent had opened. From the vent flowed magma, red-hot liquid rock oozing up from the planet's molten core. Inexorably, this magma flow descended the slope and hissed into the waters of the lake.

The explosion had dumped gray powdery ash knee-deep, turning the once-beautiful lakeside into a moonscape. Knocked down by the blast, dead trees lay splintered and half-buried in the ash. Thatched, corrugated, and clay roofs had collapsed under the weight of the heavy blanket of ash, leaving towns clusters of hulks and ruins.

The sky was an abnormal greenish gray: abnormal, but as natural as the most azure vault of heaven. Absolutely indifferent as to whether humans found this face of nature beautiful or not, the blast of the volcano was as natural as the opening of a hothouse blossom.

Days before, the tens of thousands of Indians who had inhabited the towns around the lake had escaped, most of them east or west, using the paved road of the Pan-American highway. Only a few humans remained. Their minds had found peculiar reasons for remaining at the scene of such a catastrophe.

From the summit of a mountain one ridge south, the tribe could see the tower of fire standing over the Volcan de Atitlán. They had climbed within fifty kilometers of their destination. The huge cloud of ash spread overhead to all horizons. Within the past day, the muddy rainfalls had turned the green forest into a dreary gray mess. Even the distant Pacific, far to their south, was a leaden gray.

Weirdly enough, the air smelled like a charcoal barbecue, a burnt chemical smell that did not seem healthful. The greenish-gray sky was freakish and unnerving. Also strange was the silence. The ashen sky and ashen earth had stopped all movement and dampened all sound, so the only things they heard were their own hushed voices, the whisper of the wind past their ears, and the distant earth-deep muffled roar of the erupting volcano.

In that moment, the earth underneath their feet began to tremble. Several of Van Meers's people cried out in panic. The high fine vibration of the earth suddenly accelerated back and forth into a violent heaving. A rumbling as deep and massive as the grinding of underground mountain against underground mountain, tectonic plates slipping, a roar rose up from the earth, the ash jumping and shaking in complex strange patterns—

They danced, struggling to remain standing, the earth below them jerking left and then right as if determined to bring them down; they fell onto the vibrating ash—

In the jungle, the subterranean roar was joined by the cracking and snapping of thousands of limbs, leaves rustling and shaking and raining down, the canopy snapping back and forth, huge ancient trees swaying in the grip of the treacherous earth, trees groaning as they overbalanced and fell snapping and breaking down toward the jumping ground—

Owen danced, and Irma fell to the ground. Owen's awareness went flying out, looking for stability and for certainty, but horizon to horizon, the once-solid Earth was nothing, nothing, nothing but an illusion, it would not hold them, there was nothing fixed and certain in the world, life was uncertain and they were just so small, such tiny animals, absolutely dwarfed by a hideously capricious nature—

A kilometer further north, Kate had fallen to all fours. She raised her face toward the sky, seeing the jungle canopy ripping asunder, revealing the gray, glowering sky. She raised her head and she howled, howled like a horrified animal, howled as her mind sought a past that she dimly remembered, but it had not been like this, life had been stable, it had made sense, the earth had been a solid thing, she had known who she was and she had not been this, had not been this—

The lake surface boiled and leaped, random waves rushing headlong into each other, breaking on the muddy shore, water suddenly a mere hostage of the violently shaking earth, suddenly revealed as an insubstantial substance floating atop another insubstantial substance floating atop another, the hot liquid core of a violent planet, finding voice now—

In the volcano, the pillar of fire leaping, doubling, throwing itself high into the sky, the earthquake granting it power—

Power. New vents ripped in the southern face of the volcano, shaking, giving vent to acrid gushings of ashen smoke and spits of magma—

The western tip of the volcano's cone exploded, blowing hundreds of tons of rock kilometers—

The blast compressed a volume of air into a hard wall of a sphere. The wall beyond hearing knocked the people to the ground and they were shocked, they could not think, the earth could not be so capricious, they could not they had not been able they had never imagined that the world could be like this was not the way that the world worked it was not right they could not understand—

Dumbfounded, dropped to their seats or their knees, the people were turned into children. Awestruck.

And then the earth settled and shook no more. Once again, it seemed solid and supportive.

A peculiar silence . . . a silence more total than

deafness. Then they were aware of the distant roaring of the pillar of fire.

Van Meers picked himself from off the ground. From the vantage of the high mount, he looked around and saw that from the moonscape of the shaken ash, the green lights were rising, and from the ruined sky, the golden sparkles were descending. For the first time, he saw the green lights and the golden sparkles meet in midair, green into gold, gold into green.

A beautiful lucidity washed through him. He understood now. It was all of one mind. Their brains were just nodes, phenomena that were part of a much larger pattern.

He could touch—

The Hiyul, the great Ocean-Mind, hundreds of light-years distant. He experienced sensations and thoughts of the Hiyul a thousand years old, propagated at a large fraction of the speed of light through the beautiful medium, the sphere of being—

He had always been the One. How obvious that seemed now. The One was the Soul, the Spirit, of the planet. The Earth and all power belonged to him.

He must proceed to the lake, where he would join with the ancient vessel of his mind. He would reunite with himself and gain new strength.

Constance and Axel did not wait for the trembling to die. As soon as they could regain their feet, they sprinted down the hill, northward, running away from Van Meers in the fastest route of escape. Constance ran as fast as she could, her sore feet

inside the boots flicking clumps of muddy ash backwards. Although smaller, Axel ran faster. He turned
and called to her, his voice hollow-sounding in the
ash-dampened landscape.

Constance kept her mind as quiet as she knew
how. She would not reach out to anyone, because
she did not trust the medium. Van Meers used the
medium to attack her. Constance turned inwards
into herself and withdrew from the world in a way
that only she could understand.

She was sorry that she had ever played there. In
the old life, she had been peaceful and happy. This
new life was full of terrors that she could not
understand.

Her father had not helped her, and her mother
had turned away. Who was this boy ahead of her?
She could not trust anyone. Not even the Silver
Stars . . . she would make her mind so flat and dull
that no one would see her.

Axel watched her limping stride and tried to
decide what he should do. Something about the girl
made him feel very sad. He wanted to help her.
Uncertainly, Axel doubled back and encouraged
Constance to run with him, northward.

Kate stood slowly and watched the green lights
and the golden sparkles. Kate struggled to remember who she was and where this place was. The
memories of her life seemed like a set of jewelry;
she could wear them or put them aside. But if she
didn't wear those memories, then who was she?

Witch of death, the queen of the dead? Millions
of memories, each as important as any of hers,
crowded her mind. Misery and ecstasy, the babble

of ten thousand other minds. What did any of them matter now? They were all dead, the paradise for which they had yearned, a sweet lie. Beyond the membrane of death was nothing. Eternity was empty, life on Earth was our only share of paradise. And those still living among her people called to her, the great black network of souls that were descending, going down toward that peace more final than any other. For a long moment, Kate yearned to go down with them. She did not yearn for immortality. She was not Van Meers. She did not seek power.

It seemed to her now that all her life, she had been in love with easeful peace. The end of struggle. Tranquillity. How strongly it beckoned to her now. To be at peace, all she had to do was surrender, relax, let the great tribe of her fellows drag her down to that restful place.

It had never been about immortality. She had understood that perhaps too well. It was about perpetual youthfulness. Kate was not the product of life; Constance was the process. Immortality was too great a burden even to consider. The One was so old, so old . . .

How thin the membrane into eternity seemed. How the One yearned to slip into the other side. Kate wanted to move across the threshold.

Fugue state, ancient memories mixing with the transmortal woman, the One the Spirit of the planet, so old and tired, now, it had to admit that it was tired. The dreams between cycles seemed sweeter than the cycles.

Down into the place of rest . . .

Yet down there in the last valley before the rising

of the volcanoes, Constance was running, so small and afraid. She was turning inward.

Owen touched her, and then there was Van Meers. Kate was between the two minds. The One was reaching out to them all. Kate realized that the One had been with them all along. She did not know which was—

Did Van Meers even exist?

What of Harley? Where was Harley?

Then she felt Harley, living yet, away to the northwest. He was mourning the death of Owen.

Owen, dead? Owen was—

He was reaching out to her. She was trying to remember who Owen was to her. He had seemed important once. Now that she could touch his mind directly, she wondered if she had ever known him.

They had shared many hours of many days, but they had been creatures of separate worlds. As she touched the memories that they shared, she compared her own memories with his. A party, a goodbye kiss, a long car ride . . . every moment of every day, what had happened had meant something fundamentally different to him than it had meant to her. The whole collection of their shared experiences seemed now to distance them, not bring them together.

He loved her, but Kate no longer understood what love could mean. What was love, when two people were never able even to meet each other? The old world was just meat and mouth noises and sweaty gestures. Love was possible only now, in the new world.

Let his mind into hers. Let Owen see who she was. Let him see how close to eternity she had always been. He, who was so fixed in the present and in shapes that he could make with his hands. Let him see what it meant to be a woman who was one with the great void. Who had always understood, down to the cells of her bones, that she was just a means. She was a particle of ocean water that moved in a circle as the great wave of life washed through her.

As a man, he was limited by his urge to conquer, a construct useful for males propagating genes, but one which blinded him to the truth. The world could not be conquered. He could not be the king of the world. The world honored no kings.

Was he strong enough to see that? Then let him look through her at the vastness of the void. Eternity, outside of time. Not to be. Could he even consider it?

Owen rose from his knees and watched as the green rose from the Earth and the golden sparkles descended from the sky. Touching Kate, he felt himself entering into a new level of understanding. The earthquake had taught him something about life. Nothing was solid and sure. Everything was fluid; everything that he had ever made was ephemeral. Someday, his last surviving work, perhaps *AnNautilus,* would be burnt ash or termite-chewed dust. He himself would be dust. His only share of immortality was whatever disturbance he made in whatever wave he helped boost or dampen, as that wave flowed outwards and onwards toward infinity.

He could not hold onto Kate or Constance. What he had been trying to do had been absurd. The world had changed. He could not turn back the clock. Time did not exist. The temporal illusion was just a way of thinking about things, a mental construct helpful for animals.

Yet it mattered whether he turned north toward the power or turned south to save his own life. Nothing was final, but the process of life contained exquisitely fine shades of correctness, fine grains of good and evil. Owen mattered. Turning toward the north, he knew that he must go there. The collision there would be colossal, much more important than anything he could ever do in the south.

Because, for the first time, he sensed the awesome power of the One. The great mind had been hiding itself from him, but now he was too close. It could not act on him any longer without him knowing.

Yes. The One. Huge, mighty, chaotic. Owen realized that the strangeness of the past years had not been simply the descent into the medium. The suicides of heads of state, the machine-gunning of children in playgrounds, the hydra-headed lunacies of modern life had been partially the result of the disturbed dreams of the One. There, hidden somewhere deep, the One had been thrashing slowly in its sleep, launching dissonance into the sphere of being. Strangely, humans had become figments of its nightmares.

Yes, you. The One. Owen connected with it now. Standing up to the force of its mind was like standing before the heat radiating from the open door of a blast furnace. Yet Owen stood firm. He was not afraid, because he understood himself. He was small and young; the One was colossal and ancient. But Owen was clear, while the One was confused.

You. Owen was long, thin, needle-sharp. His mind was the lance that could pierce the great brain. Let the One know fear. Owen would come and his coming would be the death of the One.

Slowly it faded from his awareness. Owen scaled back his mind's sight until he saw Constance running toward the north. He must follow and save her. Then he touched on Van Meers. The traitor! He had been taken into the One. Van Meers was not strong like Owen. Because Van Meers was weak, he would die. Because Owen was strong, he would kill.

Scaling back further, he continued to touch on Kate's confusion. The One had poisoned her with a love of death. As Kate reached out to him, Owen allowed her into his mind. He tried to remind her of all their common bonds, but everything she touched seemed to alienate her further. It was no good. Owen was not sure how much of his wife survived.

—*Why did you run away?* he asked.

—*Ask her. She knows,* Kate answered, and then she severed the connection.

Near him was this pillar of light: Irma. As his awareness scaled back to his person, Owen swept through her, discovering that she was more similar to him than Kate had ever been. She was a fighter, clear, not confused.

Natural sight returned to his eyes. Irma, her long black hair tangled, her expression wild, was staring at him.

"Don't reach out anymore," she said. "It's a trap."

"What trap?" Owen asked. Around them, the jungle lay in great disorder. Tree limbs, twigs, leaves, fallen vines, lay tumbled on the forest floor.

"That thing is drawing us all to it," Irma said. "It's going to destroy us there."

"No," Owen said. "I'm going to destroy it."

"That's just an illusion that it's giving you," Irma said. "That thing is a million times more powerful than you. It's drawing you close so that it can connect with you perfectly, at point-blank range, and then it's going to suck every memory and thought from your head . . . and leave you like the shell of a fly after the spider has sucked out its guts."

"No," Owen said. "How would you know that?"

"I felt it too," Irma said. "But I'm a *guerrillera*. I know when it's time to attack, and I know when it's time to hide. It's pulling you toward it with the illusion that you can kill it, just so that it can more easily kill you."

"No," Owen insisted. "I have to go north."

Irma tossed her head. "Then go and die," she said. "I'm not going with you."

"Yes, you are," Owen said.

Irma stared at Owen hard. She stepped back and swung the shotgun from around her back. Without any fuss, she aimed it at him.

"No, I'm not," she said.

"Yes, you are," Owen said. "The fight is to the north. I'm going to need you."

Irma continued to stare at Owen, who stood there, gazing into her eyes with a sad, certain expression.

"You will need the help," she said.

"That's right," he said. "Let's go."

Together Irma and Owen began to hike toward the north.

They had to climb over many fallen trees and thickets of fallen limbs. Owen worried that venomous jungle snakes might lurk within the tangles of splintered wood and torn vegetation, but they didn't have time to proceed carefully. He found himself helping Irma down from tree trunks. He could feel the strength of her muscles in the tapering small of her back, underneath the sweaty fabric of her cotton shirt. Her hand borrowed his strength, as she leaned on his shoulder before hopping down.

Owen wanted to rejoin with Kate. He felt a small crawling panic as he thought about the gulf between them. He needed to bring her around to him, so that the three of them could proceed against the One. Yet perhaps he would be stronger, alone with Irma, who was such a kindred spirit. Such a clear-eyed warrior. Besides, she was so alluring, with such dark, beautiful eyes.

He found himself standing next to her, his arm around her waist, gazing into her eyes. Her lips seemed so soft and luscious. She was waiting for a kiss.

A kiss?

Yes, a kiss between a king and his new queen. Together with her, Owen could rule the new world. Kate was of the past; she was of the deathway, useless to him now. He needed a strong fighter, a woman who could help him conquer the world.

Her lips were near. He could see that one of her pearly teeth was pressed against her lower lip. The tooth of a tigress . . .

Constance, Kate's voice whispered in his ear.

Owen remembered his wife and his daughter. His head drew back. He stared into Irma's eyes, seeing something coiled underneath the darkness there that he had never noticed before. For some reason, he was reminded of a dragon.

Slowly he unfolded himself from Irma's arms. He turned his back to her, and carefully, he continued to hike northward.

Thirty minutes later, they had arrived at a break in the jungle. A muddy road cut through the mountain toward the northern crest. Irma wanted to continue straight north, but Owen decided to follow the mountain road.

He had lost contact with Kate. Once again she had disappeared. He wondered whether she was ahead of them or behind.

The light was beginning to fail. Overhead, the sky, already dark with rain cloud and ash, was blackening. Heat lightning played among the clouds at the higher elevations, so that the dark clouds had a rich texture, backlit by flickering light.

A dusting of ash covered the forest here, so the dimmed greenery was further dulled. It reminded Owen of the dusty forests near cement factories. Soon they arrived at the region of heavy ash fallout, where they began to follow the footsteps of the tribe, climbing toward the crest where the tribe had ridden the earthquake. From here they could see the last valley, and beyond it, the looming Volcan de Atitlán, flaming with a tower of magma. Ruby light glowed from the underbelly of the clouds. The tower of magma penetrated the lowest elevations of the overcast, a doleful luminosity from within.

At the top of the crest, the silhouettes of a group

of people were waiting for them. Owen feared that it was the tribe. The first individual he recognized was Hector. His blood began to heat as he prepared to combat them. As they approached, however, he could see that standing next to Hector was Kate. Their mental silence was total. If he hadn't seen them, he wouldn't have known they were there.

Owen and Irma unslung their shotguns and hiked the remaining ascent with their weapons to the fore. As they approached the group, the only sound was the distant rumbling of the volcano and the crunch of their boots on the gritty ash. Everyone except Kate was armed. Hector and the two other men stood, cradling their weapons in their arms.

Beyond the group waiting for them atop the hill, the western sky was a blood meridian. Airborne volcanic gases and ash particles were refracting the light of the setting sun, causing the western sky to glow ten times more redly than normal. To their north, Volcan de Atitlán continued to erupt, the pillar of magma smearing the sky with the ruddy light of the planet's bloody heart. It was as if the wounded planet were bleeding into the atmosphere, bloodying even the face of the sun.

Down in the valley, where the nightfall was already gathering, green phosphorescence glimmered. The Earth was descending ever deeper into the sphere of being; the visual hallucinations were almost constant now for those with eyes to see. Overhead, in the darkening clouds, golden iridescence played with the flickering of the heat lightning.

Kate had returned to her otherworldly aspect.

Her flesh was translucent; her eyes glowed with pearly softness. A spectral aurora extended from her. In the gathering darkness, she seemed to glow with a black flame that flickered with the uncertain purple and emerald sheens of a hummingbird's breast in moonlight.

Owen noticed that in the failing light, it was easier to see his own aurora. His arm looked waxen. The workings of his veins no longer looked red; it seemed that his blood had become a strange color, something like deep violet in black light. The branching of his nerves now appeared much more clear: they were firing with a gold that was the same color as the sparkles that played within the clouds overhead. This transformation did not worry him. The power of the sphere of being was firing through him. He felt that he was capable of winning any fight. The powers of darkness and uncertainty would have to give way before him. He had become a soldier of light.

Now they were close enough. Irma moved to Owen's right, where she stood facing Hector and the two other ex-tribesmen. Owen stood close enough to Kate that he could sense the coiling and uncoiling of her misgivings. He realized that there would be violence.

"So, Owen," Kate said. "Now you think that the One is the dragon that you must slay?"

"Maybe it's the ghost of a dragon that haunts the world."

"More than you know," Kate said. "It is far more the ghost of a dragon than you know. But you might want to consider that it has lived for hundreds of millions of years. Maybe it isn't so easily killed. But first maybe you'd like to address the problem within your party."

Irma tossed her hair and stepped back so that she faced Kate along with the others.

"Not necessarily you, Irma," Kate said. "But one of us, perhaps more, might not be quite what they seem. Did you know, Owen, that Harley is still alive?"

"No, he isn't," Owen said. "I saw him die."

"You saw the death of something that you thought was Harley," Kate said. "Let me show you where Harley is."

Slowly, Kate reached out to Owen. He allowed her to connect with him. This close, she was much more powerful than he had imagined. Still, he made himself relax. His own wife wouldn't hurt him, would she? Then, softly, he saw the pale translucent image of his brother standing there, next to Kate.

—*Be careful, Owen,* Harley said. *Very little is what it seems.*

Kate cut the connection.

"So who was the man who fell to his death? If he wasn't your brother, then what was he?" Kate asked. "Was it even a man?"

"I don't know," Owen said.

"It was a trick of the One," Kate said. "It was an illusion. It had no more substance than a forgotten lie. Harley walked across the bridge. He saw you fall to your death, or so he thought. And I brought him here to stand with me. I would consider, if I were you, why this one has come," Kate said, pointing her finger at Irma, "so helpful, such a strong ally, from nowhere. From nothing."

"I am a fighter," Irma said, hotly. "I'm here for the fight against the One."

"You're going to have to fight me first," Kate said. "Because before I let you take another step, I'm going into you and I will find out what it is that you are."

"I'm standing here," Irma answered.

Kate seemed to uncoil. White-hot light rocketed from her and struck Irma. Owen jumped back, startled by the sudden violence of Kate's attack. Irma did not move, however, except to hunch further down, seeking a firmer stance. Irma's body looked like a dark piece of cold iron thrust into the flames of a furnace. Owen moved to engage with them, but Kate thrust him aside.

—Do not interfere.

Irma remained motionless. A yellow light began to glow from around her. Slowly but with great certainty, the yellow light began to spread through the medium of the white-hot light, seeking to reach Kate.

"No," Kate muttered.

The yellow light doubled back within itself. Irma's body began to glow cherry-red. Owen heard Irma cough softly, as if she were choking.

The iron statue of Irma's body began to move, training the shotgun toward Kate.

Owen leapt forward and knocked the shotgun barrel upwards. The blast rang achingly near his ears. As he passed between the two, he felt that one was human, the other, inhuman.

Then he found the ground suddenly thrust up against him. Something had thrown him clear. Sensing something snap behind him, he rolled onto his back and looked up. Flames returning to their source, Kate was still standing, while Irma lay prostrate on the ground.

"That," Kate said, "was not a woman."

Kate pointed her finger at Hector. A slim light licked from the gesture to touch his head. Hector stepped up to the prostrate form of Irma. He placed the muzzle of his shotgun against the back of her head and pulled the trigger. Gray matter and blood splattered the ashen ground.

"She was ridden," Kate said. "She was a creature of the One."

Shaken, Owen pulled himself to his feet.

Harley was standing there, looking down at the ruined corpse of Irma. He reached out toward Owen, as if needing to touch him to convince himself that Owen was real. Owen reached out toward his brother in a mirror-gesture. Their fingers touched; energy sparked. Owen believed that his brother still lived. More than that, he did not know.

Kate turned toward the north, the final valley and the southern slope of Volcan de Atitlán.

—*Let's go*, she said.

NINETEEN

Descending into the last valley, Owen kept his thoughts to himself. The death of Irma had made him suspect that the creature that had worn the form of Kate was not his wife. Owen told himself that if he knew anything, then it was that his wife, Kate, was not capable of cold-blooded murder.

One of the combatants had been human, the other, inhuman. If Kate was not Kate, then she must be inhuman. That meant that Irma had been human. But if it was Irma who had been inhuman, she had hidden Harley and this was the real Harley. If Kate was ridden, then perhaps Harley was dead, and this was an illusion. Or perhaps both Kate and Irma were ridden.

So perhaps he was already in the company of the One. The creatures in the forms of Kate, Hector, and the two others could be thralls of the One. Thralls, or illusions, or a mixture of the two. If they were illusions, then the One had already taken his mind.

As in all types of warfare, in psychic warfare, range was important. Connecting with distant minds was a different experience from connecting with minds that were close. It occurred to Owen that he was being escorted deep into the killing zone. Probably the One could blast him now, fry his brain, and allow his burnt corpse to fall to the ash. But he was being escorted deeper, closer, into point-blank range. Where the One could touch him perfectly, synapse by synapse, blaze through his brain, conducting a destructive supercopy, sucking his living mind into its own. Owen tried to imagine such an existence: for all infinity, a living memory within an alien brain. Rarely consulted, latent, but ready to be activated by a bored mind, to cut and caper as the memories of a fictional character might cut and caper in a human mind. Would he even have a soul, then? Would the One eat his very soul? Was that fate worse than death?

Was the One gathering the most powerful adepts in order to destroy or enthrall them? Was he to be the eternal court jester of a monster?

Or perhaps he was wrong. Maybe Kate was Kate, his only friend. Was she capable of murder? Without pity, Owen had ridden a horse to death. In the company of the army of light, he had killed many soldiers of darkness. Maybe in the struggle to survive in this new world, they were capable of acts that neither could have done in the old world.

He yearned to reach out to Kate, to seek comfort and common cause with his life's mate, but fear kept him quiet. Silently, he descended the slippery slope down into the last valley.

An evergreen forest had covered the slope. The initial blast of the Volcan de Atitlán had knocked down the forest, the fallen tree trunks fanned in a pattern like stalks of wheat in a blown-down field. Each fallen tree trunk pointed roots-first toward the ruined cone of the volcano. The blast had stripped the branches and needles, forming a bed of ruined vegetation that the volcano had buried under a meter of ash.

In the gathering darkness, they found the easiest way to descend was to walk carefully down the center of the fallen trees. The laid-low trunks formed a straight if slippery path to the valley floor.

Nothing else moved. Anything alive above-ground at the time of the blast had been killed. Those animals that had survived underground were now buried. It was as if Owen and the others were descending through a fallen petrified forest on the dark side of the moon.

In the eerie lights of the eruption, the heat lightning, and the iridescence of the medium, Owen thought he saw a disturbance in the ash on a nearby tree. He jumped down and climbed up onto it.

Yes. They were bootprints in a pattern that he recognized. Constance had passed this way.

Owen stood up straight and looked down toward the valley floor. Carefully he extended his awareness, seeking the presence of his daughter. Immediately, several other entities contacted him. He felt surrounded by a rush of sharp inquiries. Reflexively, Owen returned to himself. He felt afraid for himself and for his daughter.

He turned around. Kate had stopped. She stood on the trunk of a tree higher up the slope and to the west. Her aurora overwhelmed the smeared redness of the last light of the dying sunset. She was staring at Owen.

He realized that he could not go any further, not without confronting her. If she was a creature of the One, then going deeper into the One's range would not improve the situation. Maybe, if he confronted her now, he could beat her here. Then he could go down, find Constance, and simply run away, surrender the field to the One, and try to survive, he and his daughter.

Owen held out one hand, a warning gesture to Hector, Harley, and the other two men. Then he extended his awareness toward Kate.

"I've been waiting," Kate said. Her voice sounded muffled in the heavy air between the ashen ground and the overcast sky.

Making contact, he found her as he had found her before, Kate, but Kate transformed, the queen of the dead. He touched the memories as he had touched them before. But now, he was not satisfied. He probed deeper into her. Now he entered, not surrendering and accepting, but aggressively, strongly, ready to fight if he discovered that she was not the person that he had thought.

Kate seemed to accept this. She seemed to expand outward and upward, opening herself to him, spreading out ever-greater against the night sky. She presented her mind to him, revealing it as something far more intense and powerful than he had known, while at the same time her ego ascended and retreated into a seemingly impossible distance. Owen continued into her, not sure if he was being welcomed or surrounded. He continued, knowing that his advance would end either in merger with his soul's mate or in his destruction at the center of an alien's trap.

Dimly he was aware that the two of them were bathed in flames. The others were stepping back. He could not sense the One, unless this mental environment where he found himself was all a construct of the One.

Either Kate, or made up of Kate. Surely this was the body of his wife, the brain, the mind . . . he committed all of himself. As much as he knew that he was still Owen, he was sure now that this was either Kate or a thing that had been made from Kate. To find out, he would have to probe the ego, now as high and faraway as a star.

Now he was totally inside: her mind had closed around him. Wholly surrounded by her, he felt surprise that she was so vast that he had a great distance to go before he could touch the ego, the diamond-brilliant center of her, now closer yet still far away.

Owen stretched himself, a long bright light, stretched and extended himself, seeking to touch that brilliant center and—

Light exploded as he joined with her.

Yes!

Yes and yes and yes . . .

Yes, it was Kate. Yes, she was his wife. Yes, she was the twin of his soul. Yes, she was his life's mate. Yes, the consummation of their marriage was far more closely perfect and far more intense than any consummation of any marriage of man and woman in the history of humanity. Yes, she was far greater and more powerful than he had ever guessed. Yes, this was the twin of his soul, showing him his own self far more faithfully than any mirror could show his face. Yes, he himself was far greater than he had ever guessed. Yes, a soldier of light, but more than that, a white-hot eruption, light itself, he towered above the world and all its struggles, for a moment perfect beauty, momentarily an angel of light, a creature of creative nature, burning white-hot, a flaming, swirling, whirling column of pure spirit.

Yes . . .

Touched by the divine, in tune with the essence of the universe. Entrusted with a sacred station, not meat robots, but incarnate angels, angels made flesh, the nervous system the wick of the holy fire of the spirit . . .

To be strong. To be true.

To offer himself a vessel to divinity.

To flow with his whole self in perfect harmony with the power that slowly spun whole galaxies, that drove the riot of spring, that loved light in all its forms.

And coming down now, sweetly, to know himself as a willing weapon of righteousness. To bend his knee and lower his head . . .

Yes . . .

To embrace mortality as his station. To know that his share of paradise was to walk in the natural world. Those more pure than he might deserve a rarer fate, but he was content with his station. No wars were holy, only some fights, so as a soldier of light, his station was to serve and then to die. Coming down, he asked for forgiveness for his errors in the fight and for the unintended slaughter of innocents. He received a knowledge of all his weapons; the most powerful and the most true, more powerful than righteous hate and unstoppable determination, was the weapon of mercy. When he might slay, to sheathe the sword. To open his hands, even to those who thought him their enemy.

Slowly returning now to a native awareness of himself. And sweetly, slowly, yes . . .

Standing there, with the mad sky above him, the ruined Earth below, Owen gazed into the other-worldly eyes of Kate.

"So now you know," she said softly.

"Yes," Owen said.

He jumped down from the tree trunk. He scrambled up onto the trunk upon which Kate stood, embraced her, and sought her lips.

Willingly, softly, she joined him in the kiss. And yes, she was Kate. Yes, he had saved her. Yes, they were still together.

As the kiss ended, Kate smiled gently and said, "You have to believe in me. When we stand together before the One, it'll try to make you doubt me. If you doubt me for one moment, it will come between us and it will destroy us."

"All right," Owen said. "I can believe that."

"I've changed, Owen," Kate said. "So have you, but I'm still yours."

"Yes," Owen said, his voice deep. "And I belong to you."

He turned to his brother, Harley, whom he saw as a figure of fire. He could see the coursing runs of his nerves and the blazing flame of his brain.

"Harley," he said.

"Yeah, man."

"I thought you died. I saw you die."

"No. I thought I saw you die. I thought I saw you falling down onto the rocks. When I saw you come back again, I thought, from death, I didn't know what to think."

"No," Owen said. "I'm not what I was, but I'm not dead yet."

"I'm glad you're here," Harley said. "We all need you."

The two brothers, one a figure of light, one a figure of flame, embraced. Owen touched Harley's mind. It was his brother. They had all survived to this moment.

—*Are you ready for the fight?* Owen asked.

—*Yes, but we need you to lead us,* Harley answered.

—*Follow me and lend me your strength.*

—*I'll follow you. Don't worry.*

He turned and took Kate's hand. Together, Owen and Kate continued their descent, hand in hand, each helping the other.

If any misgivings about Kate lingered in Owen's mind, they were deep down, far below the bottommost level of his consciousness.

Mommy and Daddy were coming! Down in the crevice of the valley, Constance huddled deep inside a tangle of fallen trees. She had found a hiding place from Van Meers and the bad men. How thirsty she was! Her throat had never been this dry. Sometimes she shivered, even though she was not cold, without knowing why.

Oh, it was better not to think! If she thought about anything, all she could remember was that awful horrible Van Meers. They had never told her that men could be that bad.

Better just to be still, keep quiet, hide, wait for

Mommy and Daddy to come save her. They were coming, she was sure. They wouldn't let their best girl stay so alone. No, not for long. They loved the princess. Even back in the old world, where she hadn't understood many things, she had understood that Mommy and Daddy loved their little princess.

This boy Axel was scared like her. He thought that Uncle Harley was his daddy. Was he her brother? She would have liked to turn inward into herself, but she couldn't leave the boy alone. He was so lonely and scared. He needed her.

Constance reached out and touched the back of Axel's fist. Called from his inner thoughts, Axel looked up. In the dimness of their hiding place, he could see the gleaming of Constance's eyes. Tremulously, he opened his fist and took her hand.

—*Sister.*

—*Brother.*

—*Don't be afraid.*

Constance felt her own mind relaxing. The boy was wonderfully clever. He knew how to do so many things. Constance could see, though, that he had learned to see things in the wicked way of the bad men. Constance tried to show Axel that it could be different. All of the old people had a way of looking at the world. They had made up names for everything. They thought that they knew how the world worked, but it was different from what they all thought. Even her mother and father were wrong.

—*What is true?* Axel asked.

—*The answer is yes,* Constance said. *You just have to be careful to ask the highest question you can think. Let me show you my friends . . .*

Constance reached out and made contact with

her friends, the Silver Stars. Twelve girls, much like her, who had lived in the old world without words. Who could see another way, one without good men and bad men and fighting and so much waste and pain.

—*You are one of us*, the oldest Silver Star told Constance. *We were like before, we are like you know. You belong to us! We love you . . . that thing is playing a wicked game. Don't worry. It doesn't matter. We'll be with you. We won't let it hurt you. We'll help the boy too.*

—*Nobody hurts the Silver Stars*, another said. *We're everywhere, except anywhere they can hurt us.*

—*Silly armies*, said another Silver Star.

Then all the Silver Stars laughed together. Constance laughed with them, but Axel didn't. He didn't understand.

Twenty minutes later, they heard a scuffling outside of the tangle of trees. Axel shouted something. He tensed himself to fight. Constance reached out and laid her hand on his shoulder.

"Don't worry," she said.

"Those are the freaks," Axel said.

"I know," Constance said. "Just let's go with them for a while. It'll all be over soon."

"You think so, because those Silver Star girls think it's OK, but how do you know they are who they say they are?"

"I know."

A man had crawled into the tangle of trees. In the darkness, his eyes gleamed like wet coal.

Van Meers and the tribe hauled themselves up the last slope. The pillar of fire of Volcan de Atitlán now stood to their northeast; directly before them spread the waters of Lago de Atitlán. Usually magnificent in its beauty, the lake now looked as violent and ruddy as volcanic Mars. Heat lightning burst and shot through the overhanging clouds, illuminating the boiling waters of the lake, reddened with the subaqueous roiling of lava.

From the great depths of the lake, the One was emerging. Its egg had steered its way up from the planet's outer core. Deep within the magma chamber of the erupting volcano, the egg had steered into a dike, a slow-flowing branch off the main chamber. At the top of the dike, the egg had rested in a laccolith, a subterranean lava-filled blister. When the moment arrived, the egg generated enough energy to cause the laccolith to burst through its roof, allowing the egg to flow easily into the bottom of the deep lake. For the first time in millions of years, the egg's surface cooled.

Now the One's egg was emerging from the lake. Physically impervious to planet-scale catastrophes, the egg would continue to protect the One.

Van Meers saw the egg emerge. Looming as large as a six-story building, the One's egg was still glowing cherry-red as it radiated heat. Roughly spherical, partially oblong, the egg looked strangely organic.

Gladness filled Van Meers. He was about to find his true power. He scrambled down from the mountain pass toward the lake. The closer he came, the more huge the One seemed. Now it was glowing a dark red, steam rising from its surface.

Van Meers ran toward the One. Then the moment came when he was only fifty paces from the looming egg. A tendril of light, soft and pale, lifted from the surface of the egg and slowly, lazily, extended itself toward him. Van Meers ran toward the tendril. In ten more paces, he made contact.

Instantly the tendril of light intensified a hundredfold. Brighter than a shaft of lightning, it connected the human brain with the alien brain.

Van Meers ceased to exist as a man. As momentum carried his mindless body forward, in a chaos-driven algorithm, the tip of the One's tendril split into billions of branches, connecting with each of the billions of dendrites in Van Meers's brain. In the half-second it took for Van Meers's brain to move through the tendril, it burned through all his synapses. In one moment, a perfect model of Van Meers's mind sprung into being in a small lobe in one corner of the One's great brain. It overwrote a module that had been copied from the Jarred, which had overwritten an elaborate, forgotten dream, which had overwritten memories from two cycles ago. In all of the One's great brain, every neuron had done duty twelve times over. Nothing was new; everything was old. Sometimes it seemed to the One that it was older than the Universe.

Stunned, Van Meers's body fell, plowing face-first into the ash. The tendril lightly played on his head, as a master might pet a dog.

How glorious! After an inexplicable glitch—a flash of harsh white light—Van Meers found himself in a paradise of his own design. It was as he had always dreamed it. He, Van Meers, was the king of the world. The Earth was perfect, a blue-and-green jewel, rich with gardens and temples. Billions of people existed to worship and adore him. Wisely, Van

Meers exercised his godlike power over the population, rewarding the good and scourging the bad.

But it was boring, really, after only just a second. Such a primitive power fantasy. He was an unworthy creature. Where was the tension and the drama? Perhaps it would be more interesting to create a nemesis.

Here, down in the subconscious, were the makings of many creatures that might serve. Beasts of predation and beasts of ghoulish hunger. Oh, yes, here was a creature that might do. . . .

Van Meers didn't understand. What was the source of these thoughts? Something unsettling was happening. Hadn't he sought and won the perfect power? Then why . . . ?

No, it was not . . . a hideousness. Van Meers felt his heart pound. Blood shocked his brain. A creature so hideous it was diabolic. Made perfectly from genetic-encoded terrors and shaded with Van Meers's own personal fears. It was the soul-eater, the vampire of his mind.

Van Meers began to run, his nemesis shadowing him. The One watched for a few minutes, then tired of this pastime. It quieted the Van Meers model and turned its attention to the Van Meers animal still sprawled in the wet ash.

Such an animal might prove useful during the transition into the new cycle. These humans were problematic. Most of them had joined the deathway network, just a few shades short of passing into eternity. Some of them, however, were thriving in the sphere of being. This Owen Keegan and this Kate Keegan, for example. How close they were! The trick inside the trap was still working, but they had detected and destroyed the Irma creature. They had seen through the gambit with the Harley animal. Altogether, the Keegans were rather more trouble than the One had expected. To fight them, the One would mold this Van Meers into a more powerful thrall and send him down to deal with them.

His mind, like this . . . and strengthen this area. A touch of that. Smoother. Cleaner. Now more power in this region . . . and . . . more power still here. And now it was ready.

Van Meers rose from the ashes. He stood, the tendril still playing about his head. His aurora burning brightly, he licked his parched lips.

He was the One, the focus of all power in the planet. Time to descend to meet the Keegans. They needed to learn their place in the grand scheme of the new world.

They had followed Constance's and Axel's footprints to the hiding place of fallen trees, and then they had followed the footprints of the thralls as they climbed from the valley up the northern slope. Now they were studying a confusion of footprints, where apparently one of the thralls had fallen from the trunk of a tree. In the dust next to the confusion were two small bootprints. For a moment, Constance had stood here, and then the thralls had picked her up again. Owen swallowed painfully. He found it bitterly hard to accept that his daughter had been taken by the One's thralls. Accepting that fact threatened to fill his heart with heavy black hate, but he resisted that brutal emotional tide. He couldn't allow hate, even for the hateful, to overpower his reason.

Kate, Owen, and the others began to climb the

slope toward the mountain pass just west of the
Volcan de Atitlán. Climbing the ash-covered fallen
trees was less treacherous than descending.
Although they were bone weary, sore, and thirsty,
they forced themselves to press forward. Owen
hoped that he had enough strength for the
encounter with the One. He felt weak and afraid.

Overhead, the clouds flashed with lightning, and
thunder began to rumble. A storm was coming.

—*Make yourself strong, Owen. You are the one that
must slay the dragon. You must attack it.*

—*That would be the battle the One would win,*
Owen replied. *That is not the battle we are going to
fight. We can't confront the One. We must help the One
confront itself.*

—*I don't understand,* Kate said.

—*The way you let me into your mind,* Owen said.
That's the way we have to let it into ours.

—*You're my husband,* Kate answered. *It's our
enemy. If we let it inside of us, it will destroy us.*

—*Only if we think of it as our enemy,* Owen said.

—*You're wrong. When the time comes, I'm going to
blast it with all of the force of my people, the billion of
them, down in the deathway.*

—*If that moment comes, you'll know it,* Owen
answered. *The One itself will beg for it. Wait for that
moment.*

—*I know that I'll know,* Kate said. *And the One is
our enemy.*

—*It thinks it is,* Owen said. *We have to allow its
attack to pass through us.*

—*I don't understand.*

—*We have to allow it to realize that it is not our
enemy.*

Owen continued to climb the mountain. He tried to prepare himself for combat. He wondered who he was and why he found himself embarked on this assault. Why hadn't the burden fallen to someone else? Why him? He had been an artist. He had never demanded much of life, only to be allowed to work on his sculptures and to care for his family. Yet this awesome responsibility and this dreadful danger had fallen to him. A trick of birth had molded his brain into something slightly different from the brains of other people. An accident with no more reason than a birthmark or any harmless genetic quirk.

Or had he been chosen? Was there such a thing as destiny?

No, he thought. It was the way of nature. Billions of specimens of a species were adapted to a given environment. A tiny percentage of the population had genetic quirks that were harmless or even counterproductive in that environment. Then the environment changed, new conditions prevailed, and it was possible that what had been a quirk or flaw was now a powerful survival trait.

That was him and Constance. Because of it, he had been able to pull Kate back from the deathway. It occurred to him that if they could put an end to the One, then they could pull the dying back from the deathway and save a billion lives.

So he had to be strong and true. It was no longer only about him, or Kate, or Constance. It was about the survival of his kind.

But were the humans truly his kind? Or was he of a new kind?

A man was coming who thought that he was a

new kind. Up until now, Owen had not understood. He had not risen in power enough to see how it was. Now that he was as powerful as Van Meers had been, he could see.

What he had known as humanity was a primitive protospecies. A new species had emerged. Owen, Van Meers, and a few others were the first specimens of this new species. They were the posthumans.

There he stood. Van Meers, aflame with a pearly light, was standing up ahead atop a ruined tree, staring at Owen, who realized that he had been sharing thoughts with Van Meers for several minutes without realizing it.

"Hello, Owen," Van Meers said.

Hector, Harley, and the other two men trained their shotguns at Van Meers, who did not seem to notice.

"I've come to help you," Van Meers said.

Owen opened his mouth to speak. He was going to engage in a dialogue with Van Meers. Suddenly he realized that Van Meers had disappeared. For a moment, he was unable to understand; then he thought that Van Meers had been an illusion.

"He was no illusion," Kate said. She scrambled over several fallen trees. Following her, Owen found Van Meers sprawled on the ground behind the tree trunk on which he had stood. His aurora had gone dark. His pale skin looked waxen and unreal in the abnormal light.

"What happened?" Owen asked.

Kate turned to him, her eyes empty. "I hit him. Didn't you see me hit him?"

"No."

"I hit him with everything I had as soon as I saw him," Kate said. "What he did to me, what he did to Constance. He deserves worse than death, but death is what I had for him. He was enthralled to the One, in any case. There wasn't much there. I—"

"I didn't see you move," Owen said.

"I hit him fast," Kate said. "It was a reflex. Nothing I planned. It just happened."

Owen stared down at the lifeless form of Erik Van Meers; then he stood.

He looked up toward the mountain pass west of the flaming Volcan de Atitlán. Whatever they had become, their future awaited them on the other side of that dark slope.

T
W
E
N
T
Y

CARRYING THE CHILDREN ABOVE THEIR HEADS, THE thralls were bringing the immature Keegan and the boy to the lakeside. Too bad the girl had been so heavily damaged. Reaching as deeply as it could, the One couldn't find her ego. She had gone soulless. Such a waste. She was one of the few humans the One might have kept. Of all the humans, her cerebral architecture was one of the most interesting.

Perhaps the One could still use the infrastructure . . . the nervous system itself was in perfect condition. It would be a simple matter to drive into the brain, to overwrite all the immature's memories, and to mold the mind into whatever the One found necessary.

A moment of study, first. It was good material. The One wanted to do an exceptionally fine job. Something that would force the Hiyul to surrender praise despite its pride. The One would show the Hiyul how to make a creature!

Perhaps it should start here in the frontal lobe, converting these cognition areas into something a

little more psionic. That would be good. The process would have to overrun the verbalization—
Wait!

The One turned its attention further afield. Something had happened to the Van Meers thrall. The One had been lightly in touch with it as it had descended to intercept the Keegans. Yes, it had made contact with the two of them. Then . . .

Nothingness.

The Van Meers thrall had ceased to exist. It had simply dropped out of the sphere of being. There was no trace of violence: no force, no ripping, no burning, nothing.

For the first time in millions of years, the One experienced terror. Never before had it seen mastery of this order. It was possible that the Keegans represented a whole new way. They were creatures who had advanced into technological intelligence outside of a sphere of being. Who knew what they could do now?

His trick inside the trap? Was it working? It was good that Owen Keegan was developing into a messiah. That would make his destruction cataclysmic: not merely a personal death, but a death of a champion, signaling death for all his kind. That would make the story worth telling. What of Kate Keegan, though? Did she or did she not belong to the One? She had absorbed all the poison of the deathway that the One had facilitated, but somehow she had metamorphosed into a unique being, something the One had never before encountered. It wanted to contact her to find out, but it would be dangerous to contact her strongly at present, with her so close to Owen Keegan.

302   JOHN DE LANCIE AND TOM COOL

Better to hold this immature Keegan as a hostage. Owen Keegan retained a strong parental instinct. He was still a creature of nature. He had not yet evolved into what the One had become: a self-defined creature, beyond the constraints of nature. Hold this immature cub that had been Constance Keegan and threaten to destroy her if the situation grew desperate enough.

How wonderful . . . how wonderful it was to experience terror again. It made the One feel primitive and young. It had forgotten the delicious extent to which terror lent a creature such monstrous reserves of power. At this moment, most of the One's brain was blazing, aflame with the need to fight.

The survival instinct was also firing within Owen. He was experiencing the reserves of energy available to men and women in survival situations. Long ago, his body should have forced him to sleep. Because he knew that if he slept, then he and his kind would die, he continued to climb, to struggle up the slippery trunks, to maneuver around and over heaps of splintered trees, to fight to arrive at the high mountain pass. His hunger-thinned, thirsty, weary body seemed a mere filament for the fiery burning of his soul. He could continue. He could gain the mountaintop and go to stand before the One.

Owen concentrated on his mind. So much disharmony, so much useless anxiety and self-doubt. He had to focus himself into an effective tool. Much as he had done for his body, Owen allowed the fire to burn through his brain. He didn't fully understand the process; he only knew that he had to bring his energies into harmony. For long minutes, he was dimly aware that he was still climbing. His mind was burning in a flame that was more white and more hot.

When the purging was finished, he felt calm and powerful. For a moment, he remembered the old Owen. The man who had packed for a voyage was like a child to the man he had become. Those old memories were like childhood memories: important, formative, but lacking the current context. The old Owen could not have stood in front of the One. Perhaps the new Owen could. He reached out to Kate, and through her to the network of the deathway.

—*They are my people,* Kate said. *Together we are going to pull the One down low and kill him.*

—*The One would be waiting for that,* Owen said. *It would give you the illusion that you were pulling it down. Then, when you were low, it would drive you so deep that you, not it, would die.*

—*You don't know that,* Kate said. *You don't understand the power of the deathway.*

—*Why do you doubt me?* Owen asked.

The volcano now loomed just ahead and to their right. Leaping upwards only to fall back upon itself incessantly, the pillar of fire looked like a demon's ladder toward a ruined heaven. Here the stench of liquid rock and abnormal chemistries thickened the air. Volcanic heat warmed the night air so that sweat broke through their skins. The night heat sucked the little moisture left in their dehydrated bodies.

Yet they climbed. They found the mountain pass.

An ash-buried roadway wound through its depths, making their progress easier, except for occasional stretches where cooled lava flows forced them to climb. Owen, Kate, Harley, Hector, and the two others topped the mountain pass.

The ground trembled with the workings of the volcano. They stood, gazing down upon the troubled surface of Lago de Atitlán. From this vantage point, they could see, there on the southern shore of the lake, the huge egg of the One.

Light was playing about the misshapen oval. Tendrils of light lifted and descended, touching objects too small to be seen from this distance. Owen wondered what the One was doing. Where were Constance and Axel?

Kate looked over to him. "They're down there with it."

"You're sure."

"Yes," Kate said.

"What . . . what is it doing to her?"

"We'll have to go down to find out."

They began to descend toward the lake. A tendril of the One lifted and began to extend itself toward them. Owen felt the urge to brace himself, but he relaxed. Like a serpent of lightning, the tendril wove back and forth, thinning itself as it stretched toward them. Harley shouted something, but the tendril did not touch them. It hung in the air above their heads, weaving back and forth, buzzing with an electric potency.

They continued to descend toward the lake. Out of the corners of their eyes, they could see shapes moving in the shadows. Owen grew aware that dozens of the One's thralls had surrounded them, escorting them down toward the lake. Owen considered the problem of the thralls' attacking them physically while the One engaged them psychically. When it came to combat, could they fight in both domains simultaneously? Owen sent a message to Hector, Harley, and Axel: while he and Kate engaged the One, they should guard against the One's thralls. Harley, Hector, and Axel brightened: they trusted Owen and Kate to fight the main fight, while they felt themselves equal to the challenge of fighting the One's thralls.

He used these last minutes to commune with his wife.

—*When it comes to the moment of truth, you'll be the left and I'll be the right,* Owen said.

—*You can be the light,* Kate said. *I'll be the darkness. We'll find out which one is the more blinding.*

—*All right.*

—*Together.*

—*Yes.*

—*Though you must allow me to go where I must in order to destroy it,* Kate said.

—*I won't let you go.*

—*You already have, Owen. If it's necessary, you'll have to let go of what I became.*

—*I won't.*

—*Then all may be lost.*

—*I won't.*

—*In the moment,* Kate said. *If you must choose between Constance and me, you must choose Constance.*

—*No.*

—*Be strong.*

Owen wanted to continue to commune with

Kate, but he found that she had wrapped herself in a silence that he could not penetrate. He sensed that she was gathering her forces for the encounter with the One. Owen reached into his own reserves of strength. He guessed that they had only a few more minutes. The tendril of light playing above their heads was growing thicker and brighter; the buzzing, more harsh.

They arrived at the valley floor. For a few minutes, tumbled-down buildings, the ruins of the town of Panajachel, blocked their view of the lake and the egg of the One. Still, the tendril of light played over their heads. They made their way through the labyrinth of ruined streets, descending toward the lakeside, until they were clear of the town.

Huge as a building, the egg of the One loomed on the lakeshore. Sundered and split canoes littered the shore, their painters half-buried in the wet ash. Dozens of thralls surrounded the egg, lifting above their heads the prostrate forms of Constance and Axel, offering them up as the focus of the One's tendrils of light.

Owen and Kate approached closer. Now the hovering tendril of light brightened to a painful intensity. Another tendril joined it, and then another and another, until a network of tendrils surrounded but did not touch them.

They stepped over painters and halves of canoe hulls, approaching so close that they could discern the walnutlike convolutions in the egg. They could see Constance's eyes rolled back in her head. They could smell an unearthly funk, the excretions of the One's millennia-old shell.

As they approached within ten meters of the

One, it loomed above them, its tendrils forming a perfect network that slowly descended.

And the One made contact.

A pure light, an ecstasy of flight, a consuming climax. The One burned through Owen's mind, exciting all his memories and accelerating every mental region. Owen allowed it to join with him.

—*Yes. Connect. I am here.*

A copy of his mind erupted in the One's mind. Having touched the thrall of Van Meers, Owen had expected this. In the split second before the One attempted to destroy his human brain, Owen excited the copy of his mind in the alien brain.

—*I am here. I am one. I am two. I am four, eight, sixteen . . .*

Owen wrested control of the enthrallment. Having cooperated with the duplication of his mind, he willed each copy to make another copy, the copies to make copies, making copies . . .

—*I am thirty-two, sixty-four . . .*

Within moments, Owen had willed the creation of hundreds of his doppelgängers within the One's brain, stunning the ancient mind. Expecting resistance, it had encountered cooperation; seeking to enthrall, it found itself host to a legion of minds.

Like a black tide, Kate entered. She followed the flow of Owen into the alien's mind. She helped to interconnect the growing host of Owen inside the One's mind. As the One tried to destroy these copies, Kate connected them with the deathway network. A billion human minds were joined here, lending their strength to Owen's doppelgängers.

The One thrilled with an ecstasy of fear. It couldn't destroy these minds; they were too strong.

They had embraced so many regions of its own mind. It could not destroy them without destroying too much of itself. Far earlier than it had planned, the One indicated its power over Constance Keegan.

—*Leave me now or I will destroy your cub.*

Owen followed the gesture of the One touching his daughter, finding Constance's mind quiet, almost comatose. The One's contact with her was like a sword poised over her cerebral cortex. Owen tried to place himself between the One and Constance, but it moved too quickly, countering his thrust. The poisoned tip of the One's mind descended so slightly, just touching the membrane surrounding Constance's mind.

Instantly Owen stopped the process of making doppelgängers. The final number of them was 610. As they had grown, they had placed themselves strategically throughout the alien's mind. They were engaged fully, interlocked in an intimate grip against which the One heaved and surged. It found itself in a predicament that it had never expected.

—*Allow me to destroy these or I will kill the cub.*

—*No,* Kate said. *You cannot. If she dies, then we shall kill you.*

Kate allowed the deathway network to surge more strongly into the One's mind, rushing in like a flood of black water. The billion humans who had almost sunk down into oblivion because of the interference of the One now invaded its mind. Now with the force of a vengeful hate, they were pulling down the One toward oblivion. Death. The passage into nothingness.

—*No, Kate,* Owen said, but he hesitated from

stopping her. He could not break with her in the presence of the One. She must attack with all her dark force.

A harmony chimed through the One. It discovered a hidden layer under its moves, a self-delusion inside the trick inside of the trap. For millions of years, weary of life, it had wanted to sink down into blessed oblivion, yet it had been too weak and afraid to end itself. It had needed the agency of another power to kill its incessant self.

How kind of the humans to perform this service and give it sweet relief. Willingly, the One allowed itself to be pulled down, deeper and deeper into the deathway. The membrane into eternity was so close and thin. What a blessing finally to pass through it.

Down the deathway the One sunk, calming itself, fully embracing the mass of humanity, as it approached the limits of existence. Another iota of effort further and it would arrive at the end.

Joined with the deathway network, Kate descended with them. From his distance, Owen remained connected. He was afraid that Kate would go so low that he would lose her. The One had not yet surrendered Constance. Although he could not allow them both to pass into eternity, it was a struggle to maintain the contact. He would have to bring Constance and Kate away in the moment before the One transitioned into eternity.

A long wave of deathly calm passed through the community of humanity. On the threshold of death, the One suddenly inverted itself. Towering up strongly, it ignited immense reserves of power. Brightly burning, the One let slip the embrace of the deathway network, which sunk down below it.

Now the One rippled out to all horizons and began to push the deathway network lower.

It was exactly the trap that Owen had foreseen, but which he had lacked the discipline to stop, so sincere had seemed the One's desire to pass into eternity. Now Kate, Constance, and the bulk of humanity were low and descending lower, down toward the threshold into death.

No, he could not allow it. Owen erupted to the heights of his powers and confronted the One.

—*No*, he said. *You cannot. You are old and sick with the fear of death. These ones are young. We have not yet lived in our time. You have no right to steal our world from us.*

—*This world is my world,* the One answered. *I chose it hundreds of millions of years ago. It is of no consequence to me that freaks of nature have evolved here, infesting my planet.*

—*We are creatures of this world,* Owen said. *This is the planet that has given us birth. We only seem like freaks because you refuse to acknowledge that life is ever-evolving. You think there is nothing new. You dare to believe that you are the crown of creation. You are not. History is never-ending. We, the new and young, don't demand your death. It is you who have demanded ours.*

On the cusp of thrusting the bulk of humanity into oblivion, the One hesitated and considered what Owen had said.

—*What a strange idea,* the One thought. *It is something . . . new? Yet I am the crown of creation, the ultimate—*

—*No, you are only a sick, old animal.*

—*I am beauty.*

—*You are hideous and foul. You should see yourself as we are able to see you.*

—*I would like to see myself. Perhaps your mind is bright enough to reflect the real beauty. Would it be possible to assume your mind, to see myself as you see me?*

—*Yes,* Owen said.

—*No,* Kate said. *Don't let it, Owen.*

—*Show me then,* the One answered. *Let me into you fully, without tricks, without stratagems. Allow me to see myself. It's been so long. Sometimes it pains me to see myself in the distant mirror of the Hiyul; the Jarred do not flatter me, either. How magnificent it would be to see myself, gloriously close, magnificently radiant in the admiration of you lesser creatures. Perhaps you might serve, as the children once served before they died so mysteriously. Will you show me myself?*

—*Come as you are.*

Maintaining half its attention as pressure on the deathway network, the One entered the front of Owen's mind. Owen reached down and made strong contact with Kate.

—*Now,* he said. *Now, allow it into us, just as you allowed me.*

—*No,* Kate said.

—*Don't be afraid,* Owen answered. *We're stronger than your fears.*

The One entered Owen's mind, assuming control over his entire being and turning to look at itself. Self-absorbed for hundreds of millions of years, the One could see a deep and detailed image of itself reflected by the pure art of Owen's mind, the sacred place where his soul intertwined with ideal forms and true shapes. It saw itself, an ugly confusion of layered memories, locked in a murderous embrace with millions of innocents. Caught in the act of mass murder, its hideousness was undeniable, but the One recoiled and began to erase these memories even as they happened.

Relentlessly Kate followed it. With the subtle power of her insight, she found ghostly traces of guilty memories. Kate fired the repressed memories, exciting the regions of the One's mind that it sought most to suppress. Evil works in evil days, crimes, sins of omission and sins of commission, casual slaughters, the violation of innocents, betrayals of loves . . . Kate forced the One to relive the years when it had massacred its children, leaving it the sole surviving specimen of its race. The extermination of the dinosaurs, simply for the sake of drama. The mental savaging of the distant Sandral people, because it had been bored one cycle. Other sins that the One had wanted forever forgotten . . .

Kate shared with the One this bitter wisdom: any immortal creature, even if it struggled toward the good in this imperfect universe, must over time commit long series of crimes until the burden of its guilt was crushing. The logic of an imperfect universe made life bearable only for the innocent young, the amoral, and the amnesiac. Only what was young could be truly beautiful. Perpetual youth was the way of nature and, thus, so was death.

She forced it to confront the fact that it was an amoral monster by choice, the most absolute of cowards. The One's subconscious self-loathing exploded with a geometric rapidity, until finally it embraced the knowledge that it was a monster.

—Nothing lasts forever, Kate said. *We are creatures of this world. We live for a time, we give birth to new hope, and we die. Immortality is a perverted delusion. You have been wrong for millions of years. The better part of yourself has known it.*

—But I am weak!

—Here, Kate said quietly. *I have the strength.*

A greatness welled from Kate, a dark and wise beauty, rising to stellar heights. Owen joined her, so that the two intertwined and towered above the One and all the world. Man and woman, husband and wife, embracing their own mortality, unafraid of death, they moved with a cosmic authority, a swirling force of nature. The membrane into eternity was on the wrong side of the One. Owen and Kate allowed the One to see that clearly, now, for itself. Finally the One understood that it belonged—and yearned to be—beyond the realm of life. It was wrong for it to live.

Power shocked through the brain of the One, a massive cerebral seizure, as the old mind refused to defend itself, and Owen and Kate burned through it, purging ancient neurons of their ghostly dreams. Whole universes began to collapse, empires to fall, millions of ghosts to fade, as the brain of the One failed. With an agonizing convulsion, the ego died, and then outlying sectors, die-hard models, and forgotten realms of memory collapsed to nothingness. The last model to cease was the model of the Hiyul. In its dying moment, it launched a wave of joy, reporting to its maker, light-years away, that the work was complete, the art, although flawed, reflecting a sly glimmer of the perfect.

Natural sight returned to Owen's eyes. He felt

dazzled. He had expected night, but light filled the sky. The east beyond the volcano glowed with a ruby red far more beautiful than a normal sunrise. Owen stood. Mists hung from the slopes of the mountains to the west of the lake. He could hear the lapping of the waves upon the ashen shore.

He heard a cracking sound. He looked up at the egg of the One, where huge fissures were opening in its convoluted surface. Owen glimpsed Constance, sprawled on the ash where she had fallen. The others were nowhere to be seen. He stumbled toward the still form of his daughter.

Constance seemed cold and lifeless as he picked her up. An awful stench alerted him. Behind him, the egg was opening, dark matter oozing from the interior. Burdened by the weight of his daughter, he climbed the beach until he passed the high-water mark etched on the volcanic ash. He kept moving until he arrived at a half-buried seawall, where he sat, Constance's head lolling on his shoulder. Owen reached out to Kate, but didn't find her.

An awful flower, the egg continued to open. The remains of the One, a massive brain encased in an unnatural egg, spilled into the volcano-soiled waters and onto the ashen beach. The One was as dead as if it had died a million years ago.

Owen turned his attention to Constance. Her eyes were still rolled up into the back of her head.

"Constance," he said. "Constance."

When she didn't respond, Owen touched her throat and felt her pulse, subtle under her chilled flesh. Opening his mind, Owen sent a message into Constance's mind.

—*Princess,* he said. *Wake up. Daddy's here.*

For a long moment, there was no response. While Owen waited hopefully, he could sense the close-by presence of his daughter. He hugged the poor child. She had suffered so much, but finally he was here with her.

—*Constance,* he called.

He allowed the love he felt to radiate about him. His daughter. His child. He, Owen, recreated anew. More like him than any other creature, and yet far different. Given to him in a sacred stewardship, to care for, to protect, to empower, to go forward when his time to walk was no more.

"Daddy?"

Her voice, so sweet and small, sounding close to his ear.

"Daddy?"

Her child-small limbs, coming to life and embracing him with the purity of a child's love.

"Daddy?"

Owen's voice was gruff with emotion. "Yes, darling. I'm here."

He had to see her face, but she wouldn't lessen her embrace. Seated on the half-buried seawall, Owen realized that she needed to feel him more than he needed to see her. He had to have faith that she was well. He hugged her and rocked back and forth.

"It's all right," he said. "I'm here now."

Through tear-filmed eyes, he looked at the ruin of the egg of the One. A woman came walking around one of the huge relaxed petals. She seemed to be studying the ruins of the ancient beast. Then she turned and began to walk up the beach.

Kate smiled as she walked with the sure grace of

a queen. Her grime-filmed face was relaxed as she smiled a weary, satisfied smile.

Kate sat down next to Owen. She placed her right hand on Constance's shoulder.

"Mommy's here, darling," she said softly.

Constance released her father and clung to her mother. Kate hugged her and stroked her back. Finally Owen could see Constance's face, her blue eyes sparkling as she gazed at her father and smiled.

"That's better, Daddy," she said.

"Yes, darling."

"Don't leave Constance alone again," she added accusingly.

"No, darling. I'll be here."

"I made new friends. The Silver Stars. They took care of me and hid me while the One went looking for me. He had my body, but the Silver Stars helped me hide from him, even when I was so close."

Owen reached out in the direction that Constance indicated. He touched twelve high, bright silvery beings. They were far beyond anything that had happened that day. To Owen, that creatures such as these existed was the final proof of the absoluteness of his victory. He had slain the dragon, so that children could play, not knowing or caring about dragons. The Silver Stars laughed merrily at his foolish pride: perhaps someday their friend's old father would understand.

Owen put his arms around both his wife and his daughter. His lips were close to Kate's ear.

"I thought you had gone," he said.

Kate tossed her hair and turned her face to smile at him.

"Not today," she said. "Some day. But not today."

"No, not today," Owen answered. "And not for many years, I hope."

Kate shrugged and pointed with her chin at the ruin of the One.

"No," she answered. "Who would want to live forever?"

"Where were you? I couldn't feel you."

"I had to attend to the people," Kate said. "When the network broke up, I had to help some of them. Look."

She gestured. Owen followed the gesture, touching hundreds and then thousands of his fellow humans. They were moving in all directions. The deathway network, formed because of the One's influence, had disintegrated. People all around the world were forming new communities, following many different ways. Those who had insisted on clinging to the deathway were already gone.

Owen returned to his natural sight. The cloud cover was beginning to part, revealing a bluer sky. Reflecting both the blueness and the scattered cloud cover, the lake of Atitlán turned emerald green.

A man carrying a burden came walking from the direction of the ruined town. After a minute, Owen could see that it was Hector, laboring to carry a huge wooden bowl slopping with water. He walked up to them and turned the bowl to present the long handle of a gourd to Owen.

"Harley and I had to chase a few people away," Hector said. "There was a riot there for a moment. I don't think you noticed, but it was a real rumble. We had to protect you. On the way back, I found some water. Are you thirsty?"

"Yes. Thanks, Hector. Where's Harley? Where's the boy?"

"Harley's still chasing some of the hard cases. I think the boy is with him."

Owen scooped out fresh water, offering it to Constance's lips. She drank thirstily. Owen offered the second cup to Kate, and the third he drank himself. The fresh cool water tasted more delicious than anything he had ever drunk. Kate splashed the water on Constance's face and began to rub her muddy face clean.

"She's a pretty girl, after all," Kate said.

"The best girl," Owen said.

"Constance is the best girl," Constance agreed with the complacent, sure tone of a child.

Owen looked toward the east. A man and a boy were walking by the shore toward them. It was Harley and Axel. Harley reached out and placed his hand on Axel's head, as Axel raised his arm and pointed toward the disintegrated shell of the One. Owen reached out to them.

—*Are you all right?*

—*Everything's fine,* Harley answered. *Axel was just giving them too much hell. I had to pull him back.*

—*Butt-munch freak-heads,* Axel said.

Owen sensed that both his brother and the boy were relaxing. They were fine. The dangers of this day were past. The army of light was still engaged with rising networks of brutes, far off over the murky horizons, but here, today, no one would dare challenge them. Here and now, they were supreme.

Owen felt his own self relaxing. He had done all that he could. The man that he had been, the family that he had tried to save, no longer existed. The old world was gone. But he had refused to let go of what he had loved; only what he loved had survived the transformations. He had managed to carry the people they had become forward into the new world. What he had loved had changed, but it had survived.

Kate was watching him, thinking his thoughts. For a moment, he perceived them all as standing whirlwinds of energy. When the view of the light of day returned, he saw that Kate was smiling, a smile that he shared with her as intimately as they shared their profound mutual understanding.

—*Nothing is the same*, was the thought they shared. *Nothing is constant. Yet I am here with you for a little longer.*

Owen dipped his hand in the bowl of fresh water and helped his wife tend to their daughter.

BIOGRAPHICAL NOTE:
TOM COOL

TOM COOL is a true name.

During his service in the U.S. Navy, Tom made four aircraft-carrier battle-group deployments, supported naval operations in waters near the ex-Soviet Union, studied Central American guerrilla warfare, planned the stand up of two joint intelligence centers, and developed software for the Defense Advanced Research Projects Agency. In 1999, he retired as a commander.

His novels include: *Infectress*, Baen, January 1997 and *Secret Realms*, Tor, May 1998. His short story "Universal Emulators" was included in David Hartwell's *Year's Best Science Fiction 3*.

A native of Pittsburgh, he majored in the creative writing program at Pennsylvania State University, graduating in 1976. He earned a Master of Science, Computer Science, at the United States Naval Postgraduate School, Monterey, California, in 1987.

He and his wife, Eva Raquel Chock de Cool, a Chinese descendant from Bocas del Toro, Panama, and their two children, Raquel, 13, and Alexander, 11, live in Panama and Austin, Texas.

BIOGRAPHICAL NOTE:
JOHN DE LANCIE

JOHN DE LANCIE is an internationally celebrated actor, producer, and writer. He has played Q, the omnipotent prankster, in eleven episodes of *Star Trek: The Next Generation; Star Trek: Deep Space Nine* and *Star Trek: Voyager.* His film credits include *Multiplicity* (1996), *Evolver* (1995), *Fearless* (1993), *The Hand That Rocks the Cradle* (1992), *The Fisher King* (1991), and *The Onion Field* (1979). His television credits include *Legend* (1995), *The Thorn Birds* (1983), *Black Beauty* (1978), and *Days of Our Lives* (1982–1986, 1989), with guest appearances on *Dave's World* (1993), *L.A. Law* (1986), *MacGyver* (1985), and *The Twilight Zone* (1985).

A graduate of the Julliard Drama School, John was a member of the American Shakespeare Festival at Stratford.

His stage credits include performances with the Mark Taper Forum in *Terra Nova* and *Aunt Dan and Lemon,* with the Seattle Repertory Company in *Saint Joan, Taming of the Shrew,* and *Lion and the Portuguese,* and with the South Coast Repertory Company in *Man and Superman, Childe Byron,* and *Golden Girls.*

Together with co-owner Leonard Nimoy, he has

produced and recorded a series of audio tapes and stage productions of classic science fiction stories under the company name Alien Voices.

John and his wife, actress and singer Marnie Mosiman, and their two sons live in southern California. The family enjoys sailing their forty-five-foot ketch, *Nepenthe*.